THE CONTAINMENT ZONE

To Katie —
Danielle
Singleton

Also by Danielle Singleton:

Safe & Sound
Do No Harm (Joseph #1)
The Enemy Within (Joseph #2)
Price of Life

Connect with the author online:

www.daniellesingleton.com
@auntdanwrites
www.facebook.com/singletondanielle
www.daniellesingleton.wordpress.com

The Containment Zone

Danielle Singleton

ISBN: 1499204434

*****

To Amanda:
For The Friendship

"A sister shares childhood memories and grown-up
dreams."

ACKNOWLEDGMENTS

My first thank you is and will always be to my Lord and Savior Jesus Christ.

This book is dedicated to my sister, Amanda, who also happens to be my publicist. Thank you for your support, your friendship, and for not thinking your little sister is crazy for wanting to write books for a living.

I struggled with this story more than my others – the words wanted to fight me every step of the way. And, because of that, an extra special thank you to Madre and Amanda for putting up with my struggles and near-constant worry that I would never actually finish the book.

To my Reading Committee – thank you so much for giving of your time and expertise to help polish and refine my stories into finished novels. Y'all are awesome. Thank you also to Milton Wilkins for your book title suggestions (I apologize that the acknowledgment is so belated!). And to Ruth Dunn, Allen Hartley, and Thomas Smith for your character name ideas – they were much appreciated!

My deepest thanks to the true heroes who fight to protect the United States and give me the freedom to be an author: America's soldiers, sailors, airmen, and marines. God Bless y'all and your families.

And, of course, thank you to the best big puppy in the world, Gus.

I hope y'all enjoy the story!

The Containment Zone

*****

"Our pleasures were simple – they included survival."

Dwight D. Eisenhower

PART I

ONE

A seven year old little girl with pigtails and sparkling blue eyes was the first one to say something to Luke Russell about the spots on his face.

"What's that?" young Sophia asked, scrunching up her cheeks and pointing her finger at the nose of the man doing repair work in her school. The weather that September in Shorewood, Minnesota was unseasonably hot, and the school district had sent its in-house electrician over to Minnewashta Elementary to make sure the air conditioning was working properly.

"What's what?" Luke asked, taking a break from work to wipe sweat from his brow.

"Those dots," Sophia replied, pointing again at the man's nose. "The ones all over your face." The little girl's missing front teeth meant that each word was pronounced with a lisp, something the forty-two year old father remembered well from when his own kids were that age.

"I don't know, honey. I don't have any spots, last I checked."

The second grader kept looking at him, intent on figuring out the mystery, until her teacher called her back to the line for recess. "Leave Mr. Russell alone," the woman scolded, smiling sympathetically at him from down the hall. With a population just over 7,000, Shorewood was the kind of town where everybody knew each other. It also didn't hurt that Luke's children still attended the school.

Dots on my face, he thought. *Kids sure do have active imaginations.* Russell forgot about the encounter and went back to work, tweaking and tightening the central air system to keep it running through the rest of the Indian summer. No one else mentioned anything looking amiss about him, but then again Luke didn't talk to anyone else during the rest of his time at the school. After checking in at the front office that morning and eating lunch with his nine year old son LJ, Russell was left alone with his work for the day.

It wasn't until he returned home that afternoon that little Sophia's mention of the dots on his face returned to Luke Russell's mind. After taking a shower to clean up from a sweaty, dirty day at the school, Luke used his towel to wipe the steam off the bathroom mirror. Once clear, he saw that the girl hadn't been imagining things after all. Red dots, about the size of his pinky nail, were scattered all over his face, neck, and the upper part of his chest.

"What the hell?" Russell asked aloud, touching on the spots with his fingers. "That's so weird." Luke's skin didn't itch, and he otherwise felt fine, but the rash looked horrible. *I wonder if I was allergic to something in the air vents at the school,* he thought, continuing to press on the red dots with confusion and surprise. After a few minutes, Luke decided to take a Benadryl and see if that made it any better.

****

At 5:30pm that afternoon, Cindy Russell arrived home from her job as an office receptionist to find her children playing in the yard with other neighborhood kids and her husband napping on the living room couch. It wasn't an uncommon occurrence, especially since the local government often needed Luke to work night shifts to fix electrical problems without disrupting other municipal activities.

Forty-five minutes later, with dinner finished cooking, Cindy called her children inside and walked into the living room to wake up her husband.

"Dinner's ready, babe," she said, touching him on the shoulder and turning on a lamp next to the couch. "Oh my God – Luke! What happened?"

"Huh? What?" he replied, drowsy from his medicine-induced sleep.

"Your face!" his wife said. "You have a rash all over it."

Luke lifted up his t-shirt and looked down, noting to his own dismay that the strange circular dots had spread down to cover his whole chest and the upper level of his ribcage. "Yeah . . . I dunno. Some little girl at the school noticed it first this afternoon, but I think it's gotten worse since then."

"Does it itch?" Cindy asked, leaning down to get a closer look.

"No, thank goodness. It's weird, right?"

"Very." Cindy continued to stare at her husband with the same look on her face that young Sophia displayed earlier that day. "Have you taken anything for it?"

Luke nodded. "Some Benadryl. That's what made me fall asleep."

"Do you have the rash anywhere else? Does anything else hurt or feel funny?"

"What's going on?" asked Madison, the Russells' eleven year old daughter. She had finished washing up after playing and joined her parents in the living room. "Ewww! Dad! Yuck!"

"What?" LJ said, the little boy running in to see what cool thing was making his sister upset.

"Both of you go into the kitchen," their mother ordered, shooing the two children away from their father. "Go eat your dinner before it gets cold."

"But – "

"Go," Luke said, ending any argument before it began.

After Madison and LJ left the room, Luke finally addressed his wife's question. "I have a pounding headache," he said. "And my joints hurt. It honestly feels like the flu, honey, except for the rash part."

"Hmm . . . well, you stay here and rest. Are you hungry? I'll bring you a plate. We'll check your temperature, and I'll see if I have any flu medicine left over from last year."

TWO

Later that night, with her two children fed and put to bed and her sick husband still sprawled out on the couch drifting in and out of sleep, Cindy Russell began cleaning the kitchen, making school lunches, and taking care of the million other little household tasks that, if she didn't do them, would never be done.

Multi-tasking as always, Cindy also pulled out her iPhone and opened her Facebook app. "HELP!" she typed, "DOES ANYONE KNOW WHAT THIS IS?" She then added a picture of her husband's polka-dotted face and chest. "LUKE ALREADY HAD CHICKENPOX SO I KNOW IT'S NOT THAT," Cindy continued typing. "HE ALSO HAS A FEVER, HEADACHE, AND JOINT PAIN. HAS ANYONE ELSE HAD THIS BEFORE? PLEASE HELP!"

Seven likes and twenty-four comments later, the office receptionist still didn't have any good answers. Her co-worker noted that it was possible to get chickenpox more than once, but Cindy replied that the spots didn't itch. A neighbor whose daughter was a nurse suggested maybe eczema, but Luke's rash didn't match the pictures of eczema that Cindy saw online. Her aunt Louise, writing from her nursing home in Boise, said it reminded her of people she knew as a kid who got Measles. "WE DON'T HAVE MEASLES IN THE US ANYMORE, AUNT LOUISE," the younger woman wrote back incorrectly. "PLUS, LUKE HAD THE MMR VACCINE WHEN HE WAS A KID." Four people liked that comment.

Putting her iPhone down on the kitchen counter, Cindy sighed and looked over at her husband who was lying on the couch, his dinner plate resting untouched on his chest. "You're just going to have to go to the doctor, honey," Mrs. Russell said. The rash had continued to spread from Luke's face to his torso and now was beginning to creep onto his arms and legs. "I'll call them first thing in the morning to make an appointment."

****

    Luke Russell's primary care doctor at Park Nicollet Clinic in their hometown of Shorewood took one look at his rash, vital signs, and blood test results and sent him straight to the hospital. "The fever is interfering with your body's normal operations," Dr. Norris told him. "And the blood tests show some signs of early organ function deterioration. I won't sugar coat it, Luke," he added, looking his childhood friend in the eye. "It doesn't look good at all. I mean it, buddy. Don't pass go; don't collect two hundred dollars. Get to the hospital as soon as you can."

    While Shorewood had no hospital of its own, there were two both within twenty miles of the town. Dr. Norris sent Luke to Ridgeview Medical Center in Waconia, Minnesota, calling ahead to let them know that his patient needed to be admitted and examined as soon as he arrived. Cindy accompanied her husband to the hospital after making arrangements for a neighbor to watch the Russell kids after school.

    As instructed, the team at the 105-bed Ridgeview Medical Center was ready and waiting for their newest patient. Luke and Cindy were escorted past everyone in the Emergency Room and into the treatment area. "If you could just wait here," an orderly told Mrs. Russell, "we'll take him back and get him admitted. Once he has a room, we'll come get you."

    Three hours later, Cindy was finally led back through the hospital and reunited with her husband. An IV drip was hanging beside Luke's bed to help keep him hydrated, and he had bruising around his veins from multiple rounds of drawing blood. Just as his wife sat down beside the hospital bed and took Luke's hand in her own, a doctor walked into the room.

"Oh, no, don't get up, ma'am," the handsome, late-thirty-something man said. "You're fine there were you are." He smiled at the Russells as a form of introduction, and Cindy liked him immediately.

"I'm Dr. Keith Craig," he continued. "I'm an attending physician here at Ridgeview, and Mr. Russell, sir, I'm going to be taking care of you."

A weakened, pale Luke slowly closed and reopened his eyes as acknowledgement.

Walking over to check his patient's monitors, Dr. Craig asked: "Mr. Russell, is it alright if I discuss your condition in front of your wife?"

When Luke nodded yes, the doctor said: "we've taken the test results that your primary care physician sent us and run a number of our own diagnostic inquiries. Unfortunately, we're still coming up empty. While I'm obviously interested in finding out what's causing the rash and the other symptoms, my first concern right now is getting that fever down."

"So what does that mean?" Cindy asked.

"It means we're going to give him some more ibuprofen and try a few more things, including putting some cooling blankets on your husband to try to lower his body temperature. In the meantime, can you tell me of any unusual things Mr. Russell may have eaten or otherwise been exposed to recently?"

Cindy let out a deep breath and shook her head. "No, not that I can think of."

"Does he have any allergies that aren't noted on his file?"

"No."

"Anything else out of the ordinary happen in the last couple of days?"

"The lake," Luke whispered.

"The lake?"

"Oh yeah," his wife said. "He fell in the lake on Saturday while he was fishing. That's not really something weird or anything like that, though."

"This is Lake Minnetonka we're talking about?"

Mrs. Russell nodded her head in the affirmative.

Dr. Craig was inclined to agree with his patient's wife that the unplanned swim wasn't important, but he took note of the incident anyway. "Okay, well I'm going to go order up the medicine and cooling blankets as well as some more tests. Someone will be back to check in soon."

THREE

Over the course of the next several hours, Luke Russell's body was subjected to every kind of test the hospital was able to run. A CBC, or complete blood count, revealed normal white cell counts, telling Luke's doctors that he didn't have a bacterial infection. The red cell count was also in the normal range, as was Luke's platelet count. Dr. Craig was concerned that his patient might have internal bleeding somewhere, but the mean platelet volume and an ultrasound of Mr. Russell's central organs revealed no such problems. Although not part of his usual protocol, Dr. Craig also ran a blood smear to test the number, size, and shape of Luke's blood cells. Leukemia, malaria, and sickle cell disease were all ruled out at that point.

What the hell is wrong with this guy? Keith Craig wondered as he sat in an office shared by the doctors. All of Mr. Russell's symptoms matched a diagnosis of some form of Measles, but he had the MMR vaccine when he was a child and also tested negative for Measles, Mumps, and Rubella. *Plus those aren't this fast-acting or this severe.* Ridgeview Medical's go-to pathologist was stumped by his new patient's symptoms. When the clock struck 2:00am, Keith realized he had been looking at the same paragraph on his computer for the past fifteen minutes. "I've gotta get some rest," he said. The doctor trudged down the quiet hospital corridor to the on-call room and fell face first onto a bunk bed, fast asleep within seconds.

****

The nurse assigned to monitor Luke Russell was at the end of her morning rounds when she reached his room. The patient with the mysterious rash and high fever probably should've been one of her first stops, but nurse Natalie

O'Bryant knew that Mr. Russell's wife spent the night in his room and figured the other woman would've alerted her to any change in his condition that the vital sign monitors didn't catch.

As O'Bryant opened the hospital room door, she noticed that both Mr. and Mrs. Russell were still asleep. *I hate to wake them up*, she thought, *but I can't do anything in the dark.*

Flipping on the light, Natalie looked over toward the patient's wife to apologize for waking her up. What she saw, though, stopped her in her tracks.

Mrs. Russell had lifted her head up from its sleeping position on the hospital bed to reveal a face covered in little red rash marks. The nurse also noted that the dots were spreading down the woman's neck and chest.

Cindy Russell saw the look on the nurse's face and got scared. "What? What is it? I kept checking on him during the night and none of the machine alarms went off."

"No ma'am, that's not it. It's – " O'Bryant started to take a step toward Mrs. Russell, then stopped. "Umm, look in the mirror, ma'am, and you'll see. I'll be right back." The nurse left the room as fast as she could, closing the door behind her and flipping out a red flag near the top of the door frame . . . a signal to the other hospital workers not to enter the room.

"Where's Dr. Craig?" she asked another nurse.

"I don't know. I haven't seen him yet this morning."

"Listen, go to the nurse's station and page him, okay? It's an emergency."

While her co-worker rushed off down the hall, Natalie kept guard at the patient's door and tried to think through what was happening. By the time she heard 'paging Dr. Craig to Room 417, stat' over the hospital intercom, the veteran nurse had a pretty good idea what needed to be done. *One patient with an unknown disease is one thing*, she reasoned. *But two?* The woman shook her head. "They need to be quarantined."

"Who needs to be quarantined?" Keith Craig asked as he hurried down the hall.

"Both of the Russells. Mrs. Russell now has the same rash that he first reported."

"Are you sure?"

Natalie nodded. "I just saw it when I went in to check on Mr. Russell. She's where he was twenty-four hours ago."

Keith reached up to flip out the red 'no entry' flag but saw that it had already been done. "Call over to the isolation ward. Tell them we need two rooms. Also, round up several orderlies to clear the hallways while we transfer the patients." He walked over to a nearby supply cart and grabbed a mask and gloves. "I'm going to see exactly what we're dealing with here."

FOUR

What they were dealing with was two patients rather than one, meaning two rashes, two fevers, two headaches. Mr. Russell's rash now covered his entire body, and Mrs. Russell's appeared to spread farther with each passing minute.

Later that afternoon, when he ran out of ideas, Dr. Craig called over to the Mayo Clinic in Rochester, Minnesota and talked to their chief pathologist. After discussing the Russells' symptoms, the other doctor recommended transferring the patients the hundred or so miles over to the larger, more advanced Mayo Clinic.

"I agree that would probably be best," Dr. Craig replied, "but they're in no condition to go anywhere. Honestly, I've never seen anything like this and I've never seen a patient go downhill this far this fast."

The Mayo expert had critical patients of his own but promised Dr. Craig that he would try to visit Ridgeview the next day – provided Luke and Cindy Russell lived that long.

When he hung up the phone, Keith noted with dismay that Nurse O'Bryant was waiting for him.

"What now?" asked the frustrated physician.

"Their kids are here."

Dr. Craig's heart fell to his stomach and he was afraid to ask what came next. "Please tell me they're just here to visit."

Natalie shook her head with the same look that Keith knew he was probably displaying on his own face. "They've got it too," she said.

"Shit. Get them into isolation as quickly as possible." The doctor closed his eyes and let out a deep breath. "I hate to say it, but now maybe with a little more time and the tests we already ran on their parents, the kids might have a chance of surviving this thing."

****

Word soon got out in tiny Shorewood that all four
members of the Russell family were at the hospital. The next
morning at school, children in Madison and LJ's classes
made them 'Get Well Soon' cards and the teachers planned
to take them over to Ridgeview Medical that afternoon. By
lunchtime, though, the adults at Minnewashta Elementary
School had bigger problems on their minds. It was no longer
just the Russell children who needed well wishes for their
health . . . other kids were starting to get the signature rash
too.

The first ones to display any signs of illness were the
close friends of Madison and LJ and the children who lived
in the Russells' neighborhood. After calling their parents for
notification and permission, a bus full of young students
made the drive from Shorewood to Waconia and Ridgeview
Medical Center.

The small hospital was soon overrun with patients, and
Dr. Craig and his staff got word that children were starting to
show up at other area hospitals as well.

"Park Nicollet-Methodist has kids too," Keith told Nurse
O'Bryant and the other staff members assisting him on the
case. "What the hell is this thing?"

"How are they all tied together?" one of the other
doctors asked. "The Russells were first, but now with more
people sick it has to be something else going around, right?"

"Something in the schools maybe?" Natalie asked. "Mr.
Russell was working in the school on the day he first got
sick, and the kids are all students there."

Dr. Craig nodded. "Yeah, that could be it. They all have
ties to the elementary school, and Lord knows what kind of
bacteria are roaming around there. You know how kids are . .
. like walking germs. You get one sick kid at an elementary

school and the whole place turns into a petri dish of all things disgusting."

By this point, the specialist from the Mayo Clinic had arrived and joined the conversation. "I have contacts at Poison Control and the state's Emergency Response office. I can have a hazmat team there within the hour."

"I don't really know if a hazmat team is necessary . . . "

"You've blocked off an entire floor of your hospital to treat patients with a disease that is very serious and looking like it will be deadly – I don't know how much longer Mr. Russell can hang on. If it's the school, then you need to get a team in there and clean it out as soon as possible. And close the building until you do."

****

Even though many thought it was a severe, 'unnecessary' measure, school and government officials in the area agreed with the expert pathologist's recommendation to have Minnewashta Elementary closed on Friday and swept for any contaminants. Water experts were also sent out to Lake Minnetonka to check for pollutants there, since Mr. Russell fell in the lake the Saturday before he got sick. Parents were alerted to the potential danger and reason for the school closures and told to keep an eye on their children for any signs of the tell-tale rash.

One parent in the area, Pamelyn Ferrente, thought the whole thing was overblown and was frustrated by the fact that she had to miss a day of work to stay home with her son. Walking past his bedroom the next morning, Pamelyn peeked in to check on the third-grader as he was getting dressed to take advantage of the lack of school and go outside to play with friends.

Mrs. Ferrente didn't want to believe what she saw on her son, and blinked her eyes a few times to try to adjust her vision. Despite her efforts, the rash on Finn's neck and shoulders remained.

"Finn, honey, come here for a second."

The boy with curly, shaggy blonde hair pulled a t-shirt over his head and attempted to walk past his mom to play with friends.

"Mom, what? They're waiting for me!"

"It'll just take a minute. Let me look at you." She reached down and pulled the collar of his shirt away from his neck. "How long have you had this rash?"

"What rash?"

Pamelyn sighed and rolled her eyes. "The rash on your neck and chest." She took her son by the arm and led him to the half bath in the hallway. Mrs. Ferrente then stood behind Finn as they both faced the mirror. "See?" she asked, pointing out the spots covering the lower half of the boy's neck and top portion of his chest.

Finn's eyes grew wide and he reached his hand up to touch the red skin.

"No no, don't touch it," his mother corrected. "We don't want to spread it." Pamelyn paused as she took a closer look at the rash, still refusing to believe that her son could have the mysterious virus that had struck so many in his school. "Have you eaten anything weird lately?"

"No."

"Played with any strange stuff in the woods? You know what poison ivy is right?"

"Mom, I'm eight. Of course I know what poison ivy is."

"Of course, okay." She paused. "Listen, Finn, you can't go play with friends today."

"But Mom!"

Tears began to fill Mrs. Ferrente's eyes. "We have to go to the hospital. You're sick."

FIVE

Luke Russell died at 6:00pm on Friday night, four days after his symptoms first arrived and three days after being admitted to the hospital. Although he knew it wouldn't help their mental outlook, Dr. Craig broke the news to Luke's wife and children shortly after he passed away. Mrs. Russell cried, as did LJ, but it was the reaction of eleven year old Madison that Keith knew would haunt him for weeks. The little girl didn't cry, or sob, or make any noise of any sort. Instead, she closed her eyes and took a deep breath, and when she opened her eyes again they were glazed over. *She knows*, Dr. Craig had thought. *She knows it will be her turn soon.*

Later that night, after checking in again on the three remaining Russells and the rest of his mystery disease patients, Dr. Craig was looking as tired as he felt when he slumped down in a chair in the hospital cafeteria with a tray full of day-old salad and pizza. Keith hadn't stopped running around since he was paged to Luke Russell's room early Wednesday morning.

Transferring Mr. and Mrs. Russell to the isolation ward. Countless tests of blood levels and organ function and potential toxins – all of which came back negative. Even the far more accomplished doctors from the Mayo Clinic who he called for help didn't have any answers, only more questions. Then more patients started to arrive, and the problem snowballed. At the Mayo expert's suggestion, Dr. Craig and his team ran biopsies of every organ showing signs of stress, a full body scan, an EEG, an EKG, and eventually a lumbar puncture. Those were in addition to the MRI, CAT scan, and stool and urine tests that Keith performed on his own. Prior to his death, Luke Russell had been poked and prodded like a piece of cattle . . . to no avail.

None of the other patients offered any clues either. A rash followed by a fever and then an increasingly worse rash, joint aches, and other flu symptoms. Febrile seizures started to occur with more frequency, since the patients' bodies couldn't handle spending that long at that high of a temperature. Organ failure also set in for the early patients, and Dr. Craig reached the never-easy conclusion that, barring a miracle, all four of the Russells weren't going to make it. What continued to gnaw at him while he ate dinner, though, was the fact that the other patients were next.

"Cindy is twenty-four hours behind Luke. Madison and LJ aren't far behind their mom," Keith had told his team of interns earlier that day. "And the kids coming in are another twenty-four hours behind them. What we have to figure out is why."

Craig was so lost in his thoughts that he didn't notice when Dr. Massri, a friend and surgeon, sat down at the table with him.

"Earth to Keith," the other man said, waving his hand in front of Dr. Craig's face.

"Huh? Oh, sorry. Hi."

"Tough case?"

Keith nodded. "Very tough."

"I heard you've shut down the whole top floor with that family of isolation patients."

"More than just a family."

"What?"

"We've got a wave of kids coming in with it now. But yeah . . . that's the case." Dr. Craig let out a deep breath and pushed his food away from him. "I lost the first patient earlier tonight. I'm going to lose the rest of the family and at this rate half the kids from the elementary school too. And I don't have a damn clue what's causing it or how to fix it."

"Anything I can do to help?"

Keith shook his head. "I wish you could, but no. We've got people from the Mayo Clinic roaming around, and I sent blood and tissue samples down to the Centers for Disease Control to ask if they have any idea what it is. Haven't heard back yet, though."

"The CDC, huh? Wow."

Dr. Craig could see the concern on his friend's face, both for the patients and the strain the case was placing on his fellow doctor.

"Well, make sure you get some sleep, and eat more than that cardboard pizza, alright?" Massri said. "Especially until you get that rash cleared up."

"What rash?"

"There . . . on your face," the surgeon said, pointing to Keith's right cheek. "It looks like that time we went hiking and you accidently brushed up against the wrong plant."

Dr. Craig picked up his spoon and held it out as a makeshift mirror. Keith's eyes grew big and he switched the spoon to look at his other cheek, noting with horror that the red dots were on both sides of his face.

"Fuck."

He sat still for a minute, shock preventing his brain from kicking into gear.

"What?"

Dr. Massri's words snapped Keith out of his haze.

"I . . . I . . . fuck."

Craig pushed back his chair, stood up, and left the cafeteria as fast as his legs would carry him, without ever answering his friend's question.

It's airborne, he concluded as he made his way back to the isolation area. *Holy shit – it's airborne.*

****

At the same time that Dr. Craig was admitting and locking himself in the isolation ward – along with any other hospital staff who had come into contact with the

'Shorewood flu' patients – word of the outbreak was starting to spread around the medical community. Doctors at the Centers for Disease Control in Atlanta were among those working on the case late that Friday night. "Have we gotten the larger set of samples yet?" asked Dr. David Malhotra. Dr. Malhotra was in charge of the Division of High-Consequence Pathogens and Pathology at the CDC and, as such, had made a career out of studying infectious diseases.

"Not yet," one of his assistants replied. "I think the plane carrying them is supposed to land in about thirty minutes."

"Good," David nodded. Dr. Craig sent his first round of patient files down to Atlanta on Wednesday, but, now that there were more patients, the CDC wanted a broader range of test samples to work with. "In the meantime, what do we have for the big board?" While working on a previous task force, Dr. Malhotra had picked up the habit of listing common symptoms or other important facts on a whiteboard in the main lab or conference room.

"All patients first present with a rash," the same lab assistant said, writing 'rash' on the board as he spoke. "It starts off on their face and torso area before eventually spreading out to cover the extremities as well."

"Do we have a picture?" asked Dr. Sayers, the group's second-in-command.

Josh Lapinski, the most junior department member and the one with case briefing duties, nodded his head before opening his laptop and displaying photos on an adjacent wall. "Everything that could be sent electronically was emailed over this morning. So these are the patient files we have so far."

"When will the rest get here?"

"Pardon?"

"You said this is what we have so far," Sayers said. "When do we get the rest?"

"I'm told there are dozens of new patients showing up every hour. I don't know if it's going to be feasible to obtain every patient file."

"We'll get them eventually," David assured his team. "Let's focus on what we do have now though. Patient Zero – who is he?"

Dr. Lapinski hunched over his computer for a few seconds before standing back up and looking at a picture of a red and white polka dotted man on the wall. "This is Luke Russell," the doctor said. "He's forty-two years old and works as an electrician in Shorewood, Minnesota."

"Where is that?" asked Dr. Malhotra.

"Umm . . . " Josh said, looking down at his computer screen, "it's somewhere near Minneapolis I think. The file says he was fishing on Lake Minnetonka and somehow fell in, and then three days later he started showing symptoms."

"Write that on the board," Dr. Malhotra said. "Three day incubation period. Aside from the rash," he asked, "what other symptoms?"

"Fever. Headache. Joint pain. General flu symptoms it looks like. There's a note that says it presents like a hyper-aggressive form of Rubella."

"And Mr. Russell's status now?"

"He's dead. Died earlier tonight . . . four days after his rash first appeared."

"Shit."

Dr. Sayers had a mouth like a sailor, but this time his words echoed the thoughts of everyone in the room.

"Has anyone survived so far?" David asked. "Survived to recover, I mean?"

"No sir. I spoke with the lead doctor on the case and he said Patient Zero's wife isn't expected to live through tomorrow.

Malhotra nodded his head to acknowledge that he heard the answer but said nothing else for several minutes. Instead, the distinguished doctor sat still in his chair, staring at the table in front of him and slowly twirling a pen in his hand. After what seemed like an eternity, he looked up and spoke. "Approximately how many are sick?"

"Eighty-five and growing by the minute," Dr. Lapinski answered.

"And how long since the first patient showed up?"

"Luke Russell died today, so four days. Six, almost seven, days since he fell in the lake, if that is indeed the triggering event."

"And it's airborne?" David Malhotra questioned. "That's been confirmed?"

Lapinski nodded his head. "Yes. That's the only way it could be spreading . . . unless there were some other untraceable contaminant in the soil or water."

Dr. Malhotra shook his head. "The illness wouldn't be mushrooming out like this if it were a public contaminant. News reports and other files I've seen say people aren't getting sick unless and until they've come into contact with another sick person."

"That's correct," Josh said.

The CDC's lead pathologist grew quiet again, but only for a brief period this time. He then stood up and started walking toward the office door. "If you'll excuse me," he said, "I need to go speak with the Director."

"Hold on a sec, David," Dr. Sayers said. "Let me walk with you."

The two men left their wing of the CDC's headquarters and headed in the direction of the Director's office on the other side of the complex. Since Dr. Malhotra and his team often dealt with contagious or otherwise frightening illnesses, their research lab was located on the end of the facility away from where any potential dignitaries or financial donors might visit.

Dr. Sayers put his hands in his lab coat pockets and shuffled his feet as they walked.

"When word gets out about this," Malhotra said, "it's going to be an absolute nightmare."

"You gonna leave?" Sayers asked.

"Leave where?"

"The country."

Dr. Malhotra stopped walking. "I hadn't thought about it." He paused, considering the idea. "No. I'll send my wife and daughter overseas. But I think we'll be safe here. Load up on food andand hunker down. Besides, somebody has to stay and work on this."

The other physician shook his head. "I'm just picturing the opening scene from 'The Walking Dead' with everybody trying to flee. It's going to paralyze the cities."

"Kinda like the Snowjam in Atlanta from a couple of years ago. Remember that?"

Dr. Sayers laughed and shook his head. "Oh man, yeah. Two inches of snow and it took me fourteen hours to drive thirty miles home."

David turned to his colleague, his expression serious. "If you are going to leave, go now."

"You really think it'll come to that? Surely they're not going to just close the borders and write off three hundred million people."

"To save the remaining seven billion? Sure they will."

SIX

Dr. Malhotra knew that the Director of the Centers for Disease Control was as much of a workaholic as he was and would thus be at the office late on a Friday night. After explaining the situation and sharing some of the most pertinent patient details, the Director soon agreed with his top doctor's assessment of the situation. What came next, though, was a call they were both nervous to make.

The phone at the office of the Health and Human Services Secretary rang unanswered. After two more attempts, Dr. Malhotra and his boss decided that they were in enough of an emergency to call the secretary on her cell phone.

"I'm having dinner with my grandchildren so this better be important," the Cabinet member said as a way of answering her phone.

"Yes, Madam Secretary, it's very important," the CDC Director assured her. "I have Dr. David Malhotra here with me . . . he runs our infectious disease unit."

"I know Dr. Malhotra," said the HHS leader. "What's going on, gentlemen?"

"We have a highly contagious, deadly, airborne disease outbreak in a town just outside of Minneapolis," David said, not wasting any time. "We've also received reports of patients starting to show up at hospitals in Minneapolis proper and other surrounding suburbs."

"It's spreading like wildfire, ma'am," the Director added.

"Has anyone died?"

"One person so far," David said. "But there are three more people in the final stages and currently no known way to treat the illness."

"So what you're telling me is that, as of now, everyone who gets this disease is going to die?" The shock in the secretary's voice was palpable even over the phone.

"Yes ma'am. Unfortunately. The high fever exacerbates other organ failure problems to the point where the patient's body can't function anymore and completely shuts down."

After taking a deep breath, the woman asked: "what do you need from me?"

The CDC Director and Dr. Malhotra paused, looking back and forth at each other, not wanting to be the one to have to make the suggestion. Finally, the Director bit the bullet.

"We need to alert the Canadian authorities about it, since Minnesota is a border state," he began. "And it is our recommendation to close that portion of the border so whatever this is doesn't go international."

"Do you really think it's that serious?" Although herself a former cardiologist, the HHS Secretary was now a politician and concerned with how a border closure would reflect on her department.

"We do," confirmed the Director.

"Ma'am, this is Dr. Malhotra. I've been doing this for three decades and I've never seen anything spread this far this quickly."

After a moment of silent thought, the two men's boss said: "okay. I'll alert Canada and the World Health Organization – that definitely needs to happen – and I'll recommend the border closure. That's not my call, though."

"Thank you. And one more thing, Madam Secretary."

"What?"

"We also recommend an advisory for both domestic and international travel to Minneapolis."

"Do you have any idea how much damage that would do to the economy?"

"This thing is a killing machine, ma'am," Dr. Malhotra warned. "It's like the Pac Man of diseases. And it's just going to keep killing and killing and killing until it runs out of people to infect."

"I think that's a bit of an exaggeration," the HHS Secretary replied.

"With all due respect, ma'am, this is what I do every day. Infectious diseases. This is what I know. And this thing coming out of Minnesota . . . " he paused. "It shows every indication of being a pandemic unlike anything we've seen since the Spanish Flu – or maybe even the Bubonic Plague."

****

Although it took some persuading, including more than a few shared graphic photos of patients in their final stages of decline, America's leaders in Washington finally agreed to both the border closure and the travel warning. Once Canadian authorities heard the news, they were more than eager to cooperate in keeping Americans out of their country. It took all of Saturday to get everything arranged, but the new development also meant that, less than a week after the first patient showed up sick, the Shorewood Disease was now an international matter.

Across the pond from the United States, British Prime Minister Lucy Rodgers was receiving her Sunday morning news briefing. A potential labor strike in Northern Ireland, an upcoming vote on National Health Service benefits, and a rainstorm walloping the Scottish region of Fife had highlighted the list.

"Anything else?" the prime minister asked, her posh voice betraying the sixty-four year old's aristocratic upbringing. Often mocked in cartoons for her button-upped personal style, the five-foot-five Lucy wore her light brown hair in a coiffed bob, hid her honey-colored eyes behind rimless glasses, and favored skirt suits with low heels, tweeds, and other understated fabrics to the brighter outfits worn by female politicians in America.

"Yes ma'am, one more thing," said her top aide, the Downing Street Chief of Staff. "Although it's really only a curiosity at this point. Reports came in overnight that there is some new, unknown disease outbreak in the United States in a small town in I believe Michigan."

"Minnesota," another aide corrected.

"Right, yes. Minnesota."

"What kind of disease?" Rodgers asked. "How big is the outbreak?" A biology and pre-med student during her time at the University of Cambridge, the prime minister still had a strong interest in the field and displayed more enthusiasm for medical-related topics than many of the others that crossed her desk on a daily basis.

"It's a sort of flu, it seems. But with a rash that covers the patient's whole body. And it kills within four days of the first symptoms."

"Four days?"

"Yes ma'am. The Americans said it's highly contagious. We're hearing about it now because they've decided to close that portion of the Canadian border closest to the outbreak center."

"Is it really that bad?" Lucy couldn't quite wrap her head around the idea of anything requiring such a drastic measure.

The chief of staff nodded. "I'm afraid so. The Centers for Disease Control also issued a travel warning telling people to stay away from Minnesota."

Rodgers raised her eyebrows in surprise and then took another sip of the coffee sitting on her desk. "Well then, let's all hope they can get it under control soon."

Her staff knew that was their signal to leave. Like many women, the Prime Minister communicated as much with tone and body language as she did with her actual words.

"Yes ma'am. Let us know if you need anything."

****

Even though it was a Sunday, the work of the prime minister was never-ending. Staff meetings, phone calls, reports to review, speeches to write. Lucy often longed for the days before email and cell phones, since back then there was at least a way to take some time for oneself. *But not now*, she thought after escorting the attendees of her lunch meeting to the exit. *We're always on call now.*

And here we go again, Rodgers continued, walking back into her office. Given the news from that morning, she decided she needed to call her American counterpart, President Matthew Bates. Lucy knew that the US president was even more busy than usual, but she also wanted to get a more detailed update on the Minnesota outbreak and to pledge her country's solidarity and support.

The prime minister's phone's buzzer went off and her assistant's voice came through the line: "President Bates, ma'am."

Rodgers picked up the receiver next to her. "Matthew," she said, continuing the friendly relationship that the two allies had developed over the years. "What on earth is happening in Minnesota?"

The American president sighed loudly into the phone. "We don't know. I wish we did. But it's nasty, whatever it is. Every time I get an update, the number of victims is higher. We've got that section of the border closed and the CDC involved, and now we just have to let the doctors do their work and hope for the best."

Lucy shook her head in disbelief. "It sounds awful. My staff told me this morning . . . highly contagious, airborne, and almost always deadly?"

"Always deadly," he corrected. "There haven't been any survivors so far."

That new piece of information shocked the prime minister. No one? she thought. *This is even worse than I expected.* "Is there anything I can do to help? Perhaps my health secretary – "

"No, there's nothing," said President Bates, cutting her off. "Thank you, really. But no. Not right now anyway."

"You'll let me know if there's any change where that is concerned?"

"Of course."

What that, the two heads of government hung up the phone and returned to their busy Sundays, each hoping the doctors in Minnesota and at the CDC could get the situation under control.

SEVEN

The only thing that spread faster than the Shorewood Disease was news about it. Social media and the twenty-four hour news cycle meant that images and stories of sick patients soon flooded America's national consciousness. And even though they tried to prevent it, Minneapolis-St. Paul turned into the place to be for all enterprising reporters.

One such journalist, a correspondent for a major cable news network, stationed himself outside of Ridgeview Medical Center for his Sunday evening broadcast.

"Good evening," the man began, "I'm Tony Britsch, once again reporting live from outside the hospital that is treating the majority of people first infected by this unknown illness. I can tell you that the patients continue to stream into the emergency room, and I've been able to speak to a few of their family members . . . "

The news broadcast then cut to pre-recorded video of the reporter standing next to an aging man who looked like he hadn't slept in days. The banner along the bottom of the screen read 'Larry Stirrings – grandfather of patient.'

"Tell me, Mr. Stirrings," the reporter said, "how long has your granddaughter been sick?"

"It's both my grandkids," the man corrected. "They've been sick for three days now. My daughter and her husband were taking care of them at home, thinking it was just a bad batch of chickenpox or something, but then they got the notice from the school about some virus going around. And now my daughter and husband are starting to show signs of it too." He ran his hands through what remained of his hair. "The doctors say they don't know what's causing it or how to fix it. I don't know what we're going to do."

"I've heard some reports that the hospital staff who are treating patients are also starting to get sick themselves. Do you know anything about that? How do the doctors and nurses look to you?"

Larry Stirrings shook his head. "No, I don't know anything about that. I can't really focus on anything beyond my family, you know?"

The reporter nodded and gave the same look of feigned caring that newscasters were famous for worldwide. "Of course. Thank you for your time."

With the interview over, the TV screen focused back live on the reporter. "As you can see, things are very tense here in the western suburbs of Minneapolis."

"Tony," the anchor asked, "have you seen any patients leaving the hospital or heard any stories of recovery?"

The reporter shook his head side to side. "Sadly, no. In fact, the only people leaving the hospital appear to be family members of those patients who died."

"Wow. Okay, well thank you. That was Tony Britsch," the anchor added, "reporting for us live from Waconia, Minnesota."

****

As week two of the viral outbreak began, areas in the greater Midwest and beyond started to feel the effects of the disease. People who were visiting Minneapolis before the travel advisory were unknowingly infected, and they then turned around and took the disease back home with them. There was also an enormous ripple effect in the medical field because hospitals were so full with virus patients that they didn't have room for anyone else.

The infectious disease team at the CDC was discussing that one morning while running tests at their lab in Atlanta.

"Think for a minute about how busy hospitals always are," said Dr. Sayers. "Car wrecks and heart attacks and babies being born, not to mention elective surgeries and kids breaking their arms and Mr. Fix-Its needing stitches for whatever home improvement project went wrong this time. Now think about this: there's no room for those people anymore. So many patients have this weird rash virus that hospitals don't have beds for anybody else. Plus, the doctors and nurses are all getting the virus too, so even if there were room for the regular hospital patients, there's nobody healthy enough to treat them."

"So what are they doing?" one of the younger doctors asked.

"At first they were trying to bring in help from other cities and towns, but people are refusing to go now. So you've got patients dropping like flies with this virus, hospitals are either full or have no doctors, and Joe Schmo who could've survived his heart attack dying because he can't get treated. It's one big, giant clusterfuck of death."

"I think we can do without the language, Dr. Sayers."

David Malhotra's voice carried from the far end of the lab where he was working. Although he was no saint, Dr. Malhotra approached his job with an enormous amount of respect and decorum and knew all too well what could happen when people like him lost sight of the power inherent in their research and knowledge.

"Sorry," Dr. Sayers called out. Then, with a whisper and a smile, added to those around him: "I didn't think he could hear me."

The other doctors giggled and dispersed back to their respective lab stations, but their boss again got the last word.

"I hear everything, Sayers."

I just don't know everything, Dr. Malhotra thought, returning his focus to the microscope in front of him. *This thing makes no sense. Early reports were right . . . it does present like Rubella. But Rubella on steroids. And all of these people were vaccinated against it, so even that makes no sense.* The physician released a frustrated sigh. *I don't have a clue how we're going to stop this thing from taking over the whole country.*

EIGHT

Dr. Malhotra's words were more prophetic than he knew. By the end of week two, nearly all of the Midwest was under the grasp of the killer disease, and large areas of infection were starting to show up in other places around the country. Canada extended the border closing to include nearly the entire middle third of the United States – not an easy task given the amount of land connecting the two countries – and other nations starting either cancelling flights from the United States or quarantining passengers after they arrived. Mexico also announced it was considering closing its border after tens of thousands of people in the southern US decided to try to outrun the virus.

In Minneapolis and the surrounding cities and states, the disease wasn't the only problem people had to face. Even with all of the technological advances and America's status as one of the most developed nations in the world, it turned out that good, old-fashioned humans were still needed to run things. The patients dying in hospitals and homes and street corners weren't just mothers and fathers, daughters and sons. They were also doctors, and electrical engineers, and farmers, and delivery truck drivers. When all of those people died, there was no one left to replace them.

The first things people noticed – those who weren't sick, that is – was the dwindling supply of food and gas. Next came the power grid.

Modern electricity in the United States, a thing most people only thought about when the monthly bill arrived or the power went out, was comprised of a complicated and aging network of power stations, lines, and transformers that demanded around-the-clock human attention. Anywhere from twenty-five to fifty people were required to keep a single power plant running, and at the time the Shorewood outbreak began, many plants in the United States were already running on minimum manpower capacity in order to save money.

"Even without the deaths, the region would still be in a crisis because of the catastrophic levels of electricity loss."

Prime Minister Rodgers listened as one of Great Britain's leading public utilities experts gave a televised interview. "It sounds very elitist and very 'first world problems' of me," he continued, "but it's true. Fully developed, post-industrialized nations like the United States and Great Britain aren't designed to survive long without things like basic power. Areas of sub-Saharan Africa, Latin America, and Southeast Asia? Certainly. But not the United States."

The utilities expert's words didn't go unnoticed, and it wasn't the first time Lucy Rodgers and her fellow world leaders were alerted to the danger of power plant outages. A few years earlier in California, a group of criminals staged an attack on an electrical substation. After first cutting telephone cables, the group of snipers then opened fire on seventeen giant transformers that serviced the Palo Alto area. But that event of direct sabotage, combined with blackouts like the one that struck the East Coast of the US in 2003, were nothing compared to the outages then sweeping the United States.

"With even two or three crew members out," the British expert said, "a great number of power plants in the United States would not be able to operate for long. But with this kind of human capital loss?" The gray-haired man with a matching handlebar mustache shook his head. "Electricity is only a fond memory now in much of the American Midwest. Thank God it's September and not January," he added. "Because all of those people without power also don't have heat or air conditioning.

Questions of infrastructure and supplies also extended into areas beyond electricity. *How does one survive when the entire supply chain disappears?* was the question running through everyone's minds.

Electronic payment systems were mostly automated, but there were no attendants left to sell things. No managers to unlock the store doors or turn on the computer that otherwise ran the show during the day. *How does a first world economy run if no one is present to press the 'on' switch?*

In fairly short order, though, the way things usually functioned didn't matter anymore. Looting spread almost as quickly as the disease, and people started taking whatever they needed.

"Gotta do what you gotta do to survive," a woman in Cleveland told a reporter one day. "Ain't much food left anyway since no truck drivers wanna come here. If it's there, an' I need it, I take it. Street rules out here, girl." The woman then turned and entered a grocery store, intent on loading a shopping cart full of anything that she could find.

"And there you have it," the reporter told the video camera. "Street rules here in Cleveland."

The next morning, that same reporter woke up with a rash, and ninety-six hours later she was dead.

NINE

In the vast open space south of Odessa, Texas, where land was measured in sections and one could drive for hours without ever seeing another living soul, human or bovine, residents of a tiny town called Shining Light watched in horror as the world crumbled around them. Shining Light, population six hundred, was inhabited exclusively by members of the Shining Light Church. Just as many industries used to build 'company towns,' Shining Light was a 'church town' – complete with a town council that doubled as the board of deacons and a church-run private school educating all of the children. Founded to serve as 'a shining light for God in this dark, fallen world,' the town supported itself mainly with revenues from crop sales and oil reserves. Residents of the sleepy village knew that their form of local government likely violated the First Amendment's Establishment Clause, but they also knew that Shining Light was small enough and inclusive enough that anyone who might be tempted to file a complaint didn't think it was worth the bother.

To the people who lived there, Shining Light was like something out of a Norman Rockwell painting. As if the best parts of 1950s Americana were frozen in time: bustling main streets, friendly neighbors, and an appreciation for the qualitative goods of life over the quantitative ones. The cars were newer models, of course, and technology was no stranger to homes and businesses. But the place was definitely . . . something. Different. People in nearby cities – 'nearby' being a Texas term meaning 'within a two hour drive' – thought Shining Light was a cult town full of weirdos, but the six hundred residents heartily disagreed.

They also didn't quite deserve the 'weirdo' label, and weren't of the fundamentalist, prairie-dress, Warren Jeffs variety of religious communities. Rather, Shining Light was doctrinally in line with many other non-denominational Protestant churches in the United States . . . the only differences being its desire to actively mix religion and government and the strong libertarian streak that ran through the members' views on state and federal politics.

One town resident particularly troubled by the disease outbreak was the sheriff, Josiah Jones. Although Shining Light was a peaceful place with a low crime rate, Sheriff Jones was worried about the potential for looting, rioting, and other kinds of violence that he was reading about in the newspapers.

At only forty-one years old, Josiah Jones was the youngest sheriff in Shining Light history. But the thin, six-foot tall man with light brown hair and matching eyes was very well-respected in the community. Married for nineteen years to his high school sweetheart, Josiah and Mary had two teenage sons, Daniel and Isaac. But unlike his wife and most other residents of Shining Light, Sheriff Jones wasn't born there – he and his family were originally from the suburbs of Madison, Wisconsin. Always a very religious family, attending church every Wednesday and Sunday and declining some modern medical treatments, including vaccines, on religious grounds, the Jones were also fervently patriotic and believed that while America's culture and respect for traditional family values were in decline, the 1970s in the US were still better than the 1970s anywhere else. But when Josiah's mom was diagnosed with a severe form of Raynaud's Disease – a condition that caused some areas of her body to feel numb and cold in response to low temperatures or stress – the Jones family was advised to look for a place to live in a warmer climate. An assistant pastor at their church recommended they visit Shining Light, Texas. "It's as close to perfect as you'll find in the United States," the pastor had said. "Everyone is a Christian, and the town's government is run by God-fearing men. Plus it's so small and remote that nobody really cares if things are more religious than those Washington politicians and judges say they should be." The man had smiled wistfully. "I loved it there. My wife missed her family up here . . . that's the only reason we left."

So Mr. and Mrs. Jones, three year old Josiah, and his infant sister Ruth packed up their Studebaker Wagonaire and made the move from the metropolis of Madison to Shining Light, population four hundred fifty. Even though his parents originally thought the 'hick town' seemed more like a revival of *The Andy Griffith Show* than it did a legitimate place to live, the Jones family soon adjusted to the change of pace. Josiah's father landed a sales job at the local furniture store, his mom's Raynaud's calmed down in the warmer climate, and the two children were quickly enveloped into the fold as part of the Shining Light community.

A community that was now looking to Sheriff Jones for guidance on how to handle the pandemic headed straight for them. In consultation with the mayor and other town elders, Josiah sent out an email to the residents of Shining Light urging them to heed all travel warnings, make sure they stored up plenty of water and non-perishable food items, and, above all else, to try to remain calm.

That's like tellin' a baby to try not to cry, the sheriff thought after he pressed 'send' on the email. *Of course they're gonna panic. How's that sayin' go? If you can keep your wits when everyone around you is losin' theirs, then you don't understand the problem?* Josiah sighed and shook his head. *God help us all.*

****

Later that afternoon, after finishing his patrol of town, Josiah returned home to the ranch he shared with his wife and two sons. Mary was waiting for him when he arrived.

"Wanna ride with me up to Crane?" she asked, referencing a place north of Shining Light. Even though

Crane, an oil boom town, only had around 3,000 residents, it seemed like a big city compared to where the Jones lived.

"Crane? Why? Honey, I just got home."

"I know," Mary replied, "but I really think we need to buy some more food and water and fill up some gas cans before supplies really start runnin' low."

Josiah slumped down on the couch in the living room, stretched his arms over his head, and yawned. "Give me like ten minutes and then we can go."

Once on the road, a few minutes away from their house, Mary turned in the passenger seat to face her husband. "Why are we stayin'?" she asked.

"What do you mean?" Josiah replied, not taking his eyes off the road.

"Why don't we leave? I know we can't afford to fly to any of the faraway places that I've heard about some people goin' to, but we can definitely pack up the boys and drive to Mexico."

"Mexico shut its border."

"What? When?"

"Yesterday," said Sheriff Jones. Glancing over at his wife, Josiah softened his tone. "Look, honey, I know you're worried about this. I am too. But the virus hasn't reached Texas yet, and they're sayin' you can only get it if you come into contact with someone who is sick."

"Nuh uh," Mary responded, shaking her head. "It's airborne."

"Right, but it's airborne within a certain distance. It's not like it's rainin' down on us from the sky. I'm tellin' you . . . if we hole up out on the ranch and stay away from anybody else, I really think we've got a good shot at beatin' this thing."

Mrs. Jones let out a deep breath and rocked her head side to side, a sign that she didn't agree with her husband but either didn't want to fight about it or didn't think she had any good arguments on her side. "I hope you're right. And I guess if they closed the border we don't really have any other choice but to stay. And pray."

TEN

Much like the residents of Shining Light, business leaders from across the country were also scrambling to figure out their response to the disease outbreak. Stores and factories in and around the outbreak area in Minnesota quickly shut down, and the ripple effect spread across the region and the country. The disaster response and business continuity plans that corporations put in place for audit purposes were tested fully and, in many instances, for the first time.

Robert Paige, CEO of Martok Industries, was one such corporate leader dealing with the secondary consequences of the disease outbreak. Although his medical supply company was headquartered in Phoenix, one of its biggest warehouses and distribution centers was located just outside of Minneapolis in the suburb of Roseville.

Sitting in a small, rarely-used room at Martok's headquarters, the fifty-three year old Paige was joined in the company meeting by eleven other people – seven in person and another four on the phone. Each one was a required attendee in the Emergency Action Center, a leadership team established in Martok's written Order Fulfillment Service Disruption Contingency Standard Operating Procedures.

"Can we please call it something else?" the Vice President of Human Resources said before the meeting started. "That is way too long of a name."

Robert Paige nodded his head. "From here on out, for this group, it's just 'the Response Plan'. How's that sound?"

"Perfect."

Although the renamed Response Plan had been in place for as long as the CEO had been with the company, Paige wasn't aware of any other times when it was implemented. *And I would've known*, he thought, *since the plan says we have to keep this room staffed around-the-clock until the emergency situation is resolved.*

Looking over at his Vice President of Operations, Robert said: "Okay, Pete, how do we get this show started?"

"Well, it's laid out pretty clearly for us in the Response Plan. We have all of our plants operating on a centralized mainframe computer system, so we've already been sharing data between different warehouses and distribution centers. The problem there is that the mainframe isn't functioning properly because of the power outages, so all of our production is delayed. But, given that starting point, each one of you should be able to see the different incident levels listed on the sheets in front of you. For the people on the phone, this is page four of the Response Plan." He paused to give everyone time to find the appropriate chart. "Each incident level has a different response based on the seriousness of the event . . . meaning what percentage of capability has been lost and for how long. It's then my job as the VP of Ops to declare which incident level we have and you guys on the Leadership Team have to approve my recommendation."

"So where are we, Pete?" his boss asked.

"It may seem a bit extreme, but since we've lost all functional capacity up at the Roseville site, I'd put us at a solid Category Four."

The people in the room and on the phone simultaneously flipped to the next page in their packets to read what was supposed to happen in the event of a Category Four emergency. For a 'minimum manpower scenario' like the one they found themselves in, the Response Plan recommended shifting work to other facilities, hiring temporary workers if possible, and instructing non-manual personnel to work remotely.

"Well we can't hire any temps," the head of HR asserted. "So shifting the work elsewhere is really the only option I see."

"Agreed," said Mr. Paige, the CEO. "And I hope you all brought your sleeping bags, because this room has to stay staffed twenty-four hours a day until we're back up to normal operating capacity. That includes you guys on the phone . . . just because you're not in Arizona doesn't mean you can't dial in."

"Provided we still have power," one man said.

"Wait, we can't leave?" asked another.

"Not all at once, we can't," Robert Paige replied. "We'll work in shifts, just like the Response Plan recommends. But we need at least two people here at all times."

Groans were heard around the room, and many members of the Leadership Team took out their cell phones to let their families know they wouldn't be home for the foreseeable future.

****

Three days later, eight pairs of dreary eyes surveyed the Emergency Action Center, all wanting the question to be asked but not wanting to be the one to ask it. Finally, with a dramatic sigh, Robert Paige put his hands down on the table and stood up.

"I guess this is my call to make," he said, "since the Response Plan says that this group is in charge of the disaster recovery but that in the event of disagreement I have to break the tie." Taking a deep breath, he added: "shut it down. Go home. Our suppliers can't meet their obligations and, even if they could, we can't meet ours. We'll deal with the fallout when this is all over, but in the meantime . . . go home. Stay safe. Us sitting here in this room isn't going to change anything."

"That's it?" the VP of Operations asked. "Shut it all down?"

Paige nodded. "Shut it all down."

With the decision made, there were no words of dissent as the Leadership Team packed up their computers and cell phones and sent texts to their spouses saying they were headed home. Like an ever-growing number of companies in the United States, Martok Industries was closed for business.

ELEVEN

Just as Martok Industries was closing down its operations in the United States, the British Broadcasting Company's daily talk show panel was in full swing. The topic of conversation, of course, was the disease outbreak in the United States.

"It's absolute mayhem in America," one of the former Whitehall advisors said, gesturing wildly with his hands. "People have stopped going to hospitals because they're either full or all of its doctors and nurses are dead. Not to mention that no one in the hardest hit regions have had any petrol delivered in weeks, so their cars wouldn't work anyway."

"What about electric cars?" another panel member asked.

"Won't help," the first speaker replied. "Power plants aren't operating either . . . all of those workers are sick, dying, or dead too."

"So what's left? I mean for the healthy people?"

"Nothing really. Just what they can grow or make themselves, I guess. I'm telling you, it's total chaos over there."

A third member of the group joined the fray. "I have a quote here from an American astronomer that I find particularly appropriate for the situation: 'We live in a society exquisitely dependent on science and technology, in which hardly anyone knows anything about science and technology.'"

All of the show commentators nodded their heads in agreement. "So true. So true."

"Let's face it," he added, "the entirety of the continental United States has now been sent back in time several hundred years. The only people who are likely unaffected by it are those who were already living in that time period: the Amish."

"That's right; there are pockets of people in America who deliberately shunned modern life. Although I don't think that will help them any with surviving the disease. They might not care about the power outages, but this virus will probably still sweep through their communities."

"I heard it's not," a panel member countered. "I heard that none of the Amish have gotten sick."

"That's strange," the first commentator said. Then with a laugh he added: "let's hope they're not behind it all, right?"

****

Less than two miles down the road at 10 Downing Street, British Prime Minister Rodgers was in the midst of another harried day. Having just finished a conference call with her own health ministers about the likelihood of a Shorewood-type disease outbreak hitting her country, Lucy stood up from behind her desk and stretched her arms over her head, then turned to face her office window overlooking the bustling London street below. "Everyone thinks of a big pandemic in terms of an apocalypse," she said to no one in particular. "Like something out of a novel: buildings destroyed, alien spacecraft flying overhead, and only a handful of people still alive. But this thing in America . . ." Rodgers shook her head. "This is the real threat. No bombs or crumbling buildings. No outside invaders that we can band together and fight off like some redux of the movie 'Independence Day'. No . . . this is what we should've been afraid of. This is what we should've been planning for if we had only been smart enough to see the risk. How to combat a highly-infectious disease in one part of the world while simultaneously preventing its spread around the globe."

"It's our 'oh shit' moment," her Chief of Staff summarized.

A rare, bemused smile crossed the prime minister's face. "In so many words, yes."

Even though four stories and several layers of bullet proof glass separated Lucy from the street below, she could still hear the slogans being chanted by the crowd gathered outside her building.

"Redeem yourself! The end is nigh! The end is nigh! Repent and be redeemed!"

Prime Minister Rodgers watched as the group, led by a bearded, disheveled man with a bullhorn, paced back and forth in front of her offices.

"He still there?" her personal secretary asked, bringing in a tray holding tea, biscuits, and copies of the latest reports out of America.

"He is," she replied. Lucy turned away from the window and picked up her cup of tea. "Every day this week they've been out there with the same thing. The end is nigh. Not even near. Nigh."

The Chief of Staff shook his head. "I always dismissed the doomsday proclamations of the past. But given current events? The man may have a point."

Rodgers wasn't convinced. "If the Apocalypse is truly on its way then there's nothing we can do to stop it. And last time I checked, I'm a minister of government, not the church. I protect the citizenry's lives, not their souls."

"Yes ma'am, of course."

Both aides turned to leave when they heard their boss call out over her shoulder:

"Call me if either of you see the Four Horsemen, okay?"

They laughed and turned back to the exit. "Yes ma'am."

TWELVE

After monitoring the situation in Minnesota and the greater United States for two weeks, the United Nations, in conjunction with the World Health Organization, the European Union, and the North Atlantic Treaty Organization, decided enough was enough. The UN Special Committee on Worldwide Pandemic Response, or WPR for short, was formed, and an emergency meeting was scheduled. Given the size of the group attending the meeting and the high-level nature of the discussions, the decision was made for all of the representatives to meet at NATO's headquarters in the northern outskirts of Brussels. All available heads of government were to attend either in person or via secure conference call, and those countries unable to have their leader in Belgium had to send their local ambassador instead.

The stream of world leaders descending on NATO Headquarters was seemingly never ending, with waves of black sedan motorcades speeding down Boulevard Leopold III in the northeast corner of the city and entering the circular drive of the three-story, tan-colored building whose front was decorated by the flags of dozens of member nations. There had been considerable discussion among the Headquarters staff about whether or not the flags should be lowered to half-staff. In the end, NATO's Secretary-General ordered them to remain at full mast. "We may be saddened by the deaths in America," he had said, "but we are not in mourning. Now is not the time for remembrance, although that time will undoubtedly come. Now is the time for action."

Representatives from all twenty-eight members of the European Union were present at the first meeting, along with the presidents of the European Commission and European Council. NATO member states were also fully represented, including the Secretary-General and its military commander, General Brad Davis. The United Nations was further represented by delegates from Russia and China (the remaining permanent Security Council members) and Secretary-General Pravat Nantakarn. The UN leader had been at his office in New York when the viral outbreak first began, but he left the next day for a pre-planned trip back to his native Thailand and had been working out of Brussels in the weeks since.

Even though they wanted everyone present for discussion and decision making, only the Permanent Five members of the Security Council (plus Germany) and the nongovernmental organizational heads were in attendance for the first meeting of the day: a conference call with President Bates in the United States.

The conference room where the P5+1's representatives were meeting was a less-than-spectacular setting, but the shabbily-decorated and windowless room was the only space large enough to hold all of the various officials and their staffs. When Prime Minister Rodgers, Secretary-General Nantakarn, General Davis, and the other members of the core team all assembled in the room, an aide connected them with their counterpart in Washington, DC.

"Matthew? Are you there?" Prime Minister Rodgers asked.

"Yes, yes I'm here," the American replied, his voice booming through the speakerphone. "Several members of my staff as well as my military Joint Chiefs are also here with me."

"Excellent. Okay, well as you know we have the P5+1 represented here along with the Secretaries-General of NATO and the UN and NATO's Supreme Allied Commander, General Davis. We're hoping you can give us an overview of what the United States has done so far in response to the outbreak."

"Of course," said President Bates. "On the medical front, we have the CDC in Atlanta working with your European

CDC to figure out what the hell this thing is and how to stop it."

"Right," Lucy said. "We have a call with the ECDC after this one."

"Okay, then I'll leave the medical update to them. Suffice it to say that right now we still don't have a damn clue how to cure it, treat it, stop it . . . anything really." Bates took a deep breath. "On a more operational front, because of how fast the virus is spreading, we've deployed all mission-ready ships out of our naval bases in Norfolk and San Diego as well as our smaller ports in order to prevent those personnel from being exposed to the disease. Other naval groups in the Persian Gulf, Mediterranean, and Pacific have also started making their way back toward the US coasts in order to assist with humanitarian relief efforts. And my team and I are currently several stories below ground in a bunker under the White House."

"That's all good to hear," replied Prime Minister Rodgers. The people in the room with her nodded their heads in agreement.

"President Bates, this is Secretary-General Nantakarn," the UN chief chimed in. "We won't keep you any longer . . . I know we all have a lot to do. But you should be aware that the Special Committee here in Brussels hasn't yet decided how the global community is going to respond to the outbreak. Protecting as many lives as possible is our paramount focus."

"Understood," Matthew Bates replied. "Let us know when you do decide, and we'll work together to hopefully have the best outcome possible – the best given these circumstances anyway."

"Will do. Thanks."

****

Immediately following their call with the American leadership, the core members of the WPR began their second meeting of the day: a videoconference with Europe's top infectious disease experts.

Dr. Ricardo Capello and his team at the European Centers for Disease Control had been working closely with the Americans ever since the Shorewood Disease epidemic began, and the world leaders wanted to get an update on exactly what kind of beast they were facing.

An aide lowered a projection screen from the ceiling of the conference room and turned it on to connect the group in Brussels with Dr. Capello and his assistants in Solna, Sweden.

"Good afternoon," Dr. Capello said, his voice coming across an octave higher than normal because of nerves. Even though Ricardo was among the leaders in his field, the people staring back at him via video screen were the leaders of the world. *Breathe*, he reminded himself.

"Good afternoon, doctor," said Secretary-General Nantakarn. "We've all been briefed on the members of your team, but perhaps you can introduce yourselves so we know who is who."

Dr. Capello nodded. "Yes sir, of course. And we will speak in English, yes? This is okay?"

"Yes, English is fine."

"Okay. My name is Dr. Ricardo Capello. I am the Chief of Pathology at the ECDC, and I am leading the work here on this case. Originally, I come from Andorra."

"Very good," Prime Minister Rodgers said. "Everyone else?"

One by one, Dr. Capello's staff introduced themselves to the committee, each giving their name, research specialization, and home country. There was Max Mencken of Germany, Capello's deputy and a general pathologist; Elena Delacroix from France, a former professor with an emphasis on pandemics; Goran Ekstrom, a Swedish native who dealt primarily with vaccinations; and Zach Schroder, an American doing post-graduate work at the ECDC.

With the introductions out of the way, Dr. Capello took the initiative with the conversation.

"If it is okay with you all," he said, "I will describe for you what this disease is – so much as we know now – and how it is spreading in the United States."

"Perfect," Prime Minister Rodgers replied.

Stepping to the side and signaling for his team to do the same, the world leaders were then able to see a large, wall-sized map of North America with multi-colored rings encircling Minneapolis and spreading outward from there.

"We started with one patient," Ricardo explained. "A forty-two year old male named Luke Russell. He arrived at a hospital in Waconia, Minnesota with a rash, fever, headache, and joint pain. His wife soon exhibited the same symptoms, followed by their children and then students at the Russell children's school. It took only three days," Dr. Capello continued, "for the hospital staff to realize that the illness was an airborne contaminant. But by that point, as you say, the damage was done."

"What is it, doctor?" Lucy asked. "Do we know?"

"The disease? No ma'am, we do not know yet. It presents as a form of Measles or Rubella, but all tests for that – and everything else – are negative."

"Explain the map," said NATO's General Davis.

"Ah, yes, the map." Dr. Capello took a laser pointer out of his lab coat pocket to use as a demonstration tool. "This map shows the progress of the disease to date, with red indicating the epicenter, orange being the primary infected area, and then, as you see, the various shades of purple show the percentage of infection in a location." Ricardo pointed the laser at some spots of lighter purple on the map. "These cities and towns are more of a guess," he said. "We do not have complete numbers from these places because of the use of nontraditional medicine there."

"Wait, who lives in the light purple?"

"Mostly the Amish," the American doctor answered.

"Oh, okay," replied the general. "What's happening in Canada? It looks like there's some purple there but not much. Is that a result of the border closure?"

Ricardo nodded. "Yes sir, that is correct. The epicenter is very far north in the United States, but the Canadians learned of the disease and closed that border area very early."

"So is that what we need to do on a broader scale?" the British leader asked. "Set up some kind of isolation area to prevent it spreading even farther?"

Everyone in the room turned to look at Lucy Rodgers.

"What are you suggesting?" the French president finally replied. "Isolate the entire country? Is that even possible?"

"Wait a minute," the UN Secretary-General broke in. "You cannot be serious." He looked around the room. "You're all serious? You're going to close off an entire country? And not just any country – the United States of America?"

Dr. Capello cleared his throat. "If I may, sir, such isolation might be the best option. This is an airborne contaminant . . . we have no current way of slowing down the spread or treating anyone infected. Preventing contact with the sick is the only available approach."

Prime Minister Rodgers nodded her head. "I agree. Canada already closed its border a while ago, and Mexico followed suit last week. I don't see why we wouldn't extend that to air and sea travel. It only makes sense." Realizing the sudden sensitivity of the conversation, Lucy paused. "Is there anything else you have for us, doctors?"

"No ma'am."

"Okay, then we'll leave you to your research while we address this isolation issue. Thank you for your report."

THIRTEEN

With the videoconference over and all unnecessary aides dismissed from the room, Prime Minister Rodgers turned her attention back to the issue at hand. "Okay, everyone. How do we do this?"

Secretary-General Nantakarn shook his head. "Unbelievable."

Her mind made up, Lucy was having none of the other man's attitude. "Can someone please escort Neville Chamberlain from the room? The rest of us have work to do."

Hushed gasps filled the air.

"I'm not kidding. We don't have time for your hand-wringing, 'this might hurt someone's feelings' bullshit anymore. Either get on board or get out."

The career UN official glared at the British leader but didn't argue. Standing up in a huff, Nantakarn gathered his belongings and stormed out.

After the door closed, Lucy Rodgers looked around. "Anyone else?"

"Now hold on just a minute," the Russian president said. "Who died and made you Queen?"

"Seventy-six people would have to die ahead of me before I would become Queen of England."

The Russian leader shook his head. "The fact that you even know that . . . "

"Oh hush," she shot back. "I took charge because no one else was. This isn't the time for turf wars or pissing matches. We've got to get shit done. Leave it to historians to sift through the muck and figure out who gets credit and who gets blame."

"She's right," said General Davis. The Alabama native's Southern drawl warmed the air as he spoke. "If we don't get a handle on this thing, there won't be a society left for the historians to write about."

Prime Minister Rodgers nodded her head with confidence, glad to know that the only American in the room was on her side. "Okay," she said, "back to my original question. Brass tacks: how do we do this?"

Brad Davis, the sixty-one year old four-star general, unfolded his tall, six-foot-three frame from his chair and walked over to stand next to a whiteboard that was mounted against one of the walls. "Well," he said, "the good news is that we don't have to reinvent the wheel. We're not doing anything that hasn't been done before." Davis scribbled words on the whiteboard as he spoke. "Closed borders, no fly zones, and shipping embargos. No need to overthink it; that's what we're doing . . . if we're really doing this."

"Closed borders, shipping embargos, and no fly zones," the French president repeated.

"Yes sir."

"And the bad news?" asked the Chinese ambassador. She was filling in until China's president arrived the next day.

"The sheer scale of it." General Davis paused. "We're talking about a land mass and initial containment zone almost the size of all of Europe. Also, with previous embargos and border closings, it was accepted that a small amount of slippage would occur."

"Slippage?"

"People breaking the line. Smugglers and the like."

"Well then how do we prevent slippage this time?" Lucy Rodgers asked. "No slippage. Slippage is not an option."

"Give it to us straight, General," said the German chancellor. "What do you need? How many boats? How many planes?"

The West Point graduate rubbed a hand through his thinning gray hair. "To be honest, as many as we can get. Planes, ships – including aircraft carriers and monitoring radar. We'll probably also need a list of troops willing to go in and monitor the border. In shifts, wearing protective gear. But at some point there's no substitute for boots on the ground."

The politicians in the room nodded solemnly, taking it all in. Prime Minister Rodgers continued to look at General Davis, though, narrowing her eyes to assess her new strategic commander.

"He's not finished," she deduced.

Everyone's eyes snapped up. "What?"

"What are you not telling us, General?" Rodgers asked.

Brad Davis took a deep breath. During his forty year military career, he couldn't remember a more difficult set of mission circumstances. "We can't do this without the cooperation of the American military," he said. "Like it or not, right or wrong, they are light years ahead of the rest of the world in terms of military spending, technology, and capacity. The fleet of drones that the US has is exactly what we would need for this kind of operation, but the pilots are all inside the proposed containment zone and probably dead. Aircraft carriers, ammunition . . . we need all of the help we can get."

"President Bates did say that his ships stationed in other parts of the world are headed back toward the United States."

"And that's good. Critical, in fact, if this is going to succeed. I'm just saying we're going to need a lot of coordination and planning on that front, which could be difficult given the losses in leadership and other personnel that the American military is experiencing. And I'm not even going to start on the kinds of threats we're opening ourselves up to by diverting that many resources to the zone's borders."

"Shit," the German chancellor said. "I didn't think about that."

True to form, the only woman in the room continued to blaze the trail forward. "We divert all necessary resources to establishing and maintaining a sealed border around the outbreak areas," Lucy declared. "We'll be at a disadvantage because of the incapacitation of much of the US military, but, like the general said, there are also a good number of American bases overseas that can supply equipment and personnel. Each country does what it can to patrol its own territory and region, understanding that the backup police they've relied on before – the Americans – won't be there. And we manage the fallout as best we can. This is triage, people. Worst injuries go first."

****

Once the core team made the decision to create a containment zone around the United States, the rest of the countries represented in Brussels soon followed suit in agreement. The measure was drastic, they all knew that, but it was also viewed as their only option. To detain an entire country of people within its borders was an undertaking unlike any the world had ever seen, but the fear of a global pandemic also created unprecedented levels of international cooperation.

It was decided that Canada and Mexico would bear the initial brunt of securing the land borders, since they were already well on their way to doing so before the Brussels meeting occurred. It would take a total of 30,000 troops to seal off America's northern and southern borders; 22,000 for Canada and 8,000 for Mexico, with one soldier stationed every quarter of a mile. Boats and planes were also needed to monitor the seas, even though the core team planners knew that they couldn't prevent everyone from escaping.

"People will slip through," one of General Davis' top deputies said. "From a logistical standpoint, there's no way that we can stop everybody . . . especially those leaving via ship."

"You're right," the Supreme Allied Commander replied. "I don't think we can keep it from being one hundred percent effective. But everybody is so afraid of this thing – and rightly so – that anyone who might've been tempted to turn a blind eye to an escape won't."

"Yes sir, that's true, but one sick person getting out is all it would take for this to go global."

"That's why the zone has to be larger than just the United States – at least at first."

"Wait, what?" Prime Minister Rodgers had been listening to the exchange between the military commanders but now joined the conversation.

"He's right," France's president said. "There must be multiple levels of containment. America is absolutely cordoned off . . . nobody in or out. And we need some sort of buffer zone along each land border. The 'border region' of the US–Mexico line extends thirty-eight miles north and south . . . that's probably a good reference point. I'd say add Mexico and Canada to the second layer of containment, and maybe extend it out to Central America and the Caribbean for a third layer. We've got to get this thing locked down."

"Do we have the wording for the border signs yet?"

General Davis nodded. "We do." He shuffled a few papers in front of him until he found the one he was looking for. "Here we go. We've got it in English, Spanish, and French. It varies a bit based on which border it is, but the gist is the same. 'By order of the United Nations and Canada/the United Mexican States, this border is closed until further notice. All persons caught attempting to violate the border closing will be shot on sight.'"

"'Shot on sight'? Really?"

"I thought those were the orders we agreed to."

"Well, yeah," the French president said. "But 'shot on sight' just sounds, I don't know, strange."

"I agree it's not something you normally see on a sign, but there can't be any uncertainty or ambiguity here. There must be a clear warning." Davis paused. "We're also going to airdrop millions of paper versions of it all across the United States."

"And what about the seas?" Lucy asked.

"I've been thinking about that," responded General Davis. "It's not so much that we don't want people to leave the United States as it is that we don't want them to enter anywhere else."

"So?"

"So we devise a system wherein everyone can know whether or not a plane or ship or box of food or what-have-you is safe. Make a stamp or a sticker or something . . . put the UN logo on it. Hell, make it a smiley face with an 'A-OK' watermark in the middle of it. Whatever. But some way to denote that the person, vehicle, or item originated outside the containment zone. Anything not having the stamp gets sent straight to quarantine."

The rest of the team exchanged head nods, raised eyebrows, and the occasional grin.

"I like it," Prime Minister Rodgers replied. "That'll work."

With their basic plan designed and an iron-clad gag order enforced, the world leaders knew they needed to wait until the security forces were in place before announcing the quarantine. Otherwise, everyone still alive in the United States would make a run on the borders. The press conference was set for three o'clock the next afternoon.

FOURTEEN

American President Bates and his staff were given advance notice of the border closure, but not much. UN Secretary-General Nantakarn called the White House at 8:45am Eastern Time (2:45pm Central European Time), and the press conference announcing the containment zone began 9:00am. With his senior staff and Cabinet members already gathered in the bunker below the White House, the officials' shock had not yet subsided when they watched along with the rest of their countrymen as the United Nations declared that they were now prisoners in their own land.

"This is outrageous!" the US Secretary of State cried out, slamming his hands down on the oak table in front of him. "They can't do this. They didn't even consult us!"

The Vice President joined in the outburst. "This is completely unprecedented. Closing us off from the rest of the world? And who does this little shit think he is?" he asked, pointing to Secretary-General Nantakarn on the TV screen. "He was here, in the United States, when all of this started. Then he leaves and closes the door behind him? Motherfucker."

The Secretary of Education cleared his throat. As a former history and politics professor at Georgetown University, he knew better than most what was and wasn't without precedent. "Umm, technically," he said, "this is not the first time the United States' borders have been closed to interaction with outsiders. President Jefferson signed the Embargo Act of 1807 to prohibit American ships from departing for foreign ports. And prior to World War Two, President Roosevelt denied entry visas to a group of Jewish refugees, causing them to be sent back to Europe."

The White House Chief of Staff, himself also a student of US history, disagreed with the Education Secretary. "First of all, the Embargo Act was a total failure by all standards –

so much so that we still ended up declaring war on Britain in 1812. Secondly, the 'St. Louis Affair' was far more complicated than you make it seem. To admit those refugees would be to deny entry to the German and Austrian citizens ahead of them on the visa waitlist, and the ship was supposed to go to Cuba anyway."

The Secretary of Defense, sitting in a chair in the corner, shook his head and sighed. "This is why people think elite professors are out of touch with reality . . . because you are. We've all been condemned to die and you two peckerheads are debating stuff that happened anywhere from seventy to two hundred years ago. Personally," he said, "I'm more interested in the Vice President's second point. How the hell did that Thai midget weasel his way out of the country? You're right: he is a little shit."

****

Although their emotions were running high, after a few minutes President Bates and his leadership team settled down enough to begin planning the United States' own response to the latest turn of events. Picking up the phone, the president reached out to General Brad Davis. Although Davis was the Supreme Allied Commander Europe (SACEUR) and thus reported directly to NATO's Secretary-General, he was also a US Army officer and someone who President Bates knew he could count on to fairly consider the American point of view.

"Davis?" he said when the general answered the phone.

"Yes sir, Mr. President. What can I do for you?"

"I don't know if you're around any other members of this 'WPR' or whatever you're calling it, but we need to discuss the American military's role in your containment zone process."

Davis nodded. "Yes sir, we do. The politicians are tending to their own domestic work at the moment, but I can communicate your position to them and then set up a conference call with the larger group if need be."

"That would be great, thanks." President Bates paused. "Listen, General, let me start by saying that I understand why you all decided to put the blockade in place. NATO and the UN have a job to do; citizens to protect. I get it."

"That's good to hear, sir," replied Davis. The containment zone situation in general and this phone call in particular put the man from the small town of Wedowee, Alabama in an uncomfortable position, and he could hear the tension in his own voice. He was an American, but living outside the country. A US military officer, but tasked with promoting the interests and following the orders of an international coalition. It had never been a problem before . . . indeed, the SACEUR had always been an American – dating all the way back to Dwight Eisenhower. *But America and NATO's interests have never been at odds, either*, Davis thought.

"I see where you're coming from," the American president continued, breaking Davis' thoughts, "but you also have to appreciate that I have a responsibility to my own country and citizens. Our country and citizens. A portion – not many, but a portion – of the American population seems to somehow be immune to this disease. I can't allow healthy people to be left to die of hunger or thirst or whatever else just because they happen to be on the wrong side of the border."

"Look, I'll make this really simple for you guys in Brussels," said President Bates. "You can't create the containment zone you want to without the help of my military. You just can't. So if you want American personnel and equipment made available to you, then you have to let us fly over our territory and conduct humanitarian aid missions without restrictions."

General Davis hesitated. "Can you define 'without restrictions,' sir?"

"Don't worry: no one potentially exposed to the virus will be going to any other countries. But the containment blockade includes a no-fly zone over the whole continental United States. That's just something I can't agree to. Listen, I'm sending all of the C-130 and C-17 crews that we have in Europe to Hickam Air Force Base in Hawaii and Muñiz Air Base in Puerto Rico. From those locations, the plan is to have cargo planes running continuous airdrops of supplies. I think the international community has a moral obligation to provide those aid materials. Food, water, clothing, medicine, etcetera."

"I agree with you, Mr. President. I think I can convince the rest of the leaders here to do that, provided we have a way to prevent exposure to the people bringing those supplies to Hawaii and Puerto Rico."

"We will. The pilots will be breathing pressurized oxygen from their on-board systems whenever they're flying over the US, and we can position the aid drop-off locations far away from the planes. I'd also like to run relief missions from Bermuda because of its proximity to the US and the 8,000 foot runway there, but I understand if Britain doesn't want them on the island."

"I doubt Prime Minister Rodgers would agree to that," Brad Davis replied.

"Okay. Understood. But, like I said, if you guys at NATO and the UN want my planes helping to enforce that no-fly zone, then those same planes have to be exempted from the no-fly with regard to survivor relief efforts."

General Davis let out a deep breath. "Alright. That's reasonable, sir. Anything else?"

"The exemption also has to extend to American naval ships and helicopters. I've got Carrier Strike Groups and Amphibious Readiness Groups in the Fifth, Sixth, and Seventh Fleets headed back here to loiter along the US coasts. Those ships can help prevent people from escaping the containment zone, but they're also going to be launching helicopters to drop aid similar to what the cargo planes do."

"Do you have a way to protect those pilots? Helicopters aren't pressurized like the C-130s and C-17s."

"No, they're not. You're right," Bates replied. "But the pilots will all wear gas masks. Look, I'm not saying there isn't a risk to the personnel involved in the humanitarian aid. But you, as the international community, have no right to tell my military what risks it can or can't take to protect its own country."

"I think that's a valid argument, Mr. President."

"I'm not kidding, Davis. This is non-negotiable. We will be running the relief missions whether you like it or not. We'll make every effort to prevent the spread of the disease, both for the global good and because we don't want to expose the people on the ships and air force bases to it. But don't stand in our way on this. You try, and in my view that's an act of war to which my forces will respond in kind."

"Understood, sir. Message received. I'll talk to my staff here and then tell the other WPR committee members when we regroup later today."

With tentative agreement from Brussels, President Bates ended his call with General Davis and set about putting the humanitarian relief wheels into motion.

****

President Bates and his staff weren't the only ones reeling from the announcement by the WPR. Reaction to the imposition of the containment zone was swift and strong around the world. Governments issued statements of support for the blockade and said they would cooperate fully with any quarantine efforts. Multinational corporations announced that their US offices would close until further notice and warned people of likely delays in shipments and services. And nowhere was more opinionated about the American blockade than the news feeds and message boards of social media websites. '#PrayForUSA' was quickly trending worldwide, with even the Pope joining in the hash-tagged call for prayers. 'WTF' also flooded people's commentary, along with a not-insignificant number of remarks that the United States deserved to be closed off and 'had it coming.'

People's reactions inside the cordoned-off zone were decidedly angrier. Those who still had power, internet, or cell phone service quickly took to websites like Facebook and Twitter to air their grievances. 'What the fuck, UN? Leavin us all 2 die. I hope u die 2,' a comment by a famous pro basketball player, was quickly shared and repeated by hundreds of thousands of his fellow Americans.

General Davis, the top military officer at NATO, was keeping an eye on the social media reaction as a security measure. Given the number of guns and other ammunition in the hands of private American citizens, not to mention the police forces and stateside troops, an army could easily be raised to confront and overpower the troops stationed at the Canadian and Mexican borders that were now under his command. Davis' only saving grace in that regard – if one could call it that – was that so many people were already sick, dying, or dead that the thought of an organized escape would probably be too much for them to handle. But the four-star general and tactical leader of the containment efforts knew that his troops simply couldn't get in position in time and in large enough numbers to try to stop everyone from breaking the blockade . . . at least not yet anyway. *But we'll get most of them*, he concluded. Davis was also reluctantly prepared for what 'getting most of them' might entail, up to and including shooting down planes, sinking ships, and firing on civilians. *They're not civilians*, the general reminded himself. *They're the enemy. They're no different than a suicide bomber wearing an explosive vest. They're the threat, and they can't be let out.*

FIFTEEN

The hundreds of millions of Americans now trapped in their own country didn't only rely on social media to express their feelings about the situation. Riots broke out in many places, looting was rampant, and some major cities resembled more of a state of nature than a civilized urban center.

It wasn't all chaos, though. Many Americans responded to the WPR's announcement by getting in touch with family and friends, settling old grievances, and adopting a 'carpe diem' approach to life. In addition, millions thought seriously for the first time about their plans for the afterlife. Priests, pastors, rabbis, and imams worked overtime to shepherd their flocks. Pastor Adam Wilhelm, president of the Southern Baptist Theological Seminary, was no different.

Ten hours after the containment zone was declared, Pastor Wilhelm held a rally at his megachurch in suburban Dallas. River's Edge Church claimed nearly 15,000 members, and there were more than that present that night.

Wow, Wilhelm thought as he sat in his chair on stage and listened to the congregation sing 'It Is Well With My Soul'. *We haven't had a weeknight crowd this big since September 11th.*

When the song concluded, Pastor Wilhelm stood up from his chair and walked toward the podium. Adam looked out over the massive group in front of him and smiled. There wasn't an empty seat in the sanctuary, and more people sat in the aisles and lined the walls of the massive room. *This is good*, Wilhelm thought. *A good night.*

He cleared his throat and began to speak.

"Good evening, everyone."

A chorus of 'good evening' echoed back from the crowd.

"What beautiful music that was! A joyful noise, indeed."

A few people clapped to applaud the work of the worship team, and Pastor Wilhelm smiled again.

"I know many of you are here," the preacher said, "because you're looking for answers. And I'll tell you right now: I don't know why we have been attacked by this vicious disease. There are people out there on the streets and radios saying that they know why this happened, and that it happened because America deserved it. That we had it coming. That our pride or our greed or our wars or our immoral lifestyles made God decide to strike us down." He paused. "Let me tell you something, brothers and sisters: they're all full of crap."

Gasps of shock mixed with chuckles of nervous laughter filled the room.

"Those people don't know what caused this to happen anymore than you or I do. They're just using what is going on as a way to advance their own agendas. What is it the politicians say? Never waste a crisis? Well, that's what those folks are doing. The last time I know of God coming down and speaking directly to a human, apart from Jesus, was on Mount Sinai with Moses. Not to say God wouldn't reveal Himself to someone now . . . I'm just saying that the odds of Him speaking directly to multiple people and saying different things each time are pretty low."

More people laughed at the pastor's remarks.

Wilhelm took a sip of water before continuing his sermon. "Alright, so we can agree that we don't know why this is happening to us. And we can agree that it's probably not worth wasting what little time we have left talking about it." He surveyed the room and saw people nodding their heads in agreement. "You know, when I was a kid, I never really liked it when the preacher would say 'if you die tomorrow, will you go to Heaven?' I guess I knew there was a chance it could happen – a car wreck being the most likely scenario. But I always kinda thought 'yeah, I'll go to Heaven because I believe Jesus is God's son and He died for my sins, but not because I'm worried I'm gonna die tomorrow.'"

The preacher stepped out from behind the podium and put his hands in his pockets. Those familiar with Wilhelm's sermons knew he was about to deliver his punch line.

"Brothers and sisters," he said, "a good number of us may very well die tomorrow. Or maybe not tomorrow, but you, we, all of us, are headed for the grave very soon. My question for you is this: where are you headed for beyond the grave? When you die – because you will – where are you spending eternity?" The pastor bowed his head. "Let us pray."

****

"Did you see this?" Dr. Capello asked his top deputy the next morning, holding up a copy of Stockholm's English-language newspaper.

"See what?"

"A news story out of America. Some preacher in Texas held a big church service last night. It says seventeen thousand people attended, and five thousand of them were baptized as Christians at the end of it."

"Seventeen thousand people at one church service? Wow." Dr. Mencken raised his eyebrows in surprise. "Although, you know, if I knew I was stuck on the wrong side of a death wall, I'd probably be clinging to whatever kind of reassurances that I could find."

"That's true," Ricardo replied. "Makes sense, especially since Christians aren't the only ones doing huge rallies and stuff like that. I read online that leaders of all of the religions are holding big events."

Dr. Delacroix, overhearing the conversation, piped in from her workstation several feet away. "I heard that a mosque in Nashville had to move their prayers outside because there were too many people to fit inside the building."

Dr. Capello shook his head in disbelief. "Everybody's searching for an answer that no one has – or at least that no one on Earth has. You know, I would normally caution against big group meetings when there is an airborne outbreak like this."

"But?" Mencken asked, wondering what made this epidemic different.

"But . . . they're probably all going to die anyway. Whether it happens in their homes or in a church makes no difference. In fact," he added, "if the religious services help them cope with everything that is happening, then all the better for them."

SIXTEEN

With the containment zone declared and the first wave of border security in place, work at NATO headquarters continued at a frenetic pace. Although the organization's large, three-story building had been overtaken by international heads of government, ambassadors, and staff, the permanent team of diplomats and military service members stationed in Brussels was also working around the clock on the biggest mission the organization had ever undertaken. One of the people missing from the NATO support staff, however, was Jennifer Brown, a former naval commander who only recently left the service for a high paying consulting job at a firm in Brussels. Until her separation from the military, Brown had been one of the longest serving members of General Davis' staff. First assigned to Brad Davis' joint task force crew nearly ten years earlier at the Pentagon, Jennifer had looked on her boss as a mentor and father figure and was still a regular dinner guest at the Davis family home in Brussels.

The morning after the containment zone decision was announced, the former Commander Brown was summoned into her old boss' office.

"Close the door please, Brown," General Davis said.

Doing as she was told, Jennifer then walked to stand at attention in front of the general's desk. Davis finished typing something on his computer before looking up.

"You're not in the Navy anymore, Brown. You can relax."

There was an uncertainty in his gray-blue eyes that Jennifer wasn't used to seeing, and the general stared silently at his former staffer for several minutes. After what seemed like a lifetime, he spoke.

"I need to know I can trust you, Brown."

The NATO leader's opening words took Jennifer by surprise. "Of course you can, sir."

Davis wasn't yet satisfied. "I need to know that if what I want to happen happens that you will never speak of it to anyone and carry it all to your grave."

What in the world? she thought. *He's never been like this before.* "Of course, sir," Jennifer repeated. "I'll do whatever you need."

Brad Davis closed his eyes and nodded his head, as if trying to convince himself that what she was saying was true.

"Have a seat, Brown," General Davis said, then took a deep breath. "I assume," he continued slowly, "given that you were in the Navy, that you know your way around a boat."

The commander's confusion grew with every second that the man seated in front of her continued his unusual behavior. "Well, yes sir," Jennifer answered. "Before being assigned to the Pentagon, I spent several years as a surface warfare officer."

Davis shook his head. "Not ships. Boats. Small, deep sea fishing sized boats."

"Uhh . . . sure, I guess." She paused. "Sir, if I may, what's going on?"

"I suppose there's no need to keep beating around the bush." The general took a deep breath. "My daughter is still in the United States. She refused to leave before now . . . kept saying some shit about staying at college with her friends and my overreacting. But she's scared enough now that she'll listen. I need you to go get her."

Brown opened her mouth to ask about the travel ban, but Davis held up his hand to stop her. "There's a private jet waiting at the airport. It will take you to Cancún. There's a deep sea fishing boat there rented under the name Abigail Adams," the general added, handing her a folder with travel information inside. "You'll sail from Cancún to Destin, Florida, and Kaylie will be waiting for you."

"What about the blockade, sir? I mean, I watched the press conference when the Secretary-General said you would sink a ship before allowing it to exit the waters of the containment zone."

"You're not exiting the zone," responded the general. "You're getting far enough away from shore that you won't be in contact with the disease, but not far enough that blockade ships will think you're trying to escape." Davis stood up from his desk and began to pace behind it. "I know I'm asking a lot here, Brown. But there's no one else I can trust to do it. And I can't leave Kaylie there to die – not when there's something I can do to save her."

Jennifer nodded and gave a brave smile for her old boss' benefit. "Permission to speak freely, sir?"

"You're a civilian. Yes, of course."

"Kaylie has become almost like a younger sister to me over the years. I'm happy to do it. I would expect no less from you, General. And I admire you all the more for it."

Davis stopped pacing and walked around the desk to shake her hand. "Thank you, Brown. More than you'll ever know, thank you."

Jennifer smiled. "You're welcome. Is the plane ready? I'll head out now if it is."

"It is," Brad Davis nodded. "Godspeed, Brown."

****

As soon as Jennifer Brown left his office, the general called his daughter in the United States. After trying unsuccessfully for years to have a child, eighteen years earlier General and Mrs. Davis decided to adopt an infant girl that they met at an orphanage while stationed in South Korea. Little Kaylie was the perfect addition to their family. She grew up to attend SHAPE High School in Brussels along with other children of Department of Defense employees before heading back to America to go to college at her mom's alma mater, Auburn University. He and his wife had been talking to her as often as possible to make sure they knew if and when the Shorewood virus hit her town; luckily, she was far enough away from Minnesota that the outbreak hadn't quite reached Auburn.

Kaylie answered her phone on the second ring.

"Hey Dad."

"Hey, honey. How are you feeling?"

"I'm fine, Dad." Brad Davis could hear the annoyance in his daughter's voice, but also knew that she appreciated her parents' concern and support.

"Listen to me, honey. I know you think I overreact and am too overbearing and all of that. But I need you to listen to me right now and do exactly what I tell you."

The pretty brunette sat up on her dorm room bed, criss-crossing her legs and tucking them up under her oversized sorority sweatshirt. The news reports out of the Midwest and now other parts of the country were scary, but not nearly as frightening as the tone in her father's voice right then. "Okay, Dad. Whatever you tell me to, I'll do it."

"Pack a couple days' worth of clothes, get in your car, and drive to Destin. Don't tell anyone you're leaving and, if you have to stop for gas or anything, don't talk to anybody. Do you understand? Don't say anything to anyone."

"Okay, Dad. I won't." Tears were threatening to break through Kaylie's eyes, if only because she had never heard her warrior father sound so scared himself.

"You know the dock at our favorite restaurant? Where all of the big boats are for sale?"

"Mmm hmm."

"Drive straight to those docks. Don't stop, don't talk to anyone, just get there as quickly as possible. Commander Brown will be waiting for you. She'll tell you our family's emergency code word. Don't say it, but do you remember it?" The code word, or words more accurately, was created when Kaylie was a little girl in case something happened to her parents and someone she didn't know had to pick her up from school. Davis made sure to include the phrase in the folder he gave Jennifer before she left.

"Yeah, of course." *Flying blue unicorns*, Kaylie thought. "Dad, you're scaring me."

"Just get to the docks, honey. You're going to go with Brown and wait this out on a boat in the Gulf. I can't get you into a non-quarantined country, but I can get you out of America."

SEVENTEEN

With his daughter on her way to safety, General Davis turned his attention back to the larger task at hand: enforcing the containment zone. True to his word, the general had fighter jets in the air and ready to intercept any planes trying to leave the United States. Mexico and Canada supplied the necessary boots on the ground, with one armed soldier or law enforcement official stationed every quarter of a mile. Drones and helicopters were positioned overhead to surveil the nearly 7,500 miles of border territory. Larger, established border crossings also had extra personnel in place to fend off any coordinated escape efforts.

Reinforcing the Mexican and Canadian forces were soldiers, sailors, and airmen drawn from NATO's large cache of troops. The NATO Response Force, or NRF, described itself as a 'coherent, high-readiness, joint, multinational force package' that could consist of up to 25,000 troops. The NRF was designed for rapid deployment on as little as five days' notice, and General Davis had activated the unit in advance of the emergency meeting in Brussels just in case they were needed. Consequently, the first wave of air, land, and sea troops were in North America assisting the Canadians and Mexicans within hours of the UN response committee's announcement.

****

While international leaders in Brussels sorted out the logistics of their containment plan, doctors at the CDC in Atlanta continued to work tirelessly to find a medical cure for the Shorewood Disease. A few mornings after the announcement of the border closure, Dr. David Malhotra put on a mask and took a short walk outside to get some fresh air and see the sun for the first time in days. Having already sent his wife and daughter to visit his family in India, David had been living out of his office for well over a week.

Upon returning to the CDC building, Dr. Malhotra noticed that the security guard who had been stationed at the entrance to the research wing wasn't there anymore. *That's weird*, he thought. *Maybe he went to the restroom or something.* David was bothered enough by the other man's absence, though, to ask his fellow physicians about it.

"Has anybody seen Luis?"

"Who?"

"The security guard who's normally out front."

The other doctors shook their heads no. Dr. Lapinski, the most junior member of the group, walked in carrying a cup of coffee. "What about the security guard?"

"He's not there," David responded.

"Oh yeah, I heard somebody mention him at the coffee stand just now. Apparently he called in sick this morning. I'm surprised they didn't get a replacement of some sort."

Dr. Malhotra's face turned ashen white and his eyes grew as big as saucers. "It's here," he whispered.

"What?"

"The virus. We're too late. It's already here."

The pathologists looked around at each other nervously, no one knowing quite how to respond. "Let's just stay in here," Dr. Sayers suggested. "Seal the lab shut to keep it out."

David shook his head. "Won't work. We're too late. Luis has it now, which means he's been contagious for the past four days." He let out a deep breath. "It's here. Come on, help me email everything we have over to the European CDC in Sweden. They'll at least be able to build on what we've done."

"Then what?" asked Dr. Lapinski.

"Then we continue to work. Or at least that's what I'm going to do. I don't know about y'all, but I'm going to spend every last second I can doing tests and research and making sure Dr. Capello and his people over at the ECDC get all of the information we have so that they can pick up where we leave off. Y'all with me?"

The doctor's attempt at a motivational speech fell on deaf ears, but grumbled replies of "yeah" and "sure" accompanied the CDC team as they began scanning paperwork and making copies of test results. If their security guard had been in a carrier state for the past four days, the physicians quickly determined that they had anywhere from seventy-two to one-hundred-twenty hours left to live. Indeed, an outside observer would have been amazed by how well they all took the news: no crying, no hysterics, and no angry outbursts. The six doctors all seemed to skip straight to the final stage of grief: acceptance. One by one they took turns going into a small supply closet for privacy and calling their families, saying I love you's and goodbyes. A few members of the team had already lost loved ones to the epidemic, a fact that now seemed almost irrelevant as the doctors came to realize that, in the end, anyone lucky enough to survive would know more people who died than lived.

"What a shitty way to go," said Dr. Sayers as he worked to scan patient reports onto his computer.

"It's actually not too terrible," Josh Lapinski countered. "Relatively quick and, based on what I've heard, not all that painful."

Sayers shook his head. "That's not what I mean. This whole thing – everybody is dying. For what? Nobody knows. You're not dying in a war or anything where your death is in service of a greater cause. And you're not dying on your own time where people will notice you're gone and grieve your loss. We're all going to just disappear with no one around to remember us."

Dr. Malhotra breathed out hard, the force of his breath scattering loose paper off his desk. "I think we'll be remembered," he said after picking up the files. "And I think we can die while working toward a greater purpose by getting all of this information over to Europe. The result can't be changed at this point. But how we approach it can. I choose to think positively, to pray, and to hope that something I did will help end this epidemic and save the rest of the world from what the United States is going through."

****

Half a world away, Dr. Capello and his team of pathologists at the European CDC were busy processing all of the new information arriving from Atlanta. Although Dr. Malhotra had sent a quick email to his counterpart explaining the need for the data dump, the physicians in Sweden knew that there was no time to waste being sad about what was happening to the American doctors. There was work to be done.

Just as he had during the videoconference with the UN committee, Ricardo Capello led the charge in Solna. It was, after all, his lab. A native of the tiny country of Andorra, the forty-six year old Dr. Capello was a poster child for European integration. Thin, of average height, and effortlessly stylish in a way only Western Europeans seemed to know how, Ricardo spoke fluent Catalán, Spanish, French, and English and had a conversational knowledge of German. Married to an Austrian woman with two children, Dr. Capello had studied medicine at Leeds University in England before doing a fellowship in infectious diseases at Emory University in Atlanta. It was there that he met Dr. Malhotra for the first time.

Joining Dr. Capello in his lab was a core group of four other physicians, each extremely knowledgeable and accomplished in their own right. Ricardo's second-in-command, Dr. Max Mencken, was fifty-seven years old and a proud German. Mencken was also the longest-tenured pathologist at the ECDC, having been with the organization since its founding in 2004, but was passed over for the top spot in favor of the more charismatic Dr. Capello. The slight only added to an already bitter personality, and the divorced father of one adult daughter was without a doubt the least popular member of the team.

The only woman in the group, Dr. Elena Delacroix, did not help matters given her propensity to refer to Max as 'Dr. Grumpy Pants.' It was an expression the forty-four year old picked up during her time as a professor at the University of Paris, and she continued to use it despite knowing how much it irritated her colleague. The Frenchwoman took the same bon vivant approach to everything in life except her work on epidemics, for which she was exceptionally well-regarded. Despite being a classically beautiful woman, Elena had never married; something that perplexed her happily wedded boss.

"Why not take the leap?" he had asked her one day shortly after she began working in the lab.

Dr. Delacroix had shrugged her shoulders in response. "I say to myself: what is the point, hmm? There is no stigma in France to live together unmarried. I do not have or want children. I have my own career and do not need a man's money. There is no need for marriage."

Ricardo had disagreed with his new colleague's views, as had the only Swede in the group, Dr. Goran Ekstrom. An expert in vaccines with several patents to his name, the forty-six year old had grown up only an hour from their offices in Solna and considered the posting at the ECDC to be his dream job. Tall with blonde hair and blue eyes, Elena took her turn teasing Dr. Ekstrom by saying he looked like every model she had ever seen in travel advertisements for Sweden.

Rounding out Dr. Capello's team was Zach Schroder, a thirty-four year old native of Cedar Rapids, Iowa who was in his second year of a postgraduate fellowship in the lab. The disease outbreak understandably hit Dr. Schroder the hardest, and his colleagues knew that by the time the information began to arrive en mass from the American CDC, Zach hadn't been able to get in touch with his family for over a week.

"Maybe they got out," Dr. Ekstrom suggested, trying to give the younger man some hope.

Schroder shook his head. "They would've called me by now. I get it . . . they're dead. I just – " His words broke off as he tried to choke back tears. "I just want to get back to work," Zach finally said, changing the subject.

With that, the five doctors set about sorting through the piles of material that Dr. Malhotra and his team sent to them.

EIGHTEEN

"I don't understand how so many people could all die so quickly."

Dr. Mencken ran a frustrated hand over his bald head. "It's like somebody released some kind of chemical weapon or something – it spreads like wildfire and we have no way of stopping it or treating it."

Dr. Schroder's face grew pale. "Could they have? Could we be dealing with a terrorist attack? I mean, the bumps are like smallpox, right?"

Elena shook her head. "Smallpox is only very rarely spread through the air. And the symptoms of this aren't similar to any known chemical agent."

"'Known' being the key word."

"So it's a new disease. Okay. People flipped their shit over Ebola and AIDS too when those first appeared, right?" said Dr. Ekstrom. "The only thing that's different here is the scale and magnitude of infected people."

Dr. Capello nodded in agreement. "New . . . old . . . it doesn't matter. What matters is figuring it out. Getting this wildfire under control."

****

The wildfire analogy of the pathologists was appropriate. As the doctors continued to work in their research lab, members of the WPR in Brussels spoke of the Shorewood outbreak just like one would a fire – in terms of containment.

"Can we say we have it fully contained?" Prime Minister Rodgers asked one day at an early afternoon meeting. "I think it would be helpful if we could give some assurance to the public that we have the disease contained."

"You can say whatever you want," responded the Russian president. "I think what would be more comforting is if it were true."

Lucy let out a frustrated breath and rubbed her eyes beneath her glasses. The long hours and stress of the past several weeks were taking their toll on everyone. "Do we have it contained or not? General Davis, what have you heard from the quarantine camps?"

"No new cases reported in the last several days. I think we have it contained as much as it's possible to do so. But we still don't know what caused it in the first place, so there's no way to know if or when it might appear elsewhere."

It was with that sobering observation that the meeting was dismissed and General Davis went back to his office to review the latest personnel updates from the front lines in North America.

Before that work could be done, though, Davis had something more important to do. Walking into his office and closing the door, the general went to his desk, unlocked the bottom drawer, pulled out one of two satellite burner phones that he had Commander Brown purchase before she left town. Davis dialed the only number in the address book, connecting him to his former aide – and thus his daughter – thousands of miles away.

"Hello? Dad?"

The sound of Kaylie's voice brought tears to the general's eyes. "Yes honey, it's me. How are you?"

"I'm good," the young woman replied. "I got a little seasick the other day but I'm better now. Don't tell Mom that, though," she added. "I don't want her to worry."

Brad Davis smiled. Even while hiding in the Gulf of Mexico as a secret refugee, his daughter was still concerned about her mother's wellbeing.

"Dad? Are you there?"

"What? Yeah, I'm here. Sorry. I won't tell her. How are things going aside from the sickness? Are you getting along with Commander Brown? Do y'all have enough supplies?"

Kaylie smiled. "Yeah, Dad, we're fine. Just waiting for it to be over. You can only play so many rounds of 'Go Fish' before you get bored."

"I know, honey. I understand. And we're working as hard as we can to end this as quickly as possible." He paused. "Listen, can I speak to Brown for a second?"

"Yeah, sure. Jennifer? My dad's on the phone. Hey Dad?"

"Yes?"

"Thanks for getting me out."

General Davis couldn't quite describe the wave of emotion that overtook him in that moment, but it was so powerful that it forced him to sit down in his chair. "You don't have to thank me, but you're so, so welcome. There's no way I was going to let you stay. I love you, honey." Once again, despite his emotions, Davis was careful to not say his daughter's name aloud. Just in case someone walked by his office, he wanted to be able to plausibly claim that he was talking to his wife.

"Love you too, Dad."

There was a brief silence on the line before Commander Brown's voice replaced that of her shipmate.

"General, how are you sir?"

"As well as can be expected under the circumstances," Brad replied, his usual businesslike tone returning. "More importantly, how are you?"

"We're fine. I heard Kaylie tell you about the seasickness . . . not a big deal and she's completely recovered now. I'll admit I was a bit nervous for a few minutes when she said she didn't feel well, but there was never a rash or a fever so we figured out pretty quickly that it wasn't the Shorewood Disease."

"Good. I'm glad to hear it. And everything else?" he asked. "Do y'all have any neighbors around?"

"Not that I've seen," the former commander replied. She knew her boss was talking about blockade ships. Wanting to get away from the disease threat but not be mistaken for people trying to escape the containment zone, Jennifer and Kaylie – and other boat owners with the same idea – had to sail a fine line in the Gulf of Mexico. So far, though, the pair had managed to pull it off. "We're holding up just fine, sir."

The general breathed a sigh of relief. "Good. Let's hope it stays that way. I'll check on y'all again in a few days. You know who to call if there's an emergency," he added, referencing his wife. Knowing that Faye Davis couldn't keep a secret, all her husband had told her was that their daughter was alive. Brad refused to tell her how he knew that or where Kaylie was, but the girl had her parents' home phone number and knew to call if something happened.

"Yes sir," responded Jennifer. "We've got all the information we need."

"Good," Davis said again. "Thank you again, Brown. I'll never be able to thank you enough."

"Happy to do it, sir."

And with that, NATO's ranking general ended the secret conversation on his secret cell phone about the completely unauthorized, probably illegal secret mission that saved his daughter's life. An abuse of power? Absolutely. Worth it? *So worth it*, he thought.

NINETEEN

General Davis wasn't the only one taking time out of his busy day to call his family. Lucy Rodgers wouldn't win any Mother of the Year awards anytime soon – she knew that. One couldn't be a Member of Parliament and eventually Prime Minister to Her Majesty the Queen while still maintaining an active presence in the lives of both marriage and children. The former, her marriage, Lucy did strive to make more of an effort for . . . she genuinely loved her husband and, if nothing else, divorce would be a huge blow to her career. So time was scheduled with Charles and the pair made it a point to eat breakfast together every morning. Lunch, tea, and dinner were always too busy, but breakfast she could do.

The children, on the other hand, got the short stick in the draw. Lucy didn't start off with the intention to be distant with her two sons. Things just kind of evolved that way over the years as David and Phillip were sent away to school and Lucy's political career took off. It was also all she really knew: a product of the aristocracy, Lucy was also shipped off to boarding school at a young age and probably wouldn't have known what to do if there were children in the house underfoot all the time.

But now that her boys were grown and had children of their own (with more modern, 'commoner' views of parenting), Lucy did feel a degree of guilt at not being more involved in their lives. Consequently, six months earlier, she told her scheduler to make time once a month for her to call each of her sons. One hour per phone call, and always on the afternoon of the first Sunday of the month. David, her firstborn, thought the gesture was too little too late, but he answered her calls anyway. Phillip, the younger son, was grateful for the time and had even changed it to a video format, FaceTiming one another and letting his kids jump in on the call as well.

This Sunday was no different, despite everything happening, and when the clock struck 2:00pm, Lucy picked up the phone in the NATO office she had commandeered as her own and dialed David's number.

"Mother," he said, answering on the first ring. "How are you?"

Lucy was surprised by the concern in his voice. "I'm well, thank you. As well as to be expected under the circumstances." She stood up and began to pace the room, a nervous habit that she picked up while at university. "Did you receive the instructions on travelling to the Manor?"

"I did. Janet and I packed a bag for each of us and the kids and we have them waiting by the front door just in case."

"Good, good. And the masks?"

"Yes, Mother, the masks arrived with the instructions. We can go at a minute's notice."

"Good, good," the prime minister repeated. When news first broke of the outbreak in America, she had one of her aides take gas masks to her sons and their families. The packages also included instructions on going up to the family's country home in Yorkshire and identification badges allowing all of them access to Britain's military bases in the event of a similar outbreak and lockdown. Unbeknownst to Lucy, that act did more to heal her relationship with her older son than one hundred hours of phone calls ever could. David had stood in his foyer staring at the box for so long that his wife eventually asked him what was going on.

"She actually cares," he had replied, dumbstruck by the revelation.

"Of course she cares, darling," Janet had said, reaching up on her tip-toes to kiss him on the cheek. "She's your mother."

"Actually, Mother," David then said over the phone, "Phillip and Stacy and their kids are here. He brought his iPad . . . we thought maybe we could do one big video chat with everybody?"

The prime minister's eyes lit up at the idea, but she had long since forgotten – or had she ever known? – how to express that kind of joy. "Yes, that would be lovely," she responded, the same as she would if she had been offered a cup of tea.

"Alright then. We'll hang up and when you're ready you can call Phillip or however that usually works."

****

Lucy Rodgers was in an unusually good mood following her phone call with her sons, so much so that her colleagues on the response committee took notice. While the world leaders would have previously described their relationship with one another as 'cordial' or perhaps 'tense', working together under the current circumstances had been an intense bonding experience.

With all six members of the leadership committee reconvened in their usual conference room at NATO's headquarters, General Davis gave the team a brief rundown of the current blockade efforts and any manpower or supply necessities. There would be a call later that afternoon with Dr. Capello, but for now the politicians' focus was on the containment mission.

"What are we getting from the satellite images?" the British prime minister asked.

"Not much, to be honest with you," replied General Davis. "There's not much movement among the survivors – or presumed survivors, that is – and it's not like we're trying to see the bigger, easier things like destroyed buildings or weapons transport."

"How many people do we think are still alive?" asked the Chinese president.

Davis let out a deep breath. "It's really hard to say. Based on the patient reports from Dr. Capello and the news we were getting out of America before the power blackouts took hold, somewhere upwards of ninety percent of the population is dead. So what's that? Twenty-five, thirty million still alive?"

"That's more than I would have guessed."

Prime Minister Rodgers shook her head. "It just sounds like a big number. Imagine if everyone on the planet disappeared except the people in metro New York and Boston. That's how many people are left in America. And, based on those news reports, most of them are either very old or very young."

"We're going to have one hell of a time picking up the pieces there once this is all over," the French president commented.

"It's been done before," replied the German chancellor. "Look at Berlin. Look at Tokyo. At Germany and Japan as a whole. America helped rebuild us, and now we will help rebuild them."

"*After* we stop the virus," the Chinese president clarified.

"Of course."

General Davis cleared his throat. "On a different note," he said, "but in a way back to the question of the satellite images . . . I received a call from the International Space Station earlier today."

"The space station?" Lucy Rodgers asked. "Why?"

"One of the people on board is an American."

"Damn."

Davis nodded his head. "Colonel Allison Keener. Her husband and two teenagers were in Houston."

"She's a military woman," the Russian president reasoned. "Surely she is capable of processing the situation."

Prime Minister Rodgers, the only woman in the room, shook her head. "She's a mother."

"You say that like it somehow explains things."

"It does," Lucy replied. Turning to General Davis, she asked: "do we have any word on the colonel's family? Any chance they were among the first wave of people who left before the virus reached them? If they were in Texas and it originated in Minnesota . . . "

The NATO commander shook his head. "We haven't heard any reports of an astronaut's family showing up anywhere. I told her I'd have somebody look into it, but I doubt we'll find any good news."

****

Two bright spots for the WPR continued to be the knowledge that the US military was delivering food, water, and other aid to survivors inside the containment zone and that the President of the United States was safe in an airtight bunker underneath the White House. President Bates and his top aides and Cabinet members fled below ground before the containment zone was announced and had stayed in periodic contact with their counterparts in Belgium. It was agreed that the American politicians would remove themselves from any decision-making until the outbreak was over (except for relief mission efforts), if for no other reason than to avoid the wrath of their fellow countrymen who had no such bunker to hide in.

During one of the phone calls with President Bates, Lucy Rodgers noted that he didn't sound like his usual self. The reason why flashed in the prime minister's mind before she even asked the question.

"Mr. President, how long have you been sick?"

"What?" Bates said defensively. "No, I'm fine."

Lucy drew a deep breath. "Matthew – "

Everyone could hear a sigh through the phone. "Two days now," he said.

The politicians in Brussels didn't quite know what to say. "Does everyone in the bunker have it, sir?" General Davis asked.

Another sigh crossed the pond. "We do."

"How is that possible? You went underground long before the virus arrived in DC."

"We ran out of food."

"What?"

"The bunker wasn't designed to hold this many people for this long. Two of the Secret Service agents went up to the main White House kitchen to get food. They didn't come back down, but we think the food packaging or something like that was contaminated. I don't know . . . it doesn't really matter anyway."

"We can try to – "

"No, no," President Bates interrupted. "No special treatment or extraordinary measures. I don't have all that long left anyway." He paused. "General Davis, I actually do need something from you."

"Yes sir?"

"My Joint Chiefs here in the bunker have been directing the humanitarian relief efforts along the coasts. I'm turning that over to you."

"Yes sir. And don't worry, we'll continue the aid missions . . . it's in everyone's best interests for the United States to not be completely wiped out."

"Good," President Bates said. He directed his next comment to his closest friend on the WPR. "Do me a favor, Lucy?"

The pain in the man's voice shook the prime minister. "Sure," she replied. "Anything."

"After this ends, and the borders are reopened and the world returns to something resembling normal, will you see to it that I'm given a proper burial in Arlington National

Cemetery? Nothing ornate; no special monument. Just a small white headstone like the rest."

The prime minister choked back sadness in her voice. "Of course. Absolutely."

"And Lucy? Or I guess, everyone there?"

"Yes?"

"If people ask about me and what I did during this, tell them I loved my family, I loved my country, and I did the best I could with the hand I was dealt."

"You've done an excellent job, Mr. President," General Davis told his commander-in-chief. "No one could have predicted this."

Bates laughed at the general's words. "You're a terrible liar, Davis. But thank you." He paused as he was overtaken by a fit of coughing. When it subsided, he added: "now stop wasting your time talking to this sick old man. Do what you have to do to save as many as you can."

"I will," Lucy Rodgers answered. "We all will."

TWENTY

While the political and military leaders in Brussels dealt with the logistics of containing the virus, Dr. Capello and his team in Solna continued to strive towards figuring out the cause and cure for what everyone now referred to as the Shorewood Disease. It wasn't entirely fair to the small Minnesota town to saddle it with such an awful name association, but, once people started using it, the moniker stuck.

Consequently, it was 'Shorewood Disease Relief Fund' posters that began to adorn the walls and newsletters of charitable organizations, and 'Pray for the Shorewood Disease Victims' signs at churches, synagogues, mosques, and temples around the world. While much of the focus was on the work of the WPR and the ECDC, nongovernmental groups around the globe also sprang into action to assist in the pandemic response.

Private charitable organizations set up camp at international airports to offer assistance to stranded travelers – Americans and people from the various other containment zone layers who by luck or circumstance found themselves out of the country when the travel ban was implemented. US embassies and consulates were flooded with new cases to handle – only this time the refugees were Americans seeking shelter abroad instead of the other way around. Billions of private citizens opened their wallets, houses, and hearts to embrace the new class of global homeless. But no organizations even came close to matching the work and generosity of religious organizations. Churches held prayer vigils and fundraising drives, temples and mosques stayed open 24/7 to comfort those in need, and the Catholic Church became the largest single provider of food, clothing, and shelter as it opened the doors of its cathedrals, schools, and monasteries to not only stranded Americans but also anyone seeking answers in a time of such uncertainty.

Ricardo Capello witnessed that firsthand one Sunday morning while walking from his house to the office. The gorgeous Catholic cathedral that adorned a busy city street corner usually sat empty except for big holidays, and even then it was never full. But on this particular morning, worshippers from the early mass were streaming out onto the streets while others lined up to enter and attend the later service.

There are no atheists in foxholes, I suppose, the doctor thought as he weaved his way through the crowd. Capello was a Roman Catholic himself, baptized into the Church as a baby like most everyone he knew back home in Andorra. When people asked, though, Ricardo said he was more culturally Catholic than religiously Catholic. Mass was reserved for Christmas and Easter, but he crossed himself when he prayed and kept a medal of St. Luke in a drawer in his desk. *Patron saint of doctors*, Capello thought as he finally made his way out of the crowd and continued his walk to work. Something had been tugging at the physician ever since the whole Shorewood outbreak began; something telling him that maybe he too should join the others in attending mass and praying for answers to the deadly puzzle that kept him up at night. *I'd love to*, he thought. *I really would. But I just don't have time.*

TWENTY-ONE

Upon arriving at the ECDC's headquarters, a large, three story red-brick building with a trademark clock tower on top, Dr. Capello put his philosophical and religious thoughts aside and joined the rest of his team in his office across the hall from their shared lab.

Despite their best efforts, Dr. Capello and his assistants were still making little headway in trying to figure out which disease was wreaking havoc across the Atlantic. As such, they were all gathered to review their progress to date.

I would say we've made no progress, Ricardo thought, *except we are learning a lot about what it's not.* From their countless rounds of tests and hours of research, the ECDC doctors had been able to rule out almost every known illness. The team started with the obvious – Measles, Mumps, and Rubella – and then expanded into viruses and bacteria that had far less in common with the patients' symptoms. *Still no luck.*

The group ordered in brunch from Ricardo's favorite deli down the street and all grabbed whatever seats they could find, with Dr. Schroder carrying in a chair from a room across the hall.

"Tell me something good," Dr. Capello said as he opened his breakfast sandwich of knäckebröd and messmör – crisp bread and a sweet spread made of butter and whey.

"We've been able to rule out a lot," Dr. Delacroix answered before taking a bite of her yogurt.

"Rookie," said Dr. Mencken, speaking to Zach Schroder. "You've got whiteboard duty."

Zach rolled his eyes but didn't argue. Although he had been at the ECDC well beyond a year, as the youngest member of the team he knew that things like whiteboard duty would inevitably fall to him. The doctor was hungry enough, though, to bring his food with him and eat with one hand.

Scribbling 'ruled out' on one side of the wall-mounted board, he took a bite of his sandwich and turned to face his colleagues. "Wadda we got?"

"Measles," Dr. Ekstrom said. "Smallpox. Mumps. Rubella."

"Cancer," added Delacroix.

"All of them?" Zach asked.

"Yep."

"Alright," the American said, pausing to take another bite. "What else?"

"AIDS."

"Influenza."

"Mononucleosis."

"Staph infection."

"Impetigo."

"Ooh," Dr. Capello said, "nice one. I wouldn't have thought to test for that," he added, referring to a contagious skin infection caused by a combination of strep and staph bacteria.

"Any others?" Dr. Schroder asked.

His fellow doctors shook their heads in the negative.

"Okay," Capello replied. "Make a new column, Zach. We'll just leave this board up in my office and can add to it as we go along. This column is symptoms."

Schroder completed that task with ease, listing off the disease reactions that the doctors all knew by heart. Rash. Fever. Headache. Joint pain. Seizures. Organ failure. Death.

"One more column now. Time to come together and, oh, what is the word?" Ricardo asked. "Think as one?"

"Brainstorm?"

"Yes. Time to brainstorm," said Dr. Capello. He prided himself on his English and hated when a word escaped his memory. "What else could it be?"

Silence filled the room while the researchers both thought and ate.

"Den – " Dr. Ekstrom stopped mid-sentence to finish chewing. "Sorry. What about Dengue Fever?"

"The rash usually comes later on," Dr. Mencken argued. "Plus Minnesota isn't exactly a place where we would expect to find a tropical disease."

"I wouldn't expect an entire country to be quarantined either," Goran replied.

"Okay. Fair point."

"Put it on the board," Dr. Capello decided. "Let's keep this moving along. The more time we spend here, the more time we lose in the lab. Come on – just say whatever you think."

"Lupus," Zach suggested. "Shingles."

"Mercury poisoning?" asked Elena.

The physicians' eyes lit up upon hearing something that might offer a solid explanation, but Ricardo dashed their hopes with a shake of his head. "The CDC in America got water and soil samples when the outbreak started and tested for it."

Dr. Delacroix, their resident epidemiologist, said: "The only large-scale epidemic like this in modern history was the Spanish Flu. But this isn't a flu of any sort. Plus its infection and death rates are way too high."

"Did you know that the Spanish Flu wasn't actually 'Spanish' *per se*?" commented Dr. Schroder.

"Huh?"

Elena nodded her head. "That's correct . . . 'Spanish Flu' is just a nickname, and an inaccurate one at that."

"What are you talking about?" asked Dr. Mencken.

"No one knows the true origin of the 1918 flu pandemic," Zach explained. "Because it happened during World War I, government censors in many European countries and in the United States prevented newspapers from running stories about how bad the disease was. However, Spain was neutral in World War I so their papers wrote all about it . . . making people think that Spain was harder hit than everywhere else."

"Well, we certainly do not have that same issue today," quipped Dr. Ekstrom.

"The Shorewood Disease isn't a flu, you're right," Dr. Capello said, bringing the conversation back on topic. "It's more like the plague."

His team stopped reviewing the files in front of them and looked over at their boss.

"You think it's the plague?" Goran finally asked.

"Well it's a plague of some sort," Ricardo said. "If we're going by the dictionary definition of 'a highly infectious, usually fatal, epidemic disease.'"

"Yeah, but it's not the Bubonic Plague . . . we tested for that."

"No, that's true. It's not. But it kills like Bubonic Plague. Extremely high infection rates, outwardly visible symptoms – a rash instead of buboes, and death within a short number of days."

"Shit," said Dr. Schroder.

"Your American eloquence astounds me," Max commented. He shook his head. "A new strand of plague . . . let's add it to the board of possibilities."

With that done, the doctors continued their suggestions, each in turn rejected as not plausible.

"Could it be autoimmune?"

"We don't have evidence of abnormal T cells or other pathogen antibody signals."

Dr. Capello made a noise that resembled a growl and ran his hands over his eyes and up through his hair. "We're not getting anywhere with this. We might as well write 'no fucking clue' on the board and leave it at that." He paused. "Come on . . . let's all head to the lab and come back at it later with fresh eyes."

TWENTY-TWO

As he had every night since the viral epidemic began, Dr. Capello made it a point to return home to eat dinner with his family. He often went back to his office after his children were asleep, but Ricardo was determined to spend at least a couple of hours with his wife and kids each day.

"How did it go today at the lab?" Sabrina Capello asked her husband. The couple and their two kids had just sat down for dinner.

"Still no progress," Ricardo replied, filling his plate with generous servings of Wiener Schnitzel and potatoes. It was his favorite Austrian dish, and the doctor knew that his wife made it in an effort to cheer him up after another frustrating day of work. "This disease – " he shook his head. "It's unlike anything I have ever seen before. But," the doctor continued, "I spend all day thinking and talking about the virus. And after dinner I'll have to go back to work again. So enough of that for now. Tell me about you all. How was school this past week? Did you learn anything new?"

Grace, a precocious eight-year-old with her mother's ice blue eyes and her father's darker complexion, opened her mouth to answer the question but was interrupted by the phone ringing.

"I'll get it," said Sabrina, standing up from the table.

"School was great this week, Daddy," Grace said with a smile. "We are learning about Sweden and its history this year in social studies. It's neat."

"No – he is not here so stop calling!"

Mrs. Capello's voice echoed from the kitchen into the dining room and both kids jumped in their chairs when she slammed the phone back down on the receiver. "Reporters! Ugh . . . I hate them all!"

Ricardo could see the strain on his wife's face and knew that she had been lying to him about how often people were calling wanting to interview him.

Just as Sabrina sat back down at the table, the phone started ringing again.

"Leave it," Dr. Capello said. "Or, better yet, let's do this." He walked into the kitchen and unplugged the phone cord from the wall. "There. Much better."

"What if they need you at the lab?"

He shrugged and sat back down at the table. "The whole team got new burner phones to make sure we could discuss the case without our cell phones being hacked by reporters. They can get in touch with me if they need to."

After taking another bite of his dinner, Ricardo turned to his son. "How about you? How was school?"

"Fine," the twelve-year-old answered, picking at his food.

"Xavier . . . how was school?" repeated his father.

"Awful, okay? It was awful. I had my science presentation on Friday and I got nervous and screwed it all up."

"I'm sure it wasn't that bad."

"Yes it was!" The boy's eyes welled with tears. "They all said I was stupid and that I must be just like you because if you were smarter then you'd have a cure and people wouldn't still be dying."

Dr. Capello's eyes grew wide in shock and he looked over at his wife to hopefully deny what their son just said. Instead, Sabrina closed her eyes and slowly nodded her head up and down.

"I am so sorry, Xavier," Ricardo said, standing up from his chair and walking over to envelope the boy in a hug. "I'm so, so sorry," he repeated. "You're not stupid. You're very smart. And anything happening or not happening at my work has nothing to do with you."

"Kids talk about you at my school too, Daddy," Grace said quietly. "They keep asking me when you're going to fix things. You are going to fix it, aren't you?"

The little girl's words tore at the doctor's heart. "Come here," he said, motioning for his daughter to join the hug. "You too, Mom."

When the family of four was all huddled together, its patriarch said: "Of course I'm going to fix it. That's my job, and I'll do it." He paused, swallowing the lump in his throat. "But in the meantime, I think it would be best for you to go stay with your grandparents in Austria."

Sabrina, Grace, and Xavier all pulled back from the hug and stared at Ricardo.

"What?"

"Why?"

"I don't want to leave, Daddy."

The doctor sighed. "I know you don't, baby. I don't want you to go either. But I think it's the right thing to do. You'll be able to get away from all of the reporters and the mean kids and not have to be in the middle of this circus. Plus, I know your grandma and grandpa would love to spend some time with you."

Ricardo forced a smile, trying to convince himself as much as everyone else that this would be for the best. His wife's parents were good people – she had grown up with the kind of upper-middle class life he had only dreamed about as a kid – and he knew that his family would be safe there in Salzburg. Things had gotten too out of control in Solna. He had to stay, had to find the cure, but he wouldn't let his family suffer because of his job.

"It won't be for long," Dr. Capello reassured the three faces in front of him. "And it will be better this way, you'll see."

TWENTY-THREE

The conversations with his team about possible diseases had stuck with Dr. Capello during his evening at home and into the next day. Elena's comment suggesting an autoimmune disease was what particularly had him thinking. *What if*, Capello wondered, *it is a reaction to something found in the body? Maybe not a typical autoimmune disease, but perhaps it's the body's response to the toxin rather than the toxin itself that is the problem?* He knew that that was the case with the world's last pandemic, the Spanish Flu, when the strong reaction of healthy people's immune systems was what led to them dying in higher numbers.

With that example in mind, Ricardo shifted his focus from microscopes and test tubes to medical records and demographics studies. "What do all of the sick people have in common," he asked aloud, "besides the illness?"

They were all in the United States when they got sick – that was a given. But not all of them lived there, he noted. Some of the victims were foreign nationals visiting the country on business or vacation trips. *So it can't be geography*, Ricardo thought. It also couldn't be an environmental factor like soil or water since the outbreak had now spread well beyond the Shorewood-Minneapolis region.

"Anem . . . ¿què ets?" Dr. Capello whispered in his native Catalán, willing the answer to reveal itself. "Deixar d'amagar de mi."

After several hours of research, long past when his eyes turned red and glazed over from staring at his computer screen, something caught Ricardo's attention. *Vaccination records*, he read. *What if. . . ?* The wheels in the physician's head started spinning so fast that he could barely think straight.

Dr. Schroder, who happened to walk past his boss' office at that moment, saw the look on Capello's face and stepped inside. "What is it?" asked the American.

"What if it's autoimmune but not how we've been thinking?"

"What do you mean?"

Ricardo turned his computer screen so Zach could see the charts displayed on it. "I tried to find out what the outbreak victims all had in common," he explained. "The United States has one of the highest vaccination rates in the world. What if the pathogen attaches to the antibodies present in those people who were vaccinated?"

A light bulb turned on above Dr. Schroder's head. "That could explain why the elderly are less likely to get it. And kids too, since so many parents didn't get their children vaccinated after the autism scare several years ago."

A small grin threatened to break through Dr. Capello's usually stoic expression. "We still need to determine which vaccine, but I think we've got it now."

Zach smiled enough for both men combined. "What are we waiting for then? Let's go over to the lab and tell everybody else what you figured out."

****

Once they knew what they were looking for, the team at the ECDC identified the offending vaccine within hours. Measles, Mumps, and Rubella, or MMR, was a multi-dose vaccination administered to young children on a broad scale in much of the world. The comparisons to Rubella had, in fact, been accurate, since it was that portion of the three-pronged vaccine that was doing the damage. Although not understanding with complete clarity how it worked, the task force in Solna determined that a new strand of the Rubella virus was the ultimate culprit, latching on to regular Rubella antibodies and wreaking havoc in the victims' bodies.

With knowledge of their discovery in hand, Dr. Capello arranged a videoconference with the WPR in Brussels. The political and military leaders were understandably thrilled to hear that the cause of the Shorewood Disease had been identified, even if they remained confused as to the doctor's explanation.

"I don't understand," said the Chinese president. "I thought the vaccine protects people?"

"It is supposed to," Ricardo replied. "And it typically does. The MMR vaccine was first developed in the 1970s and has shielded hundreds of millions of people from the three incorporated diseases. Measles, which can be deadly, is now on a significant decline around the world. But the Shorewood Disease does not work like the viruses we are used to seeing."

"Why not?"

"Let me begin with some background on the function of a vaccine, no?" Dr. Capello said. "Patients are given a small dose of an agent that is comprised of either the live virus or, more commonly, something that resembles the virus. The body thinks it is under attack and the immune system responds to kill the invading organism. But the body also remembers that organism for the future, so that if it is attacked again it will be better able to respond. The memory is in the form of antibodies. Does everyone understand so far?"

The people in the room nodded their heads in the affirmative.

"Okay," Capello continued, "so everyone who received the MMR vaccine now has antibodies for Measles, Mumps, and Rubella stored up in their body. The Shorewood virus seeks out those Rubella antibodies, attaches to them, and mutates them into disease-causing cells."

France's president shook his head. "Science was my worst subject in school. You're going to have to explain this more."

"Imagine it this way," Lucy Rodgers said. "Envision everyone walking around in suits of armor to protect themselves against various weapons. But now, along comes a new weapon that's magnetized. So everyone wearing a suit of armor gets sucked up into space by the magnet. Poof. Gone. The only people left are the ones who didn't wear the suits of armor for whatever reason."

"How is that possible?" asked General Davis.

"Honestly, I do not know," Ricardo replied. "We have never seen this before."

"Where'd you learn all of that medical stuff?" the Chinese president asked Lucy Rodgers.

"I studied biology at university," the British prime minister replied. "I wanted to become a surgeon."

"Why didn't you?"

"I was told by my parents that doctors were a form of servants, and that members of my family were masters, not servants."

Murmurs of surprise filled the room.

"And the fact that you became a politician, a public servant, didn't bother them?" General Davis asked.

"A little, I suppose. They would have much preferred me to marry well and not work outside the home. But if I had to have a career – and I insisted that I did – then they deemed that being a member of the ruling political class would be suitable enough." Uncomfortable with the turn in the conversation, Lucy said: "but that's neither here nor there. We must focus on the task at hand. What are my action items?" the prime minister asked Dr. Capello. "I know we'll need a new vaccine of some sort and that will take a certain amount of time, even if we expedite it. But what are things that our governments' health ministries can be doing right now to help?"

Ricardo ran his hand through his hair while he thought. "First, and most importantly, stop giving people the MMR vaccine. We can come up with a new one, but right now the last thing we want is to expose more people to potential infection."

Rodgers nodded. "No more MMR. Got it."

"Secondly," Dr. Capello continued, "make sure hospitals have the equipment and personnel to handle cases should anyone slip through quarantine – or God forbid a new wave breaks out outside the containment zone."

"What are the odds of that, doctor?" asked General Davis. "Of this thing popping up in Munich or Beijing or Johannesburg?"

Capello exhaled deeply. "I can't answer that. I wish I could. But we don't know what caused the viral mutation to begin with, so we have no way of knowing the risk posed to those outside the United States of it happening again."

"Anything else we need to be doing to assist you and your medical team?" the British prime minister asked, trying to keep the call on track and the morbidity to a minimum.

"I don't think so. We're working on some instructions for doctors, hospitals, border patrol, etcetera to follow if they come in contact with a person they suspect is infected. And the quarantine centers at air and water ports will receive directions about how to document positive cases for future study." The doctor paused. "Right now, we just need to . . . how would you say . . . put our noses to the millstone and create a proper antidote."

"Grindstone," Brad Davis corrected.

"Pardon?"

"Put your noses to the grindstone," the general clarified.

"Ah, yes, the grindstone. And we will. If there is nothing else, I will return to the lab."

"There's nothing else," the French president said. "Thank you, Dr. Capello." A chorus of 'thank you' and 'good luck' followed.

"Thank you. Good day."

TWENTY-FOUR

While the doctors in Solna and WPR leaders in Brussels continued to work feverishly, the rest of the world found themselves in a rather peculiar position. Outside of the quarantined zone and thus safe, yet still feeling as if they were in the midst of a big event that somehow didn't quite touch them. Similar to modern-day, First World warfare fought on someone else's land and watched on news broadcasts, what was happening in and to America was something of a tragic curiosity for most people and the topic *du jour* at all major think tanks and universities.

"I've been truly impressed by the speed with which the international community has responded to this situation," one professor said during an evening symposium at the University of Sydney. "Almost immediately," he continued, "countries and corporations and individuals were taking steps to prevent the spread of the disease. I mean, even before the containment zone was imposed, you had airport officials quarantining all passengers coming from America."

"I agree," replied a visiting professor from Japan. "Many at the time felt like those initial measures were severe overreactions, but in reality it is those things that enabled the containment zone to be put in place and the Shorewood Disease to be isolated within the United States."

"How does one get to be that person?" the first speaker asked. "The kind of person who sees a problem and says 'we need to act on this, and act on it now'?"

"That's a great question. I think a good deal of it is instinct. In this instance, a survival instinct. But a lot also comes from confidence and competence in one's work. We saw that with the doctors at the American CDC who were the first to sound the alarm in a big way." The Tokyo resident took sip of water to clear his throat. "That's the kind of person we hope to have in positions of power and authority . .

. someone who knows what needs to be done and isn't afraid to be the one to do it."

"Right, well, just think of the consequences if the doctors were wrong. If it wasn't an epidemic and they just closed the borders for no reason."

His symposium partner shook his head. "Disastrous. Absolutely catastrophic damage to the world economy; we're talking hundreds of billions, if not trillions, of dollars. And I won't even start on what would happen to the reputations of NATO and the UN."

"Well, we're still faced with that amount of economic consequence. But I suppose the point is that we know it was worth it."

TWENTY-FIVE

Whether or not the border closings were in fact worth it was a question that continued to weigh on the mind of Lucy Rodgers. And as the known and unknown body count continued to climb, the sick feeling in the pit of the prime minister's stomach got worse. The only thing that made her feel any better was that she didn't have to face the media.

Rodgers and her fellow world leaders did not envy the public relations task assigned to the United Nations and NATO Secretaries-General. Wanting to present a united, global front, the powers that be in Brussels decided early on that the two nongovernmental figures would make all public announcements and be the only speakers at press conferences. The result was that the two distinguished career diplomats were relegated mainly to spokesmen status, while all actual decisions were being made by a core team of global powers and NATO military brass. The job was dwindled even further to just the NATO Secretary-General after a wave of public outcry at the fact that the UN's leader, Mr. Nantakarn, had escaped New York.

God help Henrik today, the British Prime Minister thought as she glanced from her desk to the small television set in the corner of her temporary office. NATO Secretary-General Henrik Steinway had just taken the news conference podium to announce a bombshell: acting under WPR orders, NATO pilots shot down a passenger plane full of people attempting to flee the containment zone.

"No flight plan was filed," Mr. Steinway was saying on TV, "so we don't have an exact passenger count. But we do know it was a full-size commercial jetliner."

Scores of reporters shouted questions back at the Secretary-General in dozens of languages, but the man, to his credit, remained stoic and calm.

"When we first announced the border closures and blockade," the NATO representative said, "we made it very clear that we do not have the capacity to quarantine large numbers of people who are potentially carrying the virus and that, as such, anyone trying to escape the containment zone would not be allowed to do so."

Steinway was known for his blunt, straight-talk approach, and Lucy knew he wouldn't pull any punches. "People were warned that they could not leave. Announcements were made. Leaflets were airdropped over American cities. Loudspeakers along the borders shout messages in multiple languages telling people that they will be shot if they try to exit. This plane had plenty of warning." NATO's civilian leader took a deep breath and then brought the message home. "We *will not* risk seven billion lives because we are too afraid to make the hard decisions or do the hard things. We are far past the time for sentimentality."

The reporters began shouting questions and Prime Minister Rodgers muted the TV with her remote control. The major announcement now over, she knew that Henrik could handle wrapping up the rest of the news conference. And he was right. People trying to escape the confines of the isolation area were a risk to the rest of the world, and Lucy felt confident that history would approve of the WPR's choices. *Even if it doesn't,* she thought, *we're doing the best we can.*

Turning in her chair, Rodgers looked over at her chief of staff who was seated on a couch in the corner. The two Britons were in the room assigned as the prime minister's private office in the wing of NATO's headquarters designated for the visiting foreign leaders. Although they all still had their own countries to run, there was an unspoken agreement that the core WPR members would remain in Brussels until the American blockade was lifted.

"Who is still alive in America?" Lucy asked her aide. "Do we know?"

Her chief of staff looked down at the notebook in his hands. "The President and his top ministers are now believed dead. We of course cannot confirm it . . . "

"But if anyone would have the capability to communicate with us, it would be them," Lucy finished the man's sentence for him.

"Yes ma'am. And given that President Bates admitted to being ill the last time you did talk to him . . . "

Lucy exhaled deeply. "Any other political leaders or military generals still alive?"

The aide shook his head no. "Not any inside the country, anyway. National Command Authority, which was the term the Americans used for the ultimate source of their military orders, consisted of the President, the Secretary of Defense, and then down through the Joint Chiefs of Staff and the commanding officers of the Unified Combatant Commands. You know, Pacific Command, Southern Command, etcetera. Africa and European Commands are still operational, but they're assisting in the containment efforts. General Davis is the highest ranking American who we can confirm is alive."

"So, as far as we're aware, the United States is without leadership of any kind, absent Brad Davis here in Brussels and a smattering of admirals and generals along the American coasts." She lowered her voice to keep people in the adjacent room from hearing her. "I know it had to be done," Lucy confided, "but I feel like we've condemned three hundred million people to die. I feel like a horrible person for doing it."

The chief of staff had experienced the same feelings but could only imagine the magnitude of them if the decision to create the containment zone had been on his shoulders. "Well, Madam Prime Minister, not that it changes things, but two hundred-seventy million of those people would die anyway. So it's really only thirty million left behind."

"'Only' thirty million that my soul will have to answer for on Judgment Day. Excellent."

"And billions upon billions that your soul will be thanked for saving." Having been Lucy Rodgers' top advisor for the past fifteen years, the man had a rapport and friendship with the prime minister unlike any other members of the staff. Sensing that his boss needed a pep talk, he switched from consolation to inspiration. "Now with all due respect ma'am, buck up. You're English. Straight back; stiff upper lip. When in doubt, say WWCD."

Lucy's brow furrowed in confusion. "WWCD?"

"What would Churchill do."

The prime minister laughed out loud. "What would Churchill do." Her laughter continued. "Probably get piss drunk and smoke a cigar."

The chief of staff shook his head. "No ma'am. Well, yes, likely so. But he would also soldier on and find a way to victory."

Lucy took a deep breath and stood up straight, squaring her shoulders. "You're right. Moment over. Let's go back to the conference room . . . it must be getting close to time for our next meeting."

****

When Rodgers arrived at the main command center, she was surprised to see new faces in the room.

"What's going on?" she asked.

"These people are from Médecins Sans Frontières," responded the French president. "They wish to go inside the containment zone."

"What? That's impossible."

"That's what I said," added General Davis. "Nobody out, and nobody in either."

"But that isn't completely true," the Frenchman replied. "Up until a few days ago the Americans were running relief missions from Hawaii, Puerto Rico, and their fleet of ships along the coasts."

"Those were only to drop off food, water, and other basic supplies," said the general. "The military personnel were specifically ordered to not engage with any people inside the containment zone."

"Besides," Prime Minister Rodgers added, "all of those flights have been on a temporary hold since last week."

"Why?" the lead doctor asked. "I didn't hear anything about that on the news."

"That's because we didn't make it public. We received reports that terrorist groups had infiltrated the supply chains and were planning to somehow taint the food and clothing we were giving to survivors in the United States."

"According to the chatter picked up by intelligence agencies," Brad Davis continued, "the idea was to make us look bad. You know, 'here, have this food aid; and by the way, it's poisoned.' Or, 'take this blanket, it'll keep you warm; just joking, it has smallpox all over it.'"

"You're kidding."

The general shook his head. "No. We haven't been able to confirm or deny the reports, but until we do we obviously have to shut down the relief flights."

The group of physicians from Doctors Without Borders didn't appear convinced. "Even if the humanitarian aid stopped, we don't want to bring any supplies like that so the terrorists wouldn't know. And we have not yet mentioned the main reason why we should go," one of them said. "We did not receive the MMR vaccine."

Prime Minister Rodgers surveyed the people in front of her. *If what they're saying is true, this could be our way to start really fixing things in America,* she thought. "How is that possible?" Lucy asked. "MMR is one of the most widely distributed vaccinations in the world."

"This is true," the group's spokesman admitted. "But in case you did not notice, we all grew up in countries that are lesser developed."

Rodgers realized that the physician was right. Every representative from Doctors Without Borders looked to be of African, Middle Eastern, or Southeast Asian descent. She was about to signal her approval of the idea when General Davis spoke again.

"It is an interesting concept, I admit, to make use of people who weren't vaccinated against Rubella. But I'm sorry, you can't go. We're having a hard enough time as it is keeping the borders secure . . . we simply don't have the bandwidth to support a medical mission like the one you've proposed."

"But we don't require any support," the man argued. "Listen to me, please. People are dying. And not just those who got the Shorewood Disease. People are dying from heart attacks and car accidents and other things they wouldn't normally die of because the doctors in America are all dead. I want to go." He looked around at his colleagues. "*We* want to go. This is what we do. Médecins Sans Frontières. Doctors Without Borders."

****

It took several more rounds of argument and discussion, but the leadership committee finally agreed to the doctors' request for a relief mission. The next morning, the group of six physicians loaded up a military transport plane with supplies, including medical necessities, food, power generators, and two jeeps for transportation. Less than twenty-four hours after they first arrived at NATO's headquarters, the team from Doctors Without Borders was headed west toward America. Flying the plane was a group of three military pilots who volunteered for the mission; when the plane got closer to the containment zone, the vaccinated pilots would don protective suits and air masks to hopefully shield them from any exposure to the disease.

"I still don't like this idea," General Davis muttered as the WPR gathered in the operations room to listen to the radio communication from the flight.

"They'll be fine," the Russian president assured him. "The worst that happens is the pilots get sick, and the doctors know that if that happens then they just drive north to the Canadian border to be quarantined. This is good," he added, giving his colleague a friendly slap on the back. "It will work."

No sooner than the Russian president finished speaking did the speakerphone on the center of the conference room table begin to crackle. "Headquarters, this is Angel Flight One," the plane's captain said. "We've just now entered American airspace and – what the – holy shit!"

The members of the WPR looked around the room in confusion. "What just happened? Where'd they go?"

"Did we lose them? Captain, are you there? We still have them on radar, right?" General Davis aimed his question at the air traffic controller seated across the room.

The young man shook his head. "No sir. I . . . I don't know what happened. The plane just disappeared."

PART II

TWENTY-SIX

Two Weeks Earlier

A faint buzzing sound invaded the depths of Dehqan Nazari's mind, an annoyance creeping into his sleep and making the twenty-five year old dream that he was being chased by a bumble bee. No matter how many times the slumbering man swatted at the bee, though, it wouldn't stop buzzing. Ringing bells soon joined the buzzing, and Dehqan woke up with a start when he realized his phone was ringing. Not his regular phone, though. His other phone; his second phone. The one he kept hidden in an air vent in his Nashville, Tennessee apartment.

The engineering graduate student scrambled out of bed and across the room, popping open the cover of the air vent and picking up the vibrating cell phone.

Five missed calls, he read. *Shit.*

"Hello?" Dehqan said, his voice still groggy from sleep.

A harsh male voice yelled back at Dehqan in his native Pashto: "'Hello?' You don't answer the phone until the sixth call and you speak to me in the language of imperialists and infidels?!"

Dehqan realized his mistake too late to fix it. Still half-asleep, it hadn't fully registered in his mind that the ringing phone was the one he used to communicate with his family back home in Afghanistan.

"I am sorry, Uncle," Dehqan replied in the correct language. "I was asleep and did not hear the phone ringing."

His uncle wasn't interested in any excuses. "You will sleep with the phone under your pillow from now on."

Dehqan sighed. "Yes, Uncle."

"What if I was calling to warn you of a fire, hmm? If I found out your oven had gotten too hot and would soon burst into flames?"

The younger man ran a hand through his thick black hair and rolled his eyes, grateful that his uncle was halfway around the world and couldn't see the look on his face. 'Fire,' 'oven,' and 'burst into flames' were code words, standing for danger, cover story, and police raid, respectively.

"I am truly sorry, Uncle. It will not happen again. But you can be glad, though, that we do not have to worry about fires for now. This disease outbreak has taken over everyone's attention."

"Yes, this is why I called," replied the older man. "You have done well as a sleeper in the United States. But tell me, this new virus, will you and our other agents be affected?"

"No sir, I don't think so. It's only people who were vaccinated for Rubella as kids. We were not so we are fine."

"Good. This is the weakest the United States will ever be. Go live now. Take over the most advanced military base you can get your hands on and convert it into headquarters for our North American operations." Dehqan could hear the gleam in his uncle's eyes from half a world away. "Think about it – as of yesterday, nobody is allowed to enter or exit the United States. I know the Americans are still airdropping food and other aid into the country, but we're working on a way to stop that. All of those weapons and all of that money are up for grabs with no one standing in our way." The Taliban commander laughed. "The infidels spent over a decade and hundreds of billions of dollars trying to force us out of Afghanistan. Okay. We'll just move to the United States!"

The comment drew laughter from his stateside nephew.

"Remember," the uncle added, "this won't be an easy population to subdue, even if it is true that the virus will kill ninety percent of it. They won't buy into our religious claims and they all love their guns. You've been undercover and behind enemy lines for several years. Now is the time to awaken and avenge your brother's death."

Upon hearing mention of his deceased younger sibling, Dehqan sat up straighter on his bed and a fierceness entered his eyes. "Yes, Uncle. Now is the time."

TWENTY-SEVEN

After hanging up the phone, the newly-crowned terrorist leader packed a duffle bag full of clothes, two guns, and what little food he had in his pantry and loaded it all in his car. Dehqan Nazari then programmed Colorado Springs into his GPS and headed west. During the seventeen hour drive, Dehqan used his Afghanistan cell phone to arrange things with the rest of his terrorist cell. Since he was using a satellite phone routed through a company in Riyadh, Saudi Arabia, Dehqan knew he could both make the calls more securely and not have to worry about outages at US cell providers.

One by one, Nazari went through his contact list and told them all to meet him at America the Beautiful Park in Colorado Springs in three days. Their eventual target would be the Cheyenne Mountain Nuclear Bunker, the former home of North American Aerospace Defense – better known as NORAD. Although NORAD's main offices were moved to a new facility several years earlier, Dehqan had done his research and knew that Cheyenne Mountain stayed on a readiness alert as a backup. *Anything we would want to do at the new place can be done at the old one*, he thought. *Plus it's about three thousand times more secure.* Built in the 1960s at the height of the Cold War, the bunker was carved out of the inside of the mountain and designed to withstand a thirty megaton nuclear explosion. *The perfect spot for our new headquarters.*

Getting into the bunker could be a logistical problem, but Dehqan decided he would deal with that issue when and if it arose. For all he knew, the facility might be unlocked and abandoned in the aftermath of the disease outbreak.

****

Seventy-two hours later, Dehqan Nazari and the other members his recently-awoken sleeper cell gathered in Colorado Springs' large public park, America the Beautiful. An open space like that wasn't typically where a group of terrorists would want to gather, but all of the usual rules no longer applied. The Shorewood Disease had arrived in the Rocky Mountain city several days earlier, and everyone not yet affected by it was hiding out in their homes. Including the police, Dehqan thought with smile. *Less than a month ago, if I had told someone that Taliban terrorists would be gathering openly in the United States . . .* he shook his head. *Unbelievable good fortune for us. Alhamdulillah. Praise God.*

Dehqan looked around the semicircle in front of him, surveying the group of men now under his command. *Surely this isn't everybody?* he thought. The team looked a lot smaller than he expected.

"Who are we missing?" Dehqan asked.

The strangers looked around at each other, none having an answer. As part of a strategy to stay undetected by government intelligence agencies, the sleeper agents had no idea who the other members of their cell were. The first time they had ever seen each other was ten minutes ago.

When no one answered him, Dehqan decided to go with a roll call. "Mohamed? Are you here?"

A rail-thin boy of no more than nineteen stepped forward. "I'm here," he answered in accented English.

"Why are you here?" the group's leader asked. "I mean, what skills do you bring?"

The teenager shuffled his feet, surprised by the question. "Uhh . . . I don't know. I was told that I would get sponsored to study in America if I would fight when they told me to."

"Where are you from?"

"Singapore."

Mohamed's presence now made sense to Dehqan. *Singapore is a Visa Waiver Program country,* he remembered from his training. *It's easier for those people to come to the US, so we've tried to recruit more heavily from there.* "You're a foot soldier," Dehqan summarized.

"Yeah, umm, I guess."

The boss nodded. "Alright. What about Xiao Cheng? Where are you?"

"Here."

Xiao was short and a bit overweight, with shaggy hair and thick-rimmed glasses. *He looks like he's never shot a gun in his life,* thought Dehqan with worry. *I asked for soldiers and they gave me hipsters.*

"I'm your computer expert," Xiao announced. "I studied computer science and programming at MIT. Get me in the same room as a system's computer, and I'll get you access to whatever you want."

Dehqan issued a rare smile of approval. "Good." He then looked back down at the list of names in his hand. "Albert?"

When no one answered, Dehqan looked up. "Is Albert here?"

Again, none of the men spoke.

"Maybe he got the disease," said Mohamed. "'Albert' does sound like an American name."

That's why the numbers are light, Dehqan realized. *Some of my men are sick.* With that knowledge in mind, he continued down the list of names, all Al-Qaeda or Taliban recruits that he had never heard of before. Dehqan had eleven agents in total, twelve counting him, including the computer programmer, an explosives expert, a sniper, and eight guys like the Singaporean teenager who had never done a live mission before. *Rookies. Great.*

Five men were missing from the team, all presumed sick or dead from the Shorewood Disease outbreak. *This is going to be harder than I thought.*

TWENTY-EIGHT

The terrorists' wish for an abandoned and unlocked Cheyenne Mountain complex went unfulfilled – at least on the unlocked part. Nestled into the Rocky Mountains and just to the south, southwest of Colorado Springs, the nuclear bunker was less-than-imposing on the outside. A few employee parking lots, a guard gate, and a tunnel opening were all that was visible to a visitor's eye. Upon arriving at the employee parking lot, Dehqan and his men saw dozens of cars and trucks. Careful examination revealed that all of the cars were empty, which meant that some people were still on the other side of the tunnel inside the bunker.

"How do we get in there?" Mohamed, the teenager, asked. "Shoot our way in?" Ammunition and firepower wouldn't be a problem, since each man was armed with both a pistol and an automatic rifle.

Dehqan shook his head. "It's too secure for that. Based on my research, we're going to have two problems: getting past the first opening without identification badges, and then getting through the blast doors."

"Blast doors?" the explosives expert asked.

Dehqan nodded his head. "Two twenty-five ton doors at the entrance. You get through one, and then just down the hall there's another one."

"So, basically," one of the men said, "we need someone to let us in. We can't force our way in."

"That's correct."

"Let's check all of the cars," Xiao suggested. "You never know . . . one of the workers might have left his ID badge in his car."

Although the car search was fruitless, the terrorists hit the jackpot with the guard at the gate just in front of the bunker's entrance tunnel. Approaching from behind, weapons drawn, Dehqan and his men found the enlisted military man slumped over at his desk, dead. Dangling from his neck was his ID badge.

Entrance ticket in hand, the twelve men easily weaved their way through the maze of tunnels and rooms and doors, searching for anything that looked like it might be a command center. They passed several more dead bodies along the way, and hastened the death of a few more.

"They will die soon anyway," said a teenager who called himself Joe. "We're just putting them out of their misery."

****

It took longer than they expected, but the group of Taliban fighters finally managed to locate the complex's main command center. Dozens of desks and computers lined the room, along with several whiteboards, televisions, and projection screens.

The first order of business was removing the dead bodies from the bunker and spraying down the entire thing with air fresheners to try to get rid of the smell. The second item on Dehqan's to-do list was setting up the group's living quarters, which would be spartan but better than nothing. Mohamed and a few of the other teenagers found some fold-up cots in a storage closet and laid them out in a small room off the side of the command center. The young men also located large stashes of food and weapons and what appeared to be the bunker's power station, which was still running smoothly on an autopilot system that they didn't attempt to understand.

While the rest of the team was busy making house, Xiao parked himself in front of one of the command center's computers and went to work. It was his job to get Cheyenne Mountain up and running again at full capacity, or at least as full of capacity as he could with only eleven other people helping him.

As promised, it took the native of the little-known country of Laos less than three hours to hack into the bunker's mainframe. Xiao was irritated, though, because he could normally break in much faster than that.

"This is a more complex system than many I've worked on before," he told Dehqan. "A single user is incapable of hacking the mainframe. I had to turn on several computers at once and pretend to be multiple users before anything would unlock."

"But we're in now?" the terrorist leader asked.

Xiao nodded. "We're in. As far as running operations of the bunker is concerned, we're fully functional. Power, lights, phones, airplane radar . . . it's all good. I will warn you, though; it will probably take me much longer to access control of any weapons."

"That's okay," Dehqan replied. "We have plenty of time. Besides, we want to lay low for a little longer anyway until we're sure that the virus kills all of the people it is going to and our commanders in Afghanistan figure out a way to stop the US military from flying aid missions over the country. Only then will we start to deal with any survivors."

TWENTY-NINE

Xiao, the computer expert, worked for a week straight before he finally hit the jackpot: the NORAD weapons' mainframe. By swiping the identification badges from dead employees and then authorizing additional fake usernames, the elite 'black hat hacker' tricked the system into thinking that the military complex was operating as intended. Although Xiao was well-known in the hacking community as being one of the best, and had even been interviewed by its flagship magazine *2600: The Hacker Quarterly*, this break-in was the hardest and most complicated of his career.

The twenty-seven year old was on his way out of the command control room to finally get some sleep when he heard yelling.

"Dehqan! Everyone! Come here!"

The teenage foot soldier in charge of monitoring the security cameras and air traffic radar stood up and waved his arms to signal everyone to join him at his desk.

Exiting the small storage closet that he turned into his office and looking around, Dehqan Nazari half-expected to see his men armed and preparing to fend off an invasion. Instead, they were all huddled around one computer screen.

The radar, Dehqan thought as he walked closer. "What is it?"

"There's a plane approaching the edge of the continent," the young man replied, pointing to a dot on the screen.

"The borders are closed, and Uncle's threat of sabotage stopped the relief missions," Dehqan said, as much to himself as the rest of the group. "No planes are allowed to enter the United States. The WPR said anyone who tried would be shot down."

"Unless they are the ones who sent it," reasoned Farzad, their weapons expert and Dehqan's *de facto* deputy.

"What?"

"Think about it. Nobody is going to risk getting shot down, right? So this plane must know that it won't be. And the only way they could know that they're safe is if – "

" – if the WPR gave them permission," Dehqan finished the sentence. "Spee bachee!" he swore in Pashto. "Son of a bitch! Xiao!"

"I'm right here," the hacker replied.

"Can we contact the plane?" Dehqan asked. "Tell them to turn around? Warn them we're prepared to fight if they don't recognize that we're in charge?"

"Talk to them?" Xiao shook his head. "No, the system isn't set up for that. But I can try to shoot it down."

The man from Laos stood smiling while the rest of the terrorist team turned to look at him in shock.

"Shoot it down? From here? How?"

Xiao walked over to his desk and sat down, pulling up several computer screens' worth of radar and sophisticated weapons coding. "It's what I've been working on ever since I got full access to the weapons mainframe," he explained. "Now, we know that we can't shoot off any of the nuclear missiles – the launch process is a bifurcated sequence with separate codes that travel with the president. I'll probably be able to crack those codes eventually; I just don't have it yet."

"Okay . . ."

"But," he said with a smile, "I do have access to other, so-called conventional weapons."

"Can you hurry up the lesson, professor?" asked Farzad. "The plane is about to enter American airspace."

"Right, sorry. Okay. I'll just talk you through it as I work. If I can shoot it down, that is." He looked up at Dehqan for approval.

"Yeah, of course. Blow it up."

"Okay. So once I've located the plane on the radar," explained Xiao, his fingers typing furiously as he spoke, "I open up and activate the missile defense system. This new coding I've been working on should trick the system into thinking that the plane is an incoming intercontinental ballistic missile and shoot it down."

"You can do that?"

The computer programmer shrugged his shoulders but gave a confident grin. "We'll see," he said, then returned to his typing and mouse clicking. "Alright, just a couple more steps and . . . it's done."

"Now what?" asked the group's leader.

"Now we wait to see if it worked."

Silence fell over the room and twelve pairs of eyes trained on the little green dot that was continuing its slow and steady march into American airspace. And then, suddenly, the dot was gone.

"Where'd it go?"

"Aha!" Xiao yelled, jumping out of his chair. "It worked! It worked!" He started dancing in circles around the room, jumping for joy.

"How do you know? The dot just disappeared."

"Which means the plane is gone!" said Xiao, still dancing. Seeing that his colleagues weren't convinced, he finally stood still and pointed at his computers. "You see the little red box in the corner of one of my screens? The one that says 'target destroyed'? Direct hit!"

Soon the rest of Dehqan's men joined in the dance party, reveling in their success. Nazari, for his part, leaned back against a desk, crossed his arms, and watched the celebration with a smile on his face. This was good; very good, in fact. *But we still have a lot of work to do. This is only the beginning.*

THIRTY

After the terrorists' celebration quieted down, Dehqan returned to his office and resumed the project he was working on before. He had found a map of the United States hanging on a wall in another room and brought it to his office to use as a planning tool. Since his ultimate assignment was to establish sufficient control over the Colorado region that he would be able to steal and use or sell the nuclear weapons housed there, Dehqan knew that he needed to get a firm grasp over his plans for the available territory. His uncle and boss in Afghanistan had called him the other day to say that he was lining up scores of volunteers to travel to America once the containment zone was lifted, but only if Dehqan could assure him that his plan for the future was viable and complete.

Out in the larger command control room, several of the terrorists' eyed their boss with a mix of jealousy and suspicion.

"He acts like he's some big hot shot who knows everything," one man said under his breath. "What makes him so special that he gets to be in charge?"

Mohamed, the teenager from Singapore, shrugged his shoulders. "Good question. He's not that much older than us."

"You guys don't know Dehqan's story, do you?" asked Farzad, the group's second in command. Not waiting for an answer, he said: "Dehqan is from Afghanistan. He grew up there among the Taliban and then lived through the war after the Americans and their allies invaded. His little brother was killed by a bomb that Taliban fighters planted to kill American soldiers."

"That's sad for him," Mohamed said, "but I still don't see how that makes him qualified to lead a mission."

"How much fighting have you actually done?" Farzad shot back. "None, right? You just told somebody you wanted to join the jihad and they sent you to America with a special cell phone and instructions to wait, right?"

The boy looked down and stubbed his toe into the carpet. "Maybe."

"Dehqan grew up in a war zone. He trained at Al-Qaeda camps in the Helmand province and fought actual battles against Americans while he was there. Then they sent him over here to the United States. He's an actual warrior."

"He fought in Afghanistan?" Joe asked in awe.

Farzad nodded. "And he lived to tell about it. He can also make a bomb out of next to nothing, so I don't recommend questioning his leadership anymore. Not unless you want to wake up and find that bomb shoved up your ass."

Both Joe and Mohamed got quiet and Farzad knew he had proven his point. "Now get back to work."

****

Dehqan could hear the men talking about him outside of his office. His second-in-command was correct: he was a fighter. He had grown up in the midst of war and already earned his stripes in battle. And it was true: he lost his brother to an improvised explosive device.

Nazari remembered the day well. *How could I forget it?* he thought. A teenager at the time, Dehqan and some other boys from his village had been playing football (American soccer) in an empty field. They knew it was safe to play there . . . after eight years of an American-led war with the Taliban, villagers had devised a way of spreading the word about where most of the bombs were buried. The boys were enjoying an afternoon full of sunshine and free of gunfire – a rarity – and had almost forgotten about the conflict raging around them. But then one of the boys took a shot that went too wide and the ball got loose. Dehqan's younger brother, Ghamay, ran after the battered brown ball as it bounced into an adjacent field.

Dehqan remembered feeling the explosion more than anything else. He saw it too, and heard it, and smelled the unmistakable mix of gunpowder and charred human flesh. But the feeling was what he remembered the most. *An earthquake*, he thought. *The ground shaking and my whole foundation, my whole life, shattering to pieces.*

His younger brother died instantly, never standing a chance against the ravages of the homemade bomb. All of the other boys were fine, save for a few cuts and bruises from flying shrapnel and the concussion effect of the blast. They were fine physically, that is. *That's not the kind of image that you just forget*, Dehqan thought.

The Nazari family responded to the death of their son with anger, turning from neutral bystanders into supporters of the Taliban's cause. America became the enemy, since there would not have been any explosions if the US military hadn't invaded Afghanistan. And Dehqan, for his part, was ordered to make amends for his wrongdoing. "You should not have let him chase the ball into the other field. He was younger. You were responsible for him," Dehqan's parents said, his father with a glare and his mother through tears. "You must atone for your failure; you must atone for his death."

And now here I am, thought Dehqan. Sold into his uncle's militia with its ties to Al-Qaeda, the teenager Dehqan was trained in simple small arms combat and put to work as a soldier. His uncle then tapped the boy for overseas work and sent him to the United States to act as a spy and a sleeper agent, ready to be activated at any moment. *This moment*, he thought. 'Justice for Ghamay' was tattooed on Dehqan's hip, despite his family's adherence to the belief that tattoos were *haram*. He did feel responsible for his younger brother's death, and the life Dehqan led in the United States, the mission he was on, was meant to avenge that death.

"Dehqan?" said Joe, breaking into his thoughts.

"Hmm?"

"The phones are ready to go for the call to Europe."

Dehqan nodded. "Okay, just a minute."

As he watched the young man turn and leave his office, Dehqan wondered what the motivation was behind his decision to join the terrorist cell. Born in America to a Saudi father and a white, Christian-in-name-only mother, Jawad, who went by Joe, had regaled the group with stories of Christmas presents as a child, his sister and her friends wearing bikinis while swimming in the family's pool, and his father excusing him from Ramadan obligations because it would've interfered with football season (American football, no less).

"Why are you doing this?" Dehqan asked him one day. "You grew up with everything in a beautiful, peaceful country. Why do you now choose to become an outlaw?"

Joe had eyed the other man defensively. "You say that like what we're doing is wrong."

Dehqan shook his head. "No, it is not wrong. I just question why someone who is seemingly so American would do something most see as 'un-American.'"

"Yeah, why are you here?" Farzad had chimed in. "Come to think of it, why aren't you dead? Did you not get the vaccine as a child?"

The teenager exhaled deeply, trying to control his temper. "We lived with my father's family in Saudi Arabia from when I was six months old to six years old. The vaccine was not required there and I did not receive it when my family returned to the US." He looked back at Dehqan. "And America may be beautiful," he added, "but it is not peaceful. Besides, what I am doing is the most 'American' thing someone could do. My government was oppressive to me and not responsive to my wishes as a citizen. So I rebelled. I'm the fucking George Washington of Americanism."

Dehqan laughed. "George Washington was a terrorist?"

"If you ask the British, sure."

The group's leader shook his head and smiled as he remembered that conversation from a few days earlier. *As long as he stays loyal and does his job*, Dehqan thought, *I don't really care what his motivation is.* Nazari then stood up and walked around his desk to the office door. It was time for his call to the WPR.

THIRTY-ONE

Half of two continents and an ocean away, the leaders gathered in Brussels were still trying to determine what happened to the Doctors Without Borders plane. Their usual method for investigating an airplane crash – sending a forensics team to the scene – was obviously out of the question, and they had no way of contacting anyone on the ground in the United States to find out what they saw.

"I don't know what happened, sir," said the airman in charge of radar monitoring. They were here," he added, pointing to his screen, "and we heard them radio in when they crossed into American airspace. But then all of a sudden . . . nothing."

"A plane can't just disappear out of thin air," General Davis replied. "Something must be wrong with the communications system. They have satellite phones and were given orders to call when they landed. I'm sure we'll be hearing from them soon."

****

The general's prediction failed to materialize as minutes turned to hours and the contact phone in Brussels still didn't ring. After an hour of waiting, the members of the UN special committee dispersed from their conference room and returned to either their offices or the hotel down the street that had been commandeered for their use.

Lucy Rodgers was one of the people who stayed at NATO Headquarters. She had just closed her eyes for a quick power nap when her chief of staff knocked on her office door.

"Excuse me, ma'am, the Chancellor of the Exchequer is on the telephone."

"What does he want?"

"Something about business contracts not being enforced. I'm not sure exactly. He said it'll only take a couple of minutes."

Prime Minister Rodgers leaned back in her chair and stretched her arms over her head. Sleeping on office couches and cheap hotel mattresses was taking its toll on her joints. "Fine," she replied. "Put him through."

The man in charge of Britain's banking and currency came on the line a few seconds later. "Good afternoon, Madam Prime Minister. How is Brussels?"

"Stressful," Lucy replied, not in the mood for small talk. "I was hoping you could keep domestic matters under control while I'm stuck dealing with this shit storm."

"I apologize, I do. This has just gotten to a point where it's above my pay grade."

"Alright. What is it?" Rodgers asked.

"We're running into a lot of trouble with businesses having their operations interrupted by the American blockade."

"Hundreds of millions of people are dying and you're worried about Joe Bloggs not getting his Amazon order on time?"

The economist was a bit taken back by his boss' sharp tone. "Umm, well, it's a little bit bigger than a few Amazon orders." He paused and tried to regroup his thoughts. "I know your time is very important, more so now than ever, so I'll boil it down for you. We've gotten formal complaints from thirty-one companies, with gross revenues in excess of 400 billion pounds. Corporations based in other countries are claiming that their contracts need to continue to be fulfilled without delay or disruption, saying that the *force majure* clauses in the contracts don't apply. Or, at the very least, that payments must continue to be made even though production and fulfillment cannot."

"I'm not a barrister," Lucy said. "Remind me again what these contracts say?"

"It's the 'act of God' clauses, ma'am," the head of the Exchequer explained. "They generally say that companies are off the hook for any disruptions caused by war, strikes, floods, etcetera."

"How in the bloody hell would this not count? We're in a global state of emergency."

The chancellor sighed. "Yes ma'am, but my understanding is that they're splitting hairs with the wording. They're claiming that it's not an act of God because the blockade is man-made and it's not an act of government because the containment zone was imposed by the United Nations, not the United Kingdom."

"You've got to be shitting me."

The cabinet member was stunned into silence by the reply of his usually calm, reserved boss.

"What do you need from me?" asked Lucy.

"An act of Parliament stating that our response to the American blockade is indeed an official act of the British government."

Rodgers rolled her eyes and let out a frustrated growl. "This is absurd. This is why people hate corporations and hate lawyers. Fine. Do it. Pass whatever you need to pass. Messenger it over to me if you need a signature."

"Thank you, ma'am."

"Don't thank me. I'm dealing with real problems and these companies are acting like children. They're being the little twit in the back of the classroom saying 'no, the sun isn't orange. It's tangerine.'"

The chancellor struggled to stifle a laugh. "We'll get it done, Madam Prime Minister. I just needed your approval to go forward."

"That's all?"

"Yes ma'am."

"Good. Goodbye," Lucy replied, then hung up the phone.

****

No sooner had she finished her call with the Chancellor of the Exchequer than one of the aides to General Davis knocked on Lucy's door.

"Excuse me, Madam Prime Minister?"

"Yes?"

"We received a call on the main switchboard from someone claiming to be inside the containment zone. The caller says he has knowledge about the plane that crashed."

Lucy's head shot up. "That flight wasn't announced to the public."

The soldier nodded. "Yes ma'am, we know. That's why we're asking the core team to reconvene in the conference room so you can all participate in the phone call."

Prime Minister Rodgers immediately stood up from her desk and joined the leaders of the rest of the WPR in a mad dash through NATO headquarters.

Upon arriving in their assigned conference room, the politicians found Brad Davis and his top deputies waiting for them.

"Is the person still on the phone?"

"He is," the general said. "Are y'all ready?"

When they nodded their approval, one of the military aides pressed a button to take the caller off of hold.

"This is Prime Minister Rodgers of the United Kingdom," Lucy said, taking the lead, "and I'm joined by the Supreme Allied Commander Europe, General Davis, along with the leaders of France, Germany, China, and Russia. With whom are we speaking?"

"The man who shot down your plane."

A hush swept through the room, followed by a wave of anger. A barrage of "why," "how could you," and "how dare you" in multiple languages were hurled in the direction of the speakerphone.

The only reply they received was the sound of Dehqan Nazari laughing.

General Davis was the one person in the room who hadn't yet responded. "What's your name, son?" he asked.

"My name is not important. The only names you need to know and say are Muhammad and Allah."

"Shit," Lucy whispered under her breath. "Terrorists."

NATO's commanding officer remained unfazed. "You may not think your name is important, but it would be helpful for us to know what to call you. I am assuming we will be talking more in the future?"

Dehqan was surprised by the calm in the other man's voice. *I guess he has a point.* "We will be," he responded a few seconds later. "And you may call me Dehqan."

"Dehqan," Davis repeated with a nod. "Got it. I'm Brad Davis, although you can call me General. Now Dehqan . . . is that of Afghan origin?"

"I know what you're trying to do old man and it won't work. My name is Dehqan, I shot down your plane, and I will shoot down any others that you attempt to send into my airspace."

"Your airspace?" the French president asked.

"Yes, my airspace. My men and I are now in control of the military base the Americans called NORAD . . . the one inside the mountain. We have full access to the conventional weapons systems and will defend our territory."

"Which is?" Davis asked.

"What?"

"What do you consider your territory?"

Dehqan smiled. "Your primary containment zone. The United States of America is now under our control."

THIRTY-TWO

As soon as they hung up the phone with Dehqan Nazari, an argument broke out in the conference room in Brussels.

"How the hell did they shoot down the plane?" the French president questioned. "Don't they need fighter jets in the air for that? Or at least to have hijacked a military base closer to where the plane was shot down?"

General Davis broke from his usually confident demeanor and looked uncomfortable. "Usually, yes, you would be correct. But they've taken over NORAD's reserve facility at Cheyenne Mountain. That bunker has the capability to control all air and space operations in North America."

"How did they get inside the mountain?" asked Lucy Rodgers. "I thought that place was designed to withstand nuclear blasts."

Davis nodded. "A 30-megaton nuclear explosion, to be exact. But all the tunnels, cement, and steel in the world aren't good for shit if there aren't any people alive to operate the controls. For all we know, these assholes could've waltzed right in."

"But why that facility? Surely there are other military bases that might better suit their needs."

"It's a secure base of operations," the general replied. "Trying to get them out of there will be extremely difficult. Plus, think about where these people came from, if they are indeed Taliban – the mountains between Afghanistan and Pakistan. Of all the places in the United States, the Rockies are where they would be most comfortable. Where they'd feel most confident waging whatever kind of operation they're planning."

"Whatever kind of operation," Lucy Rodgers repeated. "First you don't see the plane explosion coming and now you have no idea what these terrorists are planning?"

Davis knew he had no choice but to eat crow on this one. "That's correct, ma'am. We're in the dark right now."

"Well isn't that bloody fantastic."

"Could they be bluffing about having control of all the weapons systems?" the Russian president asked.

The general crossed his arms over his chest. "It's possible. My gut tells me no, but I wouldn't completely rule it out."

"You wouldn't completely rule out anything," said the German chancellor.

"We're working as quickly and diligently as possible to determine what happened," responded General Davis. "It is made much more difficult, though, by the fact that we're trying to conduct an investigation on a crash that happened thousands of miles away."

"I'm sure you'll find a way," Prime Minister said.

At the other end of the conference table, the Russian president cleared his throat. "I have someone who may be able to help with the NORAD takeover problem."

"Who?"

The Soviet spy-turned-politician let out a deep breath, hesitant to reveal the information. "During the Cold War," he said, "we had an agent working in your NORAD facility. Boris Stanlovich. In America, he was called Bo Stanley. Boris helped design the bunker itself and provided information about its activities and other things we thought useful."

General Davis couldn't believe what he was hearing. *Fucking communists*, he thought. "You had a spy in NORAD? You're telling us that a Soviet agent not only had access to but also was involved in the designing of our most secure military facility?"

A grin worked its way across the Russian president's face. "Yes. That is what I'm telling you."

"Where is this Boris character now?" asked Prime Minister Rodgers, attempting to diffuse the argument between the former Cold War adversaries.

"In Russia. I'll have him brought here to advise us."

"Excellent. In the meantime," Lucy said, "General Davis, you and your team can continue working on finding out exactly what the hell happened to that plane."

"Yes ma'am," Davis replied, knowing that was his cue to leave. The general stood up to his full height before snapping to attention, nodding his head in salute, and leaving.

****

With the military officer out of the room, more questioning and finger pointing ensued.

"We can't look at this as an isolated problem," the representative from China said. "If they got access to the missile system at NORAD, what else can they get their hands on?"

"Shit, you're right," Lucy replied. "What about the American CDC? Their stockpiles of diseases and biological weapons?"

Germany's chancellor shook his head. "The CDC was shut down weeks ago. After they found out they had gotten the virus, their infectious disease research team locked themselves in that section of the building and shut the air vents. So, no, the terrorists shouldn't be able to get at any of that."

"Besides, these guys are computer hackers, not biological weapons experts," the French president added.

"I think, at this point," Lucy responded, "it would be best to assume that the terrorists have the human capital to do whatever they want to."

"What about intelligence files? Defense research projects, weapons designs, and the like?"

Prime Minister Rodgers let out a frustrated sigh before picking up the phone and calling General Davis back into the room.

"What do you know about your Pentagon?" she asked. "Are there Al-Qaeda fighters roaming around looking at classified weapons designs?"

"Well, ma'am, to be honest with you . . . I don't know. Satellite images show the Pentagon complex resembling a ghost town . . . much like the rest of the country. But I can tell you that the majority of the US government's intelligence files are secure."

"And how do we know this?"

"The NSA and CIA have firewalls built in to cause them to essentially self-destruct in the event of an invasion or other catastrophic event."

"Self-destruct?" Rodgers asked, not believing her ears. "You mean like in a cartoon? Toss the message in the rubbish bin and it explodes?"

"I don't think the buildings exploded, but all of the files were erased, yes ma'am."

"Do we know this for certain?" asked the Chinese president.

General Davis nodded his head. "Yes sir. It was the first project I worked on when I was assigned to Washington before coming here to NATO."

The military man's words helped soothe some of the politicians' fears, but not all. *First a pandemic and now a terrorist attack*, Lucy thought. *If bad things come in threes, I don't want to know what's going to happen next.*

THIRTY-THREE

A few minutes after the terrorist leader finished his phone call with the world leaders in Europe, Mohamed walked into his office.

"Umm, Dehqan?"

"Yes?"

The teenager hesitated, fidgeting his hands and shuffling his feet on the carpet. "Umm, not that blowing up the plane and taking over this place wasn't cool and all, but some of the guys are wondering what we're supposed to do now."

Dehqan looked up from the card table functioning as his desk. "What do you mean 'what are we supposed to do'? You each have a job assigned, do you not?"

"No, no, we do. We do. You're right. It's just that, well, we're claiming to have control of the US but really we're just holed up in a mountain. And eventually they're going to lift the blockade. Wouldn't it make more sense to try to conquer as much physical territory as possible before we have UN commandos breaking down the doors?"

Dehqan knew that Mohamed's question was valid, albeit naïve. "No," he replied, "the goal isn't to conquer as much territory as possible. We have no interest in nation building . . . that's not what we do. Our goal here, and the reason why I chose this military base in particular, is to steal America's nuclear weapons and then either use them ourselves or sell them. We have to secure the area around the bunker so that we can give Xiao enough time to hack the nuclear codes and then ultimately transport any nukes we sell, but we have no need to take over the whole US."

"Oh, okay," Mohamed responded. "But . . . what do we do while Xiao does all his computer stuff?"

Dehqan let out a deep breath. "I am in contact with our leaders in Afghanistan. They are recruiting more fighters to send to America once the travel ban is lifted. The plan is working. Don't worry. I will inform the team of our next steps when the time is right."

Although the young man wasn't satisfied with the answer, he was smart enough to not push his luck. *Especially with what Farzad said about the bomb-up-the-ass thing,* Mohamed thought. Nodding his head, the foot soldier said "okay" and left.

Alone again in his office, Dehqan knew that more people would soon be asking him for new or more interesting assignments. Despite their rotating security tasks, boredom had begun to set in for the group of terrorists locked inside the Cheyenne Mountain nuclear bunker. With no real way to pass the time between their shifts monitoring the surveillance cameras, and no way to help Xiao with his continued efforts at computer hacking, even Dehqan occasionally joined the other men in looking for things to do. Joe, raised in America, had taught the group how to play poker, although some of the terrorists objected to the element of gambling involved. Farzad fashioned a ball out of bathroom towels and duct tape, and lively games of indoor 'football' ensued every afternoon in the bunker's cafeteria.

Joe had been amazed by the soccer skills of his fellow terrorists. "You guys could all probably walk on to college teams in the US or star in Saturday morning leagues," he said after one game. "It's amazing."

Dehqan had shrugged his shoulders. "Football is a way of life where we come from. Think about it: in most of the world, football – your soccer – is the biggest sport. Here, in America, it must compete with so many other things. Your American football, baseball, basketball, ice hockey, lacrosse. The best athletes often play those sports."

"Fair point."

"Imagine if Lebron James played center back," Dehqan had continued. "If Adrian Peterson was a winger or Mike Trout was a striker."

Joe shook his head and laughed. "Man, we'd dominate."

"There you go," his boss had replied.

Dehqan smiled at the memory. *Hopefully the rotating assignments, football matches, and card games will be enough to keep them occupied.* Although poker was a flop with the group, Dehqan knew that later that night, when the soccer matches died down for the day, Mohamed and Xiao would lead the men in their favorite new card game: Egyptian Ratscrew. The fast-paced matching game, which resembled the British Beggar-My-Neighbor with elements of Slapjack thrown in, resulted in lively bouts of playing that let them all forget for a while that they were in the center of an international firestorm.

THIRTY-FOUR

A little over ten hours to the south of Cheyenne Mountain, back in the small religious town Shining Light, Texas, people had gathered to discuss how to react to the carnage around them.

Because of Shining Light's quirky mix of religion and libertarianism, its founders had long ago decided against receiving government-issued vaccinations. Before the autism scare and before opting out of vaccines became a more popular, acceptable thing to do, the residents of Shining Light said they would rather take their chances with illness than let some bureaucrat in Washington, DC decide what kind of medicines would be injected into their bodies.

Consequently, the Shorewood Disease infection rate in Shining Light was the opposite of everywhere else in the country. Whereas over ninety-percent of the rest of Americans were infected, only five percent of the town's residents were. Those people represented the few who moved to the community later in life after being vaccinated as children. Similar to Amish, Mennonite, and other 'fundamentalist' communities, the tiny Texas hamlet found itself in a bizarre version of *The Twilight Zone* – everyone around them was dying but they remained relatively unscathed.

Two weeks after the WPR's announcement to isolate the United States and just a few days after the Doctors Without Borders plane was shot down, Shining Light's leaders, including Sheriff Josiah Jones – the man who had gone searching for supplies with his wife weeks earlier – gathered in the church's fellowship hall to discuss their next steps. Food and fuel were running dangerously low, and the only reason they had electricity or water was because the town operated its own power plant and wells.

"What are we gonna do?" said one of the church deacons, asking the question on everyone's mind.

"We need to start some form of rationin'," another man called out. "And nobody who isn't from here can come here."

Pastor Jenkins, standing in front of the group near his usual Sunday morning preaching spot, shook his head. "Now Dwayne, remember what the Lord says about lovin' your neighbor."

"I do love my neighbor. That's what I'm sayin'. I'm lovin' my neighbor by savin' mine and my neighbor's resources."

Mrs. Thomas, head of the Ladies' Auxiliary, wasn't pleased with Dwayne's reply. "If Joseph and a pregnant Mary had shown up on your doorstep, you wouldn't have even let them stay in your barn!"

"People, people," said Sheriff Jones. The slender man, dressed in his khaki work uniform, stood up and walked over beside the pastor. "Let's all stay calm, y'all. Now is not the time for this kind of bickerin'."

Chastised, Mrs. Thomas and Dwayne both sat back down in their pews.

The sheriff nodded and smiled. "Thank you. I've been thinkin' 'bout what we need to do," Josiah said in a strong Texas drawl. Even though he spent the first few years of his life in Wisconsin, decades spent in Shining Light meant Josiah sounded like a Texan when he talked. "I agree that we need rationin' of some sort. And I'd like to deputize some more men to help guard the gas and power stations and places like the medical clinic and the grocery store."

"Ahem," Mrs. Thomas coughed loudly.

"My apologies. I would like to deputize some more people."

"Okay, then what?" Pastor Jenkins asked.

The town's mayor walked in at that moment, slamming open the sanctuary doors. "Sorry sorry sorry sorry," he said, holding his hands up in the air in apology. "I couldn't get my truck to start." Joining the sheriff and the pastor in the front of the church, he continued: "y'all already start without me? Great. Where we at?"

Mrs. Thomas, who was also the school's principal and a former English teacher, grimaced in her pew.

"Glad you got your truck runnin', Mayor," said Josiah, shaking the man's hand. "We've decided to work out some kind of rationin' system for food, water, and gas. And I'm gonna deputize some more folks to help guard the supplies."

Mayor McGowan nodded. "Good." The large, heavyset man with bushy gray hair and deep blue eyes was well liked in town but also not much of a decision-maker. He said delegation was his management style, but most knew that McGowan simply wanted the title without any of the accompanying work.

"Shouldn't we do something to let people know we're still here?" asked Shining Light's resident physician. The town doctor was soft-spoken but very intelligent, and, as such, when he talked people listened.

"Waddaya mean, Doc?"

"Well, before we lost internet service, I was reading articles about Canada and Mexico closing their borders. And now the UN and NATO declared that nobody is allowed to enter or exit the country. They're trying to cut off the spread of the disease before it gets any worse."

"Can't blame 'em," Pastor Jenkins replied.

"So what are we supposed to do? Send a carrier pigeon?" asked Dwayne. "Phones an' internet are down."

"Not all phones," the doctor replied.

Sheriff Jones' eyes shot up. "You got a workin' phone?"

"Well, I haven't tested it but I don't see why it wouldn't work. Last Christmas, my wife got me a satellite phone to take with me when I go hunting in case I was ever out at the deer lease and a patient needed me."

The mood in the sanctuary lifted at the thought that they weren't entirely cut off from the rest of the world.

"Who do we call, though?" asked Mayor McGowan.

"The federal government probably wouldn't do any good," Sheriff Jones reasoned. "For all we know, the President and Congress are all dead."

"Which means they're gettin' just as much done as they usually do," Dwayne quipped.

A few chuckles of laughter spread through the room.

"C'mon . . . show some respect for the dead, huh?" Josiah said. Bringing the conversation back on point, he added: "the mayor asked a good question, though. Who do we call?"

"Anybody have any relatives overseas?" asked Mrs. Thomas.

Silence filled the church as no one could respond that they did.

Pastor Jenkins eyes suddenly lit up. "Maybe the government can help us," he said. "Dwayne, didn't you and your wife visit London when y'all went on that big trip last summer?"

"Yeah . . . "

"I remember Hannah tellin' my wife about your trip. Joanne was so impressed by how organized Hannah was. Havin' folders for every city y'all visited that had key words translated and itineraries and all kinds of stuff. She wouldn't quit talkin' about it for a week."

The farmer smiled. "Yeah, Hannah did make those. The binders had everythin' . . . includin' numbers for the embassies."

"Think your wife still has those folders?"

"Probably. The woman keeps everythin'."

In a rare moment of leadership, Mayor McGowan took charge. "Okay, here's what we're gonna do. It's the middle of the night in Europe right now so callin' embassies will have to wait. But Dwayne, if you can go home and find those numbers, we can have 'em for the mornin'. And Doc, you'll need to get that phone all charged up and ready to go. Sheriff, word will get out soon about the rationin', and we don't want anybody makin' a run before we get that all set up. So why don't you think of a list of guys – err, people – to deputize and we'll go now and round 'em up."

Josiah nodded. "Good plan. We're gonna need quite a few to rotate shifts. Everybody pitchin' in together."

Pastor Jenkins smiled. "Just like Jesus feedin' the five thousand."

The assembled group couldn't help but roll their eyes at the preacher's attempt to tie everything back to a Bible lesson.

"Any questions?" the mayor asked, enjoying his newfound authority.

When no one spoke up, Sheriff Jones nodded. "Alright. Doc, you meet me back here at 7:00am tomorrow with that phone. Dwayne, be here too. We'll get to work assignin' guards 'round town." He paused. "The rest of y'all, spread the word about the rationin' and tell people to save as much food, water, gas, and power as possible. And stay home. Ain't no reason to go travellin' about wastin' fuel."

THIRTY-FIVE

The next morning in Shining Light also happened to be the first Sunday of a new month, which meant that, back in Brussels, Prime Minister Rodgers was having another conversation with her two sons. Like the last time, both David and Phillip were in the same location and the whole family was able to videochat together.

Fifteen minutes into the call, Lucy noticed her chief of staff standing in the doorway. The look on his face showed that he knew he shouldn't interrupt, *but there he is anyway,* she thought.

"I'm busy," Lucy snapped.

"Yes ma'am, I know. But ma'am, the American embassy in London has patched through a call. From America."

The politician's head shot up and she turned around in her chair to look at her aide. Remembering that her sons were on the phone, she said "give me two seconds" and then turned back to the iPad screen. "I'm sorry loves, but I must go."

"We understand," David replied, without even a hint of his usual sarcasm. "Go."

With the family call disconnected, Lucy turned her attention back to her chief of staff. "Is it the terrorists again?"

"No ma'am. Survivors."

****

Prime Minister Rodgers arrived in the meeting room just as other members of the *ad hoc* leadership council were hurriedly making their way there from various parts of the NATO Headquarters building.

"Do we still have them?" Lucy asked.

A military staffer shook his head. "They said they couldn't be on hold for that long because of phone battery life or something like that. But we gave them a secure number to call back on here. We said any time after 4:00pm Central European Time, so 9:00am their time."

"Nine o'clock?" Lucy asked. "Where are they?"

"Texas, ma'am."

Lucy glanced over at the ornate clock decorating the center spot on one of the walls. It read 3:52pm.

After what seemed like an eternity, when the gold-plated clock struck 4:12pm, the phone on the center table rang. One of the NATO military officers sprang to answer it.

"This is the United Nations Special Committee on Worldwide Pandemic Response. With whom are we speaking?"

There was a long pause and a few crackling noises came through the speakerphone before the group gathered in Brussels heard a man's voice on the other end of the line. He sounded like he was a million miles away.

"Yes, hi. I'm here," Sheriff Jones said into the phone, knowing he was probably talking too loudly but wanting to make sure the other people could hear him. "I'm sorry about the delay . . . it's hard to get a signal with this phone when it's cloudy like it is today."

Josiah heard someone clear their throat and then a woman spoke. "My name is Lucy Rodgers. I'm the Prime Minister of the United Kingdom. Would you mind telling us who you are?"

The sheriff's eyes grew three times bigger when he heard who he was talking to. "Uhh, yes. Yes ma'am. Of course. I'm Josiah Jones. I'm the Sheriff of Shinin' Light, Texas."

Unbeknownst to Josiah, a room full of staffers half a world away began pulling up any and all information they could find about him and his town.

"This is General Davis, Sheriff. I'm the Supreme Allied Commander Europe and in charge of the military arm of the disease containment efforts. I know you told the embassy that you were calling from a satellite phone," he said, "but that skips over a more important question: how are you still alive? I mean, I assume you know about the Rubella vaccine being the cause of the disease?"

"Well, no sir, I didn't know that it was Rubella. But I guess that makes sense. Shinin' Light is in a remote part of the state and we keep to ourselves most of the time. You see, we're all pretty religious folks and we don't want modern culture corruptin' our families or our way of life."

The pretentious-sounding prime minister spoke again. "An Amish man in Texas is calling me from a satellite phone?"

Josiah laughed. "No ma'am. We're not Amish. Although I suppose they'd still be alive too. No, we're Protestants. But we stay away from government health stuff like vaccines, so with the exception of a few older folks and some newer residents, we're alright. About six hundred people total."

The general rejoined the conversation. "Sheriff, as you can probably tell from my voice, I'm an American too. There's something you need to know." There was a pause on the other end of the line while Davis surveyed the room for approval. "You're not alone in surviving the outbreak."

"Well, we sorta figured that."

"No . . . what I'm trying to say is that our air defense has been compromised."

"Good Lord, speak English to the man," another voice interrupted, this one with a heavy accent that sounded French. "A group of terrorists have taken control of your air command center in, where is it?"

"Colorado Springs," General Davis answered.

"Colorado Springs," repeated the French man (*the French president?* Josiah wondered). "They already shot down a plane carrying a team of doctors and supplies. They say they will do the same to any more planes that fly into the containment zone."

Josiah and the room full of Shining Light residents listening in were shocked by what they heard.

"So you're sayin' there's no help comin'?" asked the sheriff. "No supplies . . . no doctors . . . no nothin'?"

"We're considering other options now that we know an airlift is no longer possible," Prime Minister Rodgers answered.

"How long will the borders be closed?" Dwayne blurted out. He had promised to keep his mouth shut and just listen, but he couldn't keep quiet anymore.

"Who was that?" asked General Davis.

"Dwayne Beckwith, General. Part of the town council we got put together to figure out how we're gonna survive this thing. We're runnin' outta supplies, ya know."

"Yes, we know," Lucy replied. "And we're working on it. But I'm afraid we don't have an answer about how long the quarantine will remain in effect."

"Sheriff Jones," said General Davis, "do you have any military experience?"

"No sir, I don't. I joined the Sheriff's Department straight outta high school."

"I see. Well, nonetheless, I have some ideas I'd like to run by you."

The military leader's words broke up at the end of the sentence and Josiah looked down to see the low battery light flashing on the phone. "That sounds great, General. But I'm afraid it'll have to wait. We spent so long on hold with the embassy in London that the phone battery is fixin' to die. I'll charge it up overnight and call y'all back at the same time tomorrow, alright? And hopefully the clouds will've cleared out by then too."

THIRTY-SIX

The next day, promptly at four o'clock Central European Time, Josiah called back to speak with General Davis. For nearly three hours, the two men discussed a wide range of topics, from what victims of the virus experienced to which supplies were in most critical need to the general's own daughter, a freshman at Auburn University in Alabama. Needing to keep up appearances, Davis spun a web of lies for the sheriff.

"I tried to get Kaylie to leave when news broke of the start of the outbreak, but she wanted to stay with her friends. Typical college kid," the general said. "She thought I was blowing the whole thing out of proportion."

"And now?" Josiah asked.

"We haven't heard from her in five weeks," Davis lied again. "She had all of her vaccines when she was a baby, but my wife and I are still holding out hope that she somehow made it through the blockade. I know I'm not supposed to say that since I'm the one enforcing it, but – "

"She's your daughter," said Josiah. "Trust me, I get it." Knowing how horrible he would feel if he were in the same situation that he thought the general was in, Josiah quickly changed the subject and brought the conversation around to next steps. The battery on the phone was dying anyway so he needed to wrap things up.

It was then that Brad Davis told the sheriff of his idea for a reconnaissance mission. A group of men from Shining Light who were immune from the virus could travel to Colorado Springs and get a better idea of who the terrorists were and what they might want.

"They're claiming to have taken over the United States," General Davis explained, "and in a way they have since they control the airspace."

"Bull," Josiah replied, the minced oath making the military man smile. "No way some terrorist is gonna take us over. Absolutely, General. I'll round up a crew and we'll head out to Colorado tomorrow. You just tell me what you want us to look for."

"Excellent. Can you receive data on that phone? Emails and such?"

"Umm . . . I dunno. Hold on." Sheriff Jones returned a few minutes later. "Sorry, had to run down the hall and ask the doc. It's his phone. He said he's never tried it but he doesn't see why not. Email isn't workin' because the servers or whatever are down, but the doc said you should be able to text him an attachment with the information in it."

"Alright. I'll put together a mission plan and send it to you. Everything you'll need to know will be in that."

The two men hung up just as the satellite phone battery was blinking red and General Davis was being called into another meeting. Upon arriving at the biweekly videoconference with Ricardo Capello and his team in Solna, while waiting on the doctors to log-on, Davis informed the rest of the WPR about his plan for a recon mission.

"It's the most intact community left, outside the Amish," he explained. "Fewest deaths, fewest disruptions to daily life. They were so remote and isolated before that they've been able to insulate themselves from much of the impact."

Lucy Rodgers shook her head in disbelief. "You're telling me that our best bet on the inside is a bunch of separatist, religious zealot nuts in the Texas desert?"

"I think the labels are debatable, but yes ma'am that's essentially it."

"Maybe the guy on Downing Street was right," Lucy murmured. "This really is the Apocalypse."

THIRTY-SEVEN

After receiving the emailed mission plan from General Davis, Josiah's first thing to do was decide who else would be joining him on the trip. The first few were obvious choices, namely Josiah's buddies from high school whom he knew were both tough and trustworthy. Rounding out the team, though, proved to be more difficult. The sheriff found himself discussing the topic with Pastor Jenkins in the church office.

"How many are we sendin' total?" the preacher asked.

"We've got five right now. Me, Chris Masters, Jon Kitsch, Eric Schneider, and Will Oishi."

"What's Schneider doing in the group?" As an ambulance driver and medical assistant at the clinic, Pastor Jenkins hadn't expected to hear Schneider's name on a list for a military-type mission.

Josiah shrugged his shoulders. "Figured it'd be good to have somebody with medical skills in case we run into any trouble. The doc can't go since he's gotta stay and run the clinic. And every Army unit has a medic, right?"

"Yeah, I suppose so." Jenkins paused. "What about a shooter?"

Josiah laughed. "Every man and most women in Shinin' Light know how to shoot a gun."

"True, but there are only a few that I would hand a rifle and trust to cover me from a distance."

"You're talkin' 'bout a sniper," the sheriff reasoned.

Jenkins nodded. "Yep. And the best shot in town is that boy of yours."

Sheriff Jones shook his head. "No."

"He is."

"I know he is. I meant 'no' he's not goin'."

"Now Josiah," the preacher said, placing a hand on the sheriff's shoulder, "if somebody else in town had a son who was a crack shot like your Daniel is, you'd be goin' with me to talk his parents into lettin' him go with y'all."

Josiah pulled away from the man's hand. "I would not."

"Don't lie to me, Jones. Especially not in the Lord's house."

After a minute, Josiah said: "Okay, fine, yeah, I would. But this is my son. It's different."

This time the man sitting across from the sheriff didn't reply, and instead just stared back at him. For a good while, neither man budged, each digging in his own cowboy-booted heels.

Finally, Josiah relented.

"Okay, you're right. It's not different. Daniel's worth five shooters – at least." Sheriff Jones sighed. "He'll go."

The pastor nodded. "Good. Don't get me wrong, Josiah. I don't want the boy to have to go. I don't want anybody to have to go. But if we're gonna do this, then we're gonna do it right. And that means sendin' the best team out there."

****

After his talk with the pastor, Josiah left the church and headed in the direction of Will Oishi's house. Will was the first on his list to notify that he had been tapped for the recon mission. Sheriff Jones knew he must've looked ridiculous riding through the small Texas town in a golf cart, but they were all trying to conserve resources – especially gasoline. There were enough power generators stored up and Shining Light's power plant was still putting out some electricity, so the electric golf carts were everyone's new form of transportation. *And now that we'll be drivin' to Colorado . . . we're gonna need all the gas we can get*, thought Josiah.

One by one, Sheriff Jones went to the houses of the men joining him on the trip. They all readily agreed and were even a bit excited by the idea.

Someone who wasn't excited about it was Mary Jones, Josiah's wife. Particularly when she found out that their son was on the list to go.

"He's only fifteen!" she yelled at her husband.

Josiah tried to keep his voice calm and leaned back against the kitchen island. "Mary, the boy started goin' on huntin' trips with me when he was eight. He's the best shot in the family. Heck, he's the best shot in the whole town. We need him on the trip."

"Do you not hear me? He's fifteen!"

"Do you not hear me?" the sheriff yelled back. "We don't have the luxury of bein' able to coddle our children anymore. Daniel may only be fifteen, but he's got a man's body and a man's shot and we need him. We're not goin' to Colorado for a business meeting and a few dinners at Applebee's. We're goin' to find out information about the *terrorists* who are tryin' to take over our country. Daniel is goin'. And Isaac will be armed and a member of the security force here." Josiah paused and his voice softened. "We don't have any other choice. Trust me, honey, I wish things were different. I wish this outbreak never happened and our boys could still have long, happy, safe, and carefree teenage years. But that's simply not an option."

Mary chose that moment to start crying. Josiah felt bad about how upset she was, but also wasn't willing to change his mind. He wrapped his arms around his wife and kissed her on the forehead before saying: "we've gotta get ready to go." Josiah then turned to head down the hall toward the bedrooms. "Daniel? Pack a bag. You're comin' with me."

THIRTY-EIGHT

Bright and early the next morning, when the sun was just beginning to peek out above the horizon, the six members of the recon team gathered at the Jones' house. In order to save gas, all of the men would be riding up to Colorado Springs in Eric Schneider's large SUV.

"It'll be tight," he said, "fittin' us all in there. But we can do it."

The other men nodded in agreement and continued to load the trunk of the vehicle with supplies . . . mainly food, water, guns, and ammunition.

A few minutes after everyone else arrived, fifteen year old Daniel emerged from the house, still looking half asleep. Beside him trotted the Jones family's chocolate lab, Gus.

"What's the dog doin' here?" Chris Masters asked. "You can't bring him."

"No, we need to bring him," Josiah replied. "Best huntin' dog in Shinin' Light; probably in all of West Texas. He'll smell stuff and hear stuff long before we'd be able to."

Chris eyed the sheriff skeptically, continuing a rivalry that extended back to their high school days. Chris had wanted to date Mary and still thought that Josiah stole her away. "He's trained?" he asked. "The dog's not gonna bark at a squirrel and get us all killed is he?"

"Of course he's trained. Very trained. Mary says too well trained – she calls him robodog."

The other man glared at Josiah at the mention of his wife, but nodded his head. "Alright. The dog can go."

Josiah rolled his eyes and walked away to continue loading the SUV. *Of course he can go*, the sheriff thought. *I'm leadin' the mission and he's my dog. Jerk.*

****

The drive from Shining Light, Texas to the outskirts of Colorado Springs, Colorado covered approximately 650 miles and took Josiah and his team ten hours to complete. They could've made it there faster, but decided to drive a bit slower to conserve gas. The men also found themselves rubbernecking the whole time as they got their first glimpse of a post-epidemic America.

"It's like the whole country has become a ghost town," Daniel Jones commented.

"No kiddin'," replied his father. "You're takin' notes on this, right? Cuz we're supposed to report back to NATO about what we see."

"Yes sir," Daniel said. "I'm takin' notes."

Hoping to make the time go by faster with a little bit of conversation, Josiah turned around in his seat so he could see who was sitting behind him.

"How your kids doin', Will?" Josiah asked, knowing that the other man had two young daughters.

"Good. They're doin' good." He took a deep breath. "Right before all this disease stuff started, Susannah came home one day askin' why she looked different than her friends. Didn't figure race relations would come up in kindergarten, but it did."

"What'd you tell her?" asked Jon Kitsch.

"I said she's part Japanese because a long, long time ago her ancestors lived in Japan. I mean, what else am I supposed to say . . . that's the whole truth of it."

"Not to be rude, but how did your family end up in Shining Light?" Kitsch asked.

"Not rude...it's a fair question. We are kinda the token Asians in town." Will smiled. "My great-aunt, my grandfather's sister, was a good bit older than my grandpa," he explained. "She was in an internment camp during World War II. After the war ended, she got married to a guy who had been one of the guards at the camp where she was held, and he happened to be a farmer from near Shinin' Light."

"The Poindexters," Josiah said, knowing that much of the story.

Oishi nodded. "Yep. Well anyway, my grandpa moved to Shinin' Light to work on the farm, and that's how Japanese folks came to live in white bread Texas."

****

A few hours after Will Oishi's story, the recon team reached its destination. The group of men from Shining Light hadn't been quite sure what to expect when they arrived in downtown Colorado Springs, but what they saw wasn't it.

Cars abandoned in the streets.

Stray animals darting from one building to the next.

Vultures screeching overhead.

And rats. There were rats everywhere.

"Holy crap," Daniel said as soon as he exited their SUV, pulling his t-shirt up over his nose and mouth and nearly turning green with nausea. "What is that smell?"

The teenager's fellow recon team members also tried to block the stench from entering their nostrils.

"Death," Chris Masters replied, speaking through a handkerchief that he pulled from his back pocket. "That's why the vultures and rats are here . . . probably some wolves too if we looked for 'em. They're here for the bodies."

Daniel lost his battle with the nausea and vomited onto the ground by his shoes.

"That's enough, Chris," Josiah said in a harsh tone. "The smell is bad enough. We don't need your editorializin' on top of it."

The other man shrugged his shoulders. As a pig farmer, he wasn't as bothered by the rotten air as the others were. "The boy asked what the smell was . . . I was just answerin'."

At that moment, as if on cue, a wolf appeared from around a street corner and turned its green eyes and silver head toward the first living humans it had seen in weeks.

Josiah's dog wasn't on a leash at that point, but luckily he was well-trained enough that he didn't take off running at the other animal. "Stay," Josiah commanded, and watched while Gus waged an internal battle between following his instincts to chase the wolf and listening to his owner's instructions. "Quiet. Stay," the sheriff repeated.

Daniel reached for the rifle that was slung over his shoulder, but his father put his hand out and stopped him. "Leave him be. For now at least. If he becomes a threat, we'll deal with it. But he's fine right now."

The animal stared down the visitors for a few more seconds before turning his head and continuing his walk down the perpendicular street.

Chris, the pig farmer, chuckled. "See, kid, why would he want to battle for his dinner when he can walk down a block and get it on a platter?"

"Masters!"

Josiah walked over to his former classmate and stood nose-to-nose with him. "Knock. It. Off," he snarled. "People are dyin'. We might die too if we don't pay attention and do our job right. Please, for all of our sakes, respect what we're dealin' with here."

Chris glared back at the sheriff, and for a minute Daniel thought he might have to be his dad's wing man in a fight. But the farmer eventually broke eye contact took a step backward.

"You're right. I'm sorry," he added, glancing in Daniel's direction. "Let's finish the mission so we can go home."

THIRTY-NINE

After surveying downtown Colorado Springs and finding it abandoned, the group from Shining Light climbed back into their SUV and drove toward Cheyenne Mountain.

The nuclear bunker, Josiah and his team quickly learned, was literally a hole carved into a mountain. Not knowing what to expect, and thinking they would be approaching a large military base of some sort, the men followed their driving directions to within a mile of the bunker before deciding to finish the journey on foot. Josiah, Daniel, Will, and Gus the dog would try to get as close to the base as possible while Chris, Jon, and Eric stayed behind as lookouts. They could radio if anyone started driving up the road and be ready with the getaway vehicle if needed.

"Y'all keep your eyes open," Sheriff Jones said as he stuck a pistol in his belt holster and picked up his AR-15 rifle from the trunk. "Radio us if you see or hear anythin'. On Channel 3."

"Same to you," said Eric Schneider. He was positioned inside the SUV looking out over the sunroof, while Chris and Jon would watch the flank. "We'll be ready if you need us."

Josiah nodded, and then his son and Will Oishi walked up beside him. "Let's do this," said the sheriff.

A few minutes later, about one-third of a mile down the road, a guard gate and tunnel came into view.

"What is that?" Daniel asked.

"I dunno. The entrance I guess?"

"That's it?" Will Oishi questioned. "I thought this was some big important place."

Josiah stopped walking. "Hold up a second. Gus: wait. Somethin' doesn't feel right. I agree with Will – we're missin' somethin'." He looked up at the mountain rocks surrounding them. "We're like sittin' ducks out here. Danny, if you climb up that ridge right there, do you think you could cover us up to the entrance and back to the car?"

"The car, sure," the boy replied. "It's a little far for the entrance, but I'd be close enough to at least create a distraction for you if you needed one."

His dad nodded. "Good enough. Head up there."

As the teenage sniper made his way up the rocky ridge and into position, Josiah, Will, and the dog continued their walk toward the guard gate, with rifles poised and ready. When they reached the gate, though, it was abandoned. The tunnel entrance also showed no signs of life, with a garage-like door blocking the opening.

"Kitsch," Will said into his radio. "We're at the bunker's entrance. We've got nothin'. Zero signs of life."

"You're still all clear back here," Jon replied. "Get some pictures to send over to NATO."

"Will," Josiah said, his voice an octave lower than usual.

"Hold on," the other man responded as he searched his backpack for his camera.

"Oishi," the sheriff repeated. Hearing his owner's tone, Gus began to growl.

"What?"

"We're bein' watched."

Will froze and his eyes grew wide, looking over at his friend in panic.

"Up in the corner," Josiah said. "Your ten o'clock. There's a little camera that's been watchin' us the whole time."

"You sure?"

"Take a step sideways. Look . . . the camera moves with you."

****

Several stories below, deep in Cheyenne Mountain, Mohamed was in his final hour of a six-hour watch shift when things finally got interesting. He saw the Shining Light vehicle approaching and was getting ready to sound the alarm when the truck pulled to a stop about a mile outside the entrance. Mohamed watched through multiple security cameras as six men and a dog piled out of the SUV and proceeded to unload an arsenal of guns and ammunition from the trunk. That was when Mohamed called for Dehqan.

"What do you think they want?" the Singapore national asked, watching the two men and the dog on the closest screen. He could see three more still at the truck on his long-distance camera, but the sixth man had disappeared from view about ten minutes earlier.

"More importantly," replied Dehqan, "who are they? There's no way the UN would send in troops without any kind of gas masks. It'd be suicide. And how did they get here? We know they didn't fly in."

"They could be like us," Xiao reasoned, having joined his colleagues at the desk. "Already inside the US when the outbreak started and not vaccinated so they're immune."

The terrorist leader didn't think it was worth his time to figure it out. "Just kill them," he said.

Xiao shook his head. "We can't. Not without going outside and leaving ourselves vulnerable to attack."

"What are you talking about?" asked Dehqan. "I thought you hacked into the weapons system."

"Long range weapons."

"So you're telling me that you can shoot down a plane that's 2,000 miles away but you can't do anything about the guys literally on our doorstep?"

"Unfortunately, yes."

"Spee bachee." The Pashto curse fell easily from Dehqan's lips. He hadn't planned on visitors, especially those of the armed variety. "Just wait it out," he ordered. "Watch them. See what they do. They can't get inside, so we're okay for now." Nazari paused. "No one can get inside, right Farzad?"

"Right," the other man confirmed from across the room. "We're locked down."

****

Outside, Oishi and Jones stood motionless, afraid to do anything that might set off the cameras. Gus, sensing trouble, continued his low growl.

"Dad," the radio crackled. "Dad, what are you doing?" asked Daniel. "Dad, pick up."

"We're bein' watched," Josiah said into his hand-held radio. "They've got security cameras followin' our every move."

"Hold on." Slinging his rifle over his shoulder, Daniel ran across the edge of the ridge until he was within target range of the bunker entrance. "Just another second," he said to the radio.

"What's goin' on?" Chris asked from the truck.

"Start 'er up," Daniel replied. "Dad, Will, I've got you. Just turn around and walk away. If anybody comes out of the bunker, I'll get 'em. Y'all at the truck," the boy continued, "be ready to pick us all up about half a mile closer in."

The crew from Shining Light followed the orders of their youngest member, with the sheriff, his dog, and Will Oishi calmly but quickly leaving the tunnel and guard gate area and the three men in the SUV speeding down the road to the pick-up point.

When all seven were back inside the truck, Eric slammed his foot down on the gas and backed away from Cheyenne Mountain in full speed reverse, travelling well over two miles before slowing down enough to turn the truck around and drive facing forward.

"Holy shit," said Will, half in shock and half in relief. After Jon Kitsch glanced sideways at him, Oishi added: "what? Pastor Jenkins isn't here and I just got within ten feet

of terrorist headquarters. If there was ever a time when sayin'
'holy shit' was appropriate, it's now."

"No kiddin'," Daniel agreed. "Ho – "

"Holy don't you even think about it," his father cut in.
"Now wadda y'all say we go home?"

FORTY

While the men from Shining Light travelled home from Colorado and the WPR in Brussels eagerly awaited the recon mission's results, Dr. Capello and his team of physicians at the European Centers for Disease Control continued to work toward creating a new vaccine for the Shorewood Disease.

Their first order of business was to gain a better understanding of how the virus functioned. Data sent over from the American CDC, along with samples taken from some victims who were quarantined at airports in Europe, were used to study the Rubella mutation. It wasn't easy work, especially since it was the first time any of the doctors had ever known a vaccine's antibodies to backfire on recipients.

Once the doctors finally unearthed the composition and capabilities of the Shorewood virus, they set their sights on creating a vaccine. The European method for making a vaccine, using cell cultures, took approximately five to eight months. However, the egg-based approach approved by the US government took six to nine months. Dr. Capello, on the other hand, decided to go with the faster but controversial recombinant DNA method. Still in development and not yet approved by either the United States or the European Union, the recombinant DNA method could produce a vaccine in as little as six weeks. *Which is still too much time but certainly better than the other options*, Ricardo thought.

His bigger problem, though, was figuring out a way to test the vaccine prototypes on humans.

"No one will want to do it," Dr. Capello muttered to himself one night while working in the lab.

"No one will want to do what?" asked Dr. Schroder. Ricardo liked the younger man, he really did, but he also found it kind of annoying how the American doctor always seemed to be hanging out around him.

"Be the guinea pig for the vaccine," Dr. Capello said. "But don't worry about that now. It's late. Go home. Rest. You're of no good to me if you are tired."

"I could say the same to you," Zach replied.

"But you won't, because I am your boss and this is my lab."

Dr. Schroder knew that Ricardo didn't mean to sound so rude. Sleep deprivation and frustration from repeated vaccine failures had worn away at the pathologist's normally sunny disposition.

"May I ask you something, Dr. Capello?"

Ricardo nodded without looking away from the papers in front of him. "You may."

"Why'd you become a doctor?"

Capello put down the chart he had been reading and took a deep breath before spinning his stool around to face Zach. "Why do you ask?"

The younger man shrugged his shoulders. "I don't know. Just curious, I guess."

Ricardo thought for a minute before answering. "What do you know of my home country of Andorra?"

"Not much. It's between Spain and France."

"Yes, that is correct. It is a small country . . . we have less than 90,000 total citizens. But it is a rich country. We have many holiday resorts and also many banking and tax benefits."

"Hmm, interesting," Zach replied, wondering what this Encyclopedia Britannica lesson had to do with his boss' career.

"Despite that, despite the wealth and the advantages," the doctor continued, "my family was poor. My father was a sheep farmer and his father was a sheep farmer and on and on back in time. Sheep are not clean animals. Raising them is not an easy life."

"Okay . . . " responded Dr. Schroder. He noticed that his boss' accent grew much thicker when he started talking about home.

"My mother, God rest her soul," Ricardo said, crossing himself as he spoke, "did not want me to be a sheep farmer. My older brother, he had no choice as the oldest son. But I was the youngest and my dear mother wanted better for me. So she helped me study and sent applications and arranged a scholarship for me at a school in Madrid. I left home when I was fourteen."

"Wow."

Not hearing his colleague's comment, lost in his thoughts, Dr. Capello went on: "the morning that I left, my mother pulled me aside and got a jar down from a top shelf in the kitchen. She pulled out a handful of money – all that she had saved over years and years – and told me to go and make something of myself." He paused as his eyes began to fill with tears. "She got sick with the cancer the next year, and after she died I dedicated myself to becoming a doctor. A disease researcher so I could help save lives."

"Well," Zach said, "you did it."

"Did what?" Ricardo replied, his voice startled as if he just remembered that he wasn't alone in the room.

"You made something of yourself. Your mother would be proud."

The ECDC's chief pathologist shook his head in denial. "My legacy will rise or fall with the outcome of this Shorewood research. None of my other work will matter if we do not succeed in this."

Dr. Schroder studied his boss' face and realized that the older man was one hundred percent serious. "Then I guess we better get back to work."

FORTY-ONE

Early the next morning, when Zach Schroder had returned to his apartment for a few hours of sleep and the rest of his research assistants had yet to arrive, Ricardo was alone in his lab when he heard a knock on the door.

Dr. Anna Hallstrom, a native of Sweden and a fellow in the oncology department, smiled and nodded hello before walking into the room. "How is everything going?" she asked. Ricardo knew that Dr. Hallstrom would've loved to be a part of his Shorewood research group, but the Director of the ECDC had decided to keep Capello's unit small so that doctors in other divisions wouldn't get too far behind on their work with other illnesses.

"It's going," Ricardo replied. "A lot of tests; not a lot of results."

"Anything I can do to help?"

"No, we're fine. Thanks."

Ricardo expected the other physician to take that as her cue to leave, but Anna continued to linger in the lab. "Did you see that author lady on the news last night?" she asked. Ricardo knew that Dr. Hallstrom was trying to make small talk and cheer him up, but he wasn't in the mood.

"Who?" he asked, keeping a sharp edge on his tone of voice.

"Some doctor," Hallstrom said. "Apparently she wrote a book a few years ago about how vaccines don't do any good and that mainly they've been used as weapons and in eugenics experiments."

"That's absurd."

Anna shrugged her shoulders. "Absurd or not, a lot of people are buying into what she's saying. Overreach of the government and how the only people still alive in America are the ones who refused to get vaccinated for Rubella."

"That may be true in this one case," Ricardo said, reaching up to rub a sore spot on his neck, "but on the whole to say that vaccines do more harm than good . . . like I said, absurd."

Unbeknownst to Dr. Capello, Dr. Hallstrom had had her eyes on him ever since she joined the ECDC three years earlier. Anna knew that Mrs. Capello and the kids were out of town, and she figured that now might be her best shot to start something up with the handsome Andorran.

"Here," she offered, taking a step closer to Ricardo's desk. "Let me massage your neck for you."

The warning bells that would have usually gone off in the happily-married man's head were clouded by his lack of sleep, and Dr. Capello was so tired and stiff from countless days and nights spent hunched over his desk that he considered accepting Anna's offer. Indeed, if he had stayed facing forward and just allowed her to start the massage, Ricardo wasn't quite sure what would have happened.

But he didn't stay facing forward. Dr. Capello turned in his chair, intent on saying thank you, but what he saw in Dr. Hallstrom's gleaming, sultry eyes woke him out of his haze. Ricardo jumped up from his chair, putting his arm out to stop Anna from walking any closer.

"On second thought," Ricardo said, "no. I am fine."

The other doctor batted her eyelashes and smiled as she took a step closer. "Come on, Ricardo. What's the big deal? I give a great massage. I actually thought about being a chiropractor for a while before medical school. You won't regret it."

Dr. Capello shook his head and walked around to the other side of his desk to put more space between himself and the coquettish woman. "No, I believe I would regret it. If I need a massage, I will have my wife do it."

Rejected, Dr. Hallstrom's smile left her face and a harshness that Ricardo had never seen before entered her eyes. "Fine. Suit yourself," she said before turning on her heel and stalking out of his office.

Dr. Capello put his hands on his hips and shook his head back and forth, partly in surprise at Anna's advances and partly in self-retribution at how close he came to accepting them. For a moment, Ricardo was worried that Anna might try to retaliate somehow. *I've heard stories about that. An employee is rejected by a co-worker and claims harassment or something to get back at them.* "Fotre", he swore. *That's the last thing I need right now.* But a blinking red light coming from the corner of the room caused Ricardo to breathe a sigh of relief.

"Security cameras," he said with a smile. He closed his eyes and exhaled deeply, then heard a knock on his office door. Half-expecting Dr. Hallstrom to have returned, Ricardo's eyes flew open.

"You planning on joining us?" Dr. Schroder asked, leaning against the doorframe.

"Huh?" Capello said, still not quite together.

"We have a call scheduled with the WPR for right now."

"Shit! You could've started with saying that," Ricardo responded as he grabbed his notebook off his desk and followed Zach out of the room.

****

The twice weekly call between Brussels and Solna started with an update from General Davis about the reconnaissance mission to Colorado. The men from Shining Light were expected back in Texas within the next twenty-four hours, the general explained, and then they would have to wait to recharge the one satellite cell phone before calling NATO with a full report. But Sheriff Jones knew to call during the recon mission if they got into any kind of trouble, so radio silence at that point was considered a good thing.

Dr. Capello's status update came next. While trying to craft a traditional vaccine, the doctors were also working on a way to make the MMR vaccine antibodies disappear. However, that was a harder task than they initially realized.

The researchers' first theory, Ricardo explained, was a procedure called plasmapheresis. Because singling out the Rubella antibodies was beyond the bounds of modern medical science, plasmapheresis was deemed the next best option.

"It's a way to wash the blood," Dr. Capello told the politicians. "We remove the blood from the patient's body, separate blood cells from the plasma, and return the blood cells to the body. The plasma is put back in either as completely fresh plasma or a form of artificial substitute. On our lab rats, we've used a saline solution mixed with a specific protein."

"And this will work on humans?" Prime Minister Rodgers asked.

"I hope so. I don't know, but I hope so."

"Not to be the Debbie Downer," Lucy said, "but how do you plan to mass market this? We can't wash the blood of seven billion people."

"We're not there yet, ma'am. We're hoping plasmapheresis will be the cure, and then once we have that we can hopefully convert it to a vaccine."

"Wait," said the French president. "I thought this blood washing thing was the vaccine."

Dr. Capello shook his head. "No sir. They're two separate approaches. As Prime Minister Rodgers said, given the disease's level of contagiousness, it is logistically impossible to perform plasmapheresis on the number of people we would need to. We still need a vaccine."

"Good luck convincing people to get that," the Chinese president commented. "A vaccine gone wrong is what got us into this mess in the first place."

"That's not entirely true," replied Ricardo. "The MMR vaccine functioned as designed for decades and prevented many illnesses until some as-yet-unknown contaminant in Lake Minnetonka triggered the antibody reaction."

"I know that," China's leader said, "and you know that. But to the vast majority of the world's population, this happened because of a vaccine gone wrong. And they have a point, since people without the MMR shot survived." He paused. "All I'm saying is that convincing people to get this vaccine, once we have it, could be difficult."

FORTY-TWO

The gloomy prediction of the Chinese leader left a cloud over the mood at the ECDC. Dr. Mencken in particular latched onto the argument that what they were doing was pointless. "No one will want to be vaccinated," Max kept saying, even while he continued to work. "We are wasting our time if we cannot force people to receive the inoculation."

Max's colleagues tried to tune him out, but they all had to admit there was more than a kernel of truth in the statements.

Dr. Schroder could see that Goran Ekstrom in particular was taking the words to heart.

"Don't let him get to you," Zach said, slapping his Swedish colleague on the back. "There's one in every group. If he won the lottery tomorrow, he'd complain that he wasn't paid in small bills."

Dr. Ekstrom smiled. "You are probably right. He does have a point, though. Why keep working on a vaccine if the patients might not agree to get it? It makes it impossible to continue to work so hard."

Zach shook his head. "It's not impossible. It's harder, sure. But not impossible. Hell, if I can keep my chin up when it's my country that's gone to shit, anybody can."

The older doctor responded with a small laugh. "Thanks, Zach."

"You know," Dr. Schroder continued, "going into World War II, the United States' military didn't even crack the top ten of the world's most powerful armed forces. Franklin Roosevelt, our president, knew the US would need a big growth in the military in order to fight the impending war, so he told everyone that America would build 50,000 planes in the next four years." Zach paused. "Everybody thought he was crazy. Thought it was a joke. Everything that Max has been saying about this vaccine initiative, they said about the planes." A smirk worked its way across Dr. Schroder's face. "Wanna know how many planes we built? Take a guess."

"50,000."

"Nope. 100,000. 100,000 airplanes. Airplanes that flew night raids over Germany, torched Tokyo, and dropped the bombs that ended the war." He paused. "If a bunch of Rosie the Riveters can build 100,000 airplanes in four years, we can make a vaccine and a cure. And you wanna know why?"

Goran smiled again despite himself, caught up in the American's enthusiasm. "Why?"

"Because not doing it is not an option."

****

A few minutes later, the research team heard a soft knock on the laboratory door.

"Excuse me, Dr. Capello?" said Julia, the ECDC's receptionist, as she poked her head around the corner. Julia didn't speak the doctor's native Catalán and he spoke very limited Swedish, so the two decided early on to communicate in their commonly understood English.

"Yes, Julia?" Ricardo replied, looking up from the test results he was reviewing.

"You have visitors."

The doctor's brow furrowed and he looked at the blonde receptionist in confusion. "I don't have any appointments today. In fact, I asked for my team to be left alone to work and not be disturbed."

The young woman nodded. "Yes sir, I know. But I think you might want to meet with them. They're in the lobby."

"'They?' How many people is it?"

"About fifteen I would say."

Dr. Capello's curiosity was piqued. "What do they want? Did they say?"

"They said they could help with your research, but that's all they wanted to tell me with all of the reporters roaming around."

Ricardo nodded. He could understand that. He had to send his wife and kids to stay with her parents in Austria because the media firestorm in Solna was too intense. The doctor thought about it for a minute and then replied: "make them give you any mobile phones or cameras. Then take them to the auditorium on the second floor. I'll go down there when I finish what I'm working on."

The receptionist nodded. "Okay. Any idea how long that will be? Just so I can tell them?"

"A half hour or so, probably."

****

True to his word, thirty-five minutes later, Dr. Capello made his way from his third floor research lab to the second-floor auditorium usually reserved for case reviews or speeches by visiting dignitaries.

When Ricardo entered the room, though, he didn't see overzealous reporters or designer-clad investors or even what looked like other doctors and scientists. Instead, he saw . . . old people. What looked to be around fifteen to twenty retirees in their late seventies and eighties. Julia, needing to return to her receptionist duties, had left the group alone under the instruction that they not leave the room. *By the looks of it, they couldn't walk very far even if they tried,* Capello thought. *At least not without canes and walkers.*

The doctor went to the short stage in the front of the room and cleared his throat. Hesitantly, he stumbled through two sentences in Swedish: "Jag talar inte svenska mycket bra. Har någon av er talar katalanska, engelska, spanska, eller franska?"

He was trying to find someone in the group who could serve as a translator since he only knew a few phrases in Swedish.

"Je parle le français," an elderly woman replied in a quiet voice.

And so Margaret, an eighty-three year old from Stockholm who learned French as a girl while a ballerina in Paris, joined Dr. Capello on the small platform that functioned as a stage and translated for the group.

They were all friends, Margaret explained, and lived in the same neighborhood in Stockholm. Almost all were widowed, although two husband and wife pairs were among the sixteen who had journeyed out to Solna on the morning commuter train. Older and retired but all in relatively good health (Ricardo had been wrong; not a single member one of them had any trouble walking), the group decided at their card game two nights earlier that they would volunteer to help in the efforts of Dr. Capello and his team at the ECDC.

"Help how?" Ricardo asked.

Margaret smiled a smile that only eight decades of life and wisdom could produce. "We've all lived full, happy lives," she explained in free-flowing, almost-musical French. "We are old and will not live many years longer." Margaret paused and looked over at her friends, who all nodded their heads as a way of saying 'yes, continue.' "We heard on the news how you cannot do the research you need to because all of the patients with this disease either died or are in America and not allowed out."

Dr. Capello nodded. "Yes, this is true, but . . . "

"We will be your patients," Margaret concluded. "Give us the disease and test your vaccines on us."

The doctor couldn't believe his ears. *Surely*, he thought, *something was lost in translation. She can't really mean what she just said.*

But Margaret nodded and gave Ricardo her same knowing smile. Eyes betraying complete confidence and not an ounce of fear shined at him through large-rimmed glasses. "We want to do it," the woman continued. "Far better to test the vaccines on us, who will die soon anyway, than to risk not having the right medicine if this disease ever comes back."

Sensing Dr. Capello's disapproval of the idea, she added: "we will sign whatever waivers and forms that you wish. And who knows – maybe your vaccines will work on the first try and we can all reunite next year to celebrate."

She does mean it, Ricardo thought. *They all mean it.*

Looking around at the wrinkled and weathered faces seated in front of him, Ricardo saw not one sign of doubt or indecision. The good doctor was torn. On the one hand, his gut reaction told him that the idea was ridiculous. *These people are volunteering to die.* It would go against everything he as a physician believed in to intentionally infect healthy people with a killer virus. *It would be downright criminal.*

And yet . . . would it? They did volunteer, he thought. *It was their idea and I do need to test the antidote on humans to have any idea of its efficacy. Sixteen lives is nothing compared to the hundreds of millions we've lost already.*

Capello exhaled deeply and ran his hand through his hair. "Stay here," he told the group. "I need to run the idea by my superiors."

FORTY-THREE

"That is absolutely out of the question."

After three decades in public service, it took a lot to surprise Lucy Rodgers. But the request from Dr. Capello at the ECDC genuinely shocked her. "No. We've lost enough people already."

"Now Lucy," the German chancellor said, "let's at least discuss it."

"What is there to discuss? Those people would be committing suicide."

"Not the first time the elderly have volunteered for something like this," commented the French leader.

"What are you talking about?"

"Japan. After the tsunami in 2011, retired engineers volunteered to go into the Fukushima nuclear reactor to work on fixing the damage."

"Yes," Prime Minister Rodgers replied, "and the government declined the offer."

General Davis usually left policy decisions to the elected leaders, but he felt like this particular question needed his input. Clearing his throat, he said:

"You know, in World War II, the Prisoner of War camps run by the Japanese were notoriously brutal. I read an account one time that said that American medical personnel who were also being held prisoner had to try to ration off food, medicine, and vitamins among their fellow prisoners. They also had to decide who to give medical treatment to, and oftentimes the worst off were left to die in hopes of saving those who might recover."

The general took a deep breath and placed his hands down on the table in front of him. "The article quoted a Navy doctor who said 'we must do what is best for the greatest number.'" Davis paused. "We must do what is best for the greatest number. Is it painful to think of these volunteers dying? Yes. But it's more painful to think of condemning billions more people to die in the future because we were afraid to make the tough decisions now. Closing the borders was difficult, yes. And so is authorizing the use of these volunteers. But it must be done. We must do what is best for the greatest number."

****

Once approval was given to use the Stockholm retirees as test subjects, Dr. Capello knew that he wouldn't be leaving the ECDC headquarters unless healthy antidote recipients left with him. And with his wife no longer in the country, Ricardo realized that he needed a personal assistant. Dr. Capello picked up the phone on his desk and called the receptionist, Julia. Cost-cutting at the agency had turned Julia into a *de facto* administrative aide as well as receptionist. "Can you come up here for a minute? Thank you."

When the young Swede arrived, Ricardo described the situation and began to explain the kind of assistant he would need. "It must also be a person very trustworthy and dependable," he said. "Someone who will not seek to exploit their access to the ECDC for any reason."

Dr. Ekstrom, who was passing by in the hall, stopped to listen. Stepping inside his boss' office, he said: "Sorry to barge in, but I have the perfect person for you. Not to take the search away from you, Julia, but I already know an excellent candidate."

"No, no, that's fine. If you know of someone, this is good."

"Who?" asked Dr. Capello.

"My son, Liam," Goran replied. "He's eighteen and looking to earn money for university next year. He's very dependable, lives nearby with his mother and me, and he can be trusted to not tell anyone things he should not because he can see the stress and strain this research project has put on his own family."

"Eighteen, you said? Does he have his driver's license?"

Ekstrom nodded. "He does. He is in his final year of school before university. Very smart. Really, Ricardo, he'd be perfect."

"I would need him to bring breakfast before he went to school and dinner in the evenings; to take care of laundry and my mail and all of that."

"Not a problem."

Dr. Capello thought about it for a minute, then said: "okay, I'll give him a shot."

As Dr. Ekstrom broke into a smile, Ricardo turned to the receptionist. "Sorry to make you come all the way up here for nothing."

"Oh, do not worry. Happy to help I'll get back downstairs now, though, unless there's anything else you need?"

"No, thank you."

****

Liam Ekstrom, the teenage son of Ricardo's colleague Goran, turned out to be a great hire. The boy was given keys to the Capello apartment and the use of a prepaid debit card to cover any expenses. Every morning before school, Liam brought Dr. Capello breakfast, coffee, and anything else Ricardo might need for the day. Dinner was delivered promptly at 7:00pm, and twice a week Liam picked up the doctor's laundry and took it to the cleaners, delivering it back the next day fresh, clean, and folded. Dr. Capello slept on a cot that was brought into his office, never more than a few hundred feet away from his patients.

Even though he knew that he shouldn't, that he had more important things to do, Dr. Capello still found himself compelled to watch at least a portion of the news broadcast each evening. He did so while eating the dinner Liam brought him, justifying it as a necessary 'mental health break.' There was some truth to that – after all, Ricardo had been working around the clock for almost two months – but he still felt guilty about pausing his research for any amount of time. Not guilty enough to stop, though.

This night's broadcast followed the same general format, with reports on the weather and the economic markets and any major fires, accidents, or other crimes. There was also the inevitable NATO update from Brussels and one from a reporter standing in front of the ECDC – indeed, several times Dr. Capello had looked out the window and seen the same reporter below that he could hear talking on his television set.

The news broadcasts typically concluded with some sort of human interest story. Earlier, before the Shorewood outbreak, they were Ricardo's favorite part of the program. A handicapped little boy who won a sporting contest or a young mother finding a creative way to bring about a better life for herself and her children. But now, ever since the pandemic began, Dr. Capello didn't like the human interest stories. And yet, the interviews with people who escaped the US or still had family members there inspired him to keep working hard to find an answer for the deadly disease. Tonight's report was no different, as the story featured an American couple named Harrington. Brian and Lisa Harrington, the reporter said, were two weeks into a three-week cruise in the Mediterranean when the containment zone was established. Now stuck in Italy, allowed to stay there with refugee status, the Harringtons were nonetheless fighting furiously to be allowed to return home.

"Our family is still there," said Mrs. Harrington. "Our daughter and son-in-law and two grandbabies."

"We haven't talked to them since just after the borders were closed," her husband added.

"Did they have the Rubella vaccine?" the newscaster asked.

Mrs. Harrington nodded, sniffling back tears. "All of them. It was expected for my kids, and they never believed that supposed autism link when it came time for my grandbabies to be vaccinated. My daughter and I always shook our heads at the people who didn't get the vaccines for their children. The doctors said we needed it, and vaccines work. But now? Now my whole family is dead."

"You haven't been able to get in touch with any of them?" the reporter pressed.

"No. Nobody. I don't even have anything I could compare it to. They're all just . . . gone. It's all gone."

Mr. Harrington put his arm around his wife's shoulders. "Italy labeled us as refugees. I'm an American. Americans aren't refugees. We take refugees from other countries. I don't even – " He sighed. "I just . . . " Tears welled up in the man's eyes. "There are no words for this."

FORTY-FOUR

Quickly labeled the 'Stockholm Sixteen', the volunteers for vaccine testing all moved into renovated rooms in the basement of the ECDC. Solna and its surrounding areas had plenty of top quality hospitals, but Dr. Capello decided it would be best to treat the volunteers at his headquarters. Keeping the entire operation in one building would help prevent the intrusion of the press, and the ECDC was designed with top-of-the-line isolation rooms and ventilation systems. Much like its American counterpart, the European Centers for Disease Control regularly stored active versions of numerous infectious diseases and chemical and biological weapons for research, so it was equipped with air vent sealing and other capabilities beyond those found in most hospitals. *Not to mention the fact that the Swedish government won't let me bring any test vaccines into its hospitals*, Ricardo thought. Although they had reluctantly agreed to the Stockholm Sixteen project at the ECDC, Sweden's prime minister and king refused to allow any version of the live virus to leave the walls of the medical research facility.

Despite the best efforts of Dr. Capello and his team, news about the so-called 'human lab rats' spread quickly throughout Sweden, Europe, and around the globe. Reaction was mixed, with some saying the testing was murder and Ricardo should be arrested while others pointed out that patients participate in drug trials all the time.

"*Sick* patients do drug trials," one philosophy professor argued while participating in a televised roundtable on the subject. "And only after the medicines have gone through several rounds of mice and other animal testing."

"They've done mice testing," a bioethicist snapped back. "And all of the actual patients are already dead."

"He's right," a third 'expert' weighed in. A specialist in topics like game theory and non-governmental organizations such as the United Nations, the man seemed a little out of place among the group of scientists and ethicists but was nonetheless a hearty contributor. "What we need to keep in mind here is that healthy people are going to be guinea pigs. There's no way around it. Anyone infected with the Shorewood Disease is dead. So what it really comes down to is a numbers game: do we want a dozen or so test subjects or billions of test subjects? It's either test it on a few or release it untested on everyone."

The philosophy professor remained unconvinced. "Surely there must be a better way."

"And all wars can be resolved with group hugs and candy canes, right?"

"Okay, okay," the panel's moderator said. Let's try to keep the sarcasm to a minimum."

****

While the world debated the decision, Dr. Capello and his team went to work. Not knowing any better or fairer method, the doctors drew names from a hat to determine which volunteer would be the first to receive the virus and an accompanying test vaccine. One by one names were drawn, and one by one the medicines failed.

Margaret Larsson was the fourth person to be picked. With her sunny disposition, ballerina grace, and beautifully-spoken French, the eighty-three year old widow had quickly become Dr. Capello's favorite in the group. It tore him up inside to know how little chance she stood of survival. They had learned a lot and made great gains based on the results of the first three attempts, but Ricardo knew they were still not there yet.

Despite the failure of the end results, the ECDC doctors had developed what they thought was a good process for the trials. First, to eliminate any outside influence, all of the patients were put on a specific, nutritionally-sound diet. The variety of foods in the volunteers' meals was designed as a cleanse of sorts, wanting to clear any impurities from their systems. Seventy-two hours before it was their turn to be infected with the Shorewood Disease, the patients stopped taking any medicine that wasn't necessary for their survival.

"I know it's not how clinical trials are typically done," Dr. Capello told his team, "but with so few test subjects, we really don't have any other choice. We need blank slates."

On the day the virus was administered and then again when the vaccine was given, the doctors took samples of the patient's blood, urine, and other vital signs as well as pictures of his or her skin to monitor the outbreak of any rash. Those same things were then checked with regularity after the drug was injected.

The learning curve was steep. Gustaf, 'unlucky Number One' as Zach called him, died in the exact same manner that the actual Shorewood victims did, only faster. Ricardo and his staff concluded that they made the active portion of the drug too strong and spent the next four days working to create a new version. The rest of the volunteers, after holding a touching memorial service, returned to their quarantined rooms and passed the time in the same way that they had in the city center: playing cards, watching TV, some knitting and other small arts and crafts, and a lot of reading.

"It's weird," Dr. Schroder said one day.

"What is?" asked Ricardo.

"I stopped by the basement this morning on my way up to the lab. Just to check in on them and stuff."

"And?"

"And they're just chillin', acting like they aren't at the center of this huge medical experiment and media firestorm."

"I don't think they care about any of the media stuff," Dr. Capello said, his eyes still glued to the microscope on the desk in front of him.

"Yeah," Zach agreed. "But I guess the weirdest thing was that I thought they would be sadder, you know? The first three test volunteers were part of them; some of their best friends. They died just recently and the others are already back to going about their lives like nothing happened."

The younger doctor's boss lifted his head from the microscope and looked over at his colleague. "Just because they aren't wailing and crying hysterically doesn't mean they aren't sad. Grief affects every person in a different way." Ricardo paused. "But they are also older, and have more experience with death because of that."

Dr. Delacroix, who had been eavesdropping from across the room, chimed in: "besides, it's not like their deaths were a surprise. They all knew what they signed up for."

Ricardo looked at Zach but nodded in Elena's direction. "She has a point. But the bigger point, for all of us, is to try to make it where Margaret doesn't become the next victim."

FORTY-FIVE

The flurry of activity in Solna was rivaled by that in Brussels. Pressure continued to mount on the WPR as weeks turned into months and the world seemed to be in a suspended state of anticipation, waiting for the containment zone to be lifted.

The politicians who had relocated their offices to NATO headquarters also found it increasingly difficult to ignore domestic matters in their home countries. Lucy Rodgers, for her part, was sitting at her desk trying to focus on a parliamentary budget report when she heard a knock at the door.

"Come in," she said without looking up.

"Excuse me, Prime Minister," said Brad Davis, taking a step inside the office. The prime minister and the general hadn't gotten off on the best foot, but by that point had grown to be almost friends. "I don't mean to bother you," he added, "but I thought you might like to hear the good news."

Rodgers turned around in her chair. "'Good news'? Of course. It's been so long I'd almost forgotten what that sounds like."

The general responded with a smile. "We've located Colonel Keener's family."

"Colonel Keener?"

"The astronaut, ma'am."

Lucy sprang to her feet and clapped her hands together. "That's fantastic! Where are they?"

"Australia. Apparently when news about the virus kept getting worse, the colonel's husband decided to get as far away from it as possible. He and their kids have been in Sydney for nearly nine weeks now."

"Oh, that's great. You're right . . . wonderful news."

"It is, yes," Davis said, nodding his head. "I thought perhaps you'd like to join the phone call when I tell Colonel Keener?"

The prime minister smiled. "I would. Very much. Thank you."

****

The good news continued that afternoon when NATO's tactical command unit announced it had figured out a new way to deliver food and other supplies into the United States without the terrorists knowing. An estimated twenty to twenty-five million people were still alive inside the containment zone, but they wouldn't stay that way for much longer if they didn't start receiving some form of food and medical aid. With cargo plane and helicopter relief flights no longer an option, the WPR needed a backup plan.

"We're going to use trains," General Davis announced. "We'll load the trains with supplies, computer program the destination, and send them on a one-way trip into the United States."

Prime Minister Rodgers asked the question on everyone's mind: "how the hell did we not think of this sooner?"

"I'm not entirely sure, ma'am. We dropped the ball."

"But now you've picked it up again," the German chancellor said, seeking to diffuse an argument. "It'll be like the Berlin Airlift but over ground. The Soviets wouldn't allow supplies to cross through East German land to reach West Berlin, so the Allies flew in supplies. These terrorist shits won't let anything fly into the airspace, so we'll go by land."

"General, will it work?" Lucy asked. "Or will they just blow up the trains?"

"We've received no indication that they have any way of monitoring ground transport. NORAD's systems are for air and space traffic only."

The political members of the P5+1 nodded their heads in agreement, all liking what they were hearing.

"It goes without saying," added Davis, "that news of this relief mission cannot leak out to the press. We still don't know how many terrorist agents are inside America . . . we can't have them knowing about the supply trains."

****

Within forty-eight hours of the special committee's go-ahead, two staging areas were established just outside the containment zone – one in Mexico and one in Canada. Workers from each government, NATO, and the UN wore protective suits and masks and had to be scrubbed down before exiting the trains' loading areas. But the plan appeared to be working. Air cargo planes – some from overseas military bases but most hired out from shipping companies like UPS and FedEx – carried food, clothing, and other supplies from around the world to the staging areas. Once there, the cargo was transferred from planes to trucks and from trucks to the trains that would carry it all to predetermined cities in the United States.

The process of deciding what items to send and who should donate what took almost as much time and effort as the actual gathering and shipping of it all did. Foodstuffs should be kept as local as possible, it was determined, so that things could remain fresh for longer. Clothes from China – "they're coming from there anyway," people said – and gasoline from OPEC nations. Battery-powered, satellite-linked cell phones from Japan and South Korea, and railcars stuffed full of medical supplies came directly from the same European CDC that was working frantically to create a new vaccine.

One lingering problem was how to inform survivors in the US that the trains were coming.

"How will people know what it is?" one NATO official asked.

General Davis brushed off the question. "Those who have survived are hungry enough and brave enough to approach a train that suddenly appears. Plus, we can write notes on the boxcars that say what's inside and where it's coming from. Just make sure there is absolutely no media coverage of this *and* that the trains stay well clear of Colorado Springs."

Where to send the trains, though . . . therein laid the other big topic for debate. The first wave of supplies would only have enough for six trains of ten cars each. It was decided that the items should be split, with three train loads travelling south from Canada and three heading north from Mexico. With Vancouver, Ottawa, Montreal, and Winnipeg all evacuated to outside the buffer zone, Canada chose Calgary to be its launching point. Seattle, Chicago, and New York City would be the recipients. South of the containment area, the UN set up shop in Monterrey and sent supplies north to Atlanta, Dallas, and Los Angeles.

The train project was a risk, and the WPR knew it. But so many people had died from the Shorewood Disease when there was nothing they could do about it, and the leaders in Brussels refused to sit back and let the survivors die of starvation.

FORTY-SIX

One of those Shorewood survivors was Caleb Harris. A resident of Los Angeles, California, the sixty-nine year old retiree was a Vietnam Veteran and widower who passed his time in a retirement community full of other 'old geezers' as he liked to call them. Many of the old geezers in his neighborhood were still alive, since their generation got the Measles vaccine as kids before the combination MMR was created. An organic vegetable garden behind the retirement center kept the group of elderly Americans relatively well-nourished, given the circumstances, but almost two months of the global blockade and then stoppage of the air relief flights meant that even the best attempts at rationing weren't very useful anymore.

When the first supply train arrived in Los Angeles, the residents of the Mill Acres Retirement Community were some of the lucky recipients of the food, water, gasoline, power generators, and clean clothes that had filled the railroad boxcars to the brim. *First time I've ever been glad to live near the train tracks*, Caleb had thought. He was usually one of the ones cursing the conductors for blowing the whistle in the middle of the night.

The morning after the train came, Mr. Harris was out in his driveway loading up his truck. "Hey Caleb," a neighbor called out. "Where are you going?"

Harris didn't stop packing but answered: "to get my grandkids." Caleb's son was a civilian instructor at the Air Force Academy, and his daughter-in-law was 'one of them hippie health freaks' who didn't believe in traditional medicine. Consequently, Amber, Hunter, and Turner Harris, ages eleven, nine, and seven, never received the MMR vaccine. Their grandfather smiled as he remembered a conversation with his son when he announced they were having their third child.

"I'll never understand why your generation finds it necessary for your kids' names to all rhyme or start with the same letter," Caleb had said in reference to the baby's name of Turner.

"And I'll never understand why your generation wanted to name their kids 'Sunshine' or 'Moonbeam'," his son had replied.

"How do you know they're still alive?" asked the neighbor, bringing Caleb back to the present.

"Their mother was into all that alternative medicine stuff. Refused to see real doctors. I thought she was endangering the kids' health by not getting them vaccinated." He huffed in equal parts disgust and disbelief. "Turns out she knew what she was doing."

"Where are they?" the other man asked. "Your grandkids, I mean."

"Colorado Springs."

"You have enough gas for the drive?"

Harris nodded. "Yeah. I went around this morning asking people for their supply. Paying them, making trades, that sort of thing. Most everybody around here is just staying put until it's all over, so it wasn't too hard to get what I needed. Donna gave me some of your gas, by the way," he added, referring to the neighbor's wife. "She didn't tell you?"

"No, but I don't mind. Go get the grandkids. I'd be doing the same thing if I were in your shoes."

****

It took the sixty-nine year old Harris thirteen and a half hours to drive from his condo in Los Angeles to his son's home in a neighborhood just outside of downtown Colorado Springs. Only stopping for a brief power nap and the occasional call of nature, Caleb didn't see another soul during the entire trip.

I shouldn't be surprised by that, he thought as he exited the interstate and began following the surface streets toward where his grandchildren lived. *It's a lot of desert anyway, and any people still alive don't have much gas to get around.* It was still an adjustment, though, and the former Army tank gunner had stopped at six stop signs leaving his neighborhood before he realized that there was no need. No other cars on the road; no police around to enforce the traffic laws. His Cadillac sedan averaged 100 miles per hour during the rest his trip.

The eerie ghost town feeling continued as Harris drove past street after street of Colorado Springs homes with no people in them. Or at least no living people in them. Military cities like this one were particularly hard hit by the virus, since vaccines were mandatory for all new recruits.

Eventually, though, Caleb began to see life. Every so often, a fellow retiree like himself would open a front door to peer out at the first moving vehicle they had seen in weeks or months. Children, dirty and disheveled, temporarily stopped their searches for food to stare at the man driving by. The newcomer had the sudden sensation that he was at an amusement park or wildlife preserve, and half expected to hear a tour guide's voice saying 'and here, ladies and gentlemen, are examples of how early American plague survivors used to live.'

Caleb shook his head to clear his thoughts as he pulled into his son's driveway. He saw no signs of life on this particular street but grabbed his shotgun just in case. *People can start to lose their sanity when put in a situation like this*, Harris thought, having learned that lesson the hard way during two tours in Vietnam. Caleb knew he was taking a risk by leaving some food and other supplies in the truck, but he didn't see any other choice. Locking the car doors, the man set off in search of his grandchildren.

FORTY-SEVEN

The small, one-story ranch house where the Colorado Harrises lived looked nearly identical to the other cookie-cutter homes in the planned community that was named, for no apparent reason, Shady Woods. Well over half of the neighborhood's residents had direct ties to the military, which meant it was at once both transient and tight knit.

Making his way up the sidewalk toward the front door, Caleb couldn't help but admire the work his son and daughter-in-law had done to spruce up the house and otherwise make it their own. Perennials lined one side of the walkway, and a couple of dogwood trees added character to the small front yard. The shudders were also nicely painted and an American flag still flew from a pole near the front door.

There were signs of disrepair too, though. The grass had grown up to mid-calf height, weeds dotted the flowerbeds, and Caleb noticed that the blinds and shades were drawn shut tight – the children wanting to block out any signs of the chaotic world outside.

Keeping his shotgun poised and ready, the visitor from Los Angeles stepped up onto the porch and rang the doorbell. No answer. When the children still hadn't appeared after his third attempt, their grandfather started to worry. *I know they weren't vaccinated, but what if something else happened to them? If they got sick and there weren't any doctors left or if they tried to leave here and go somewhere else?* Concern rising in his voice, Caleb started to walk around the side of the house and called out the children's names.

"Amber! Turner, Hunter! It's me, Grandpa. It's okay; come outside. It's Grandpa."

The house remained silent.

Reaching the back door, Caleb decided he had no other choice but to break into the home. He hadn't driven all this way and used all of that precious gasoline to leave without knowing for sure that his grandkids weren't there. When he didn't find a key under the doormat or any of the potted plants, the athletic former military man raised his leg and, using all of his strength, kicked the door open.

A huge weight was lifted from Mr. Harris' shoulders when he entered the home . . . there were signs of life everywhere. Toys strewn across the living room in a way his daughter-in-law would never allow. Plates of fresh-ish looking food scrounged up from God-knows-where dotted the kitchen table.

"Kids!" he called out again. "Amber, Turner, Hunter! It's Grandpa! Where are you?"

A small head full of curly black hair slowly appeared from behind the doorframe of the master bedroom. Two brown eyes showed up next, and then seven-year-old Hunter bolted out of the room and down the hall into his grandfather's waiting arms. Amber and Turner soon followed, and for a minute Caleb forgot the danger lurking around the house and soaked up all of the love and happiness that filled their group hug.

"You're here!" Hunter said with a huge smile. "I told them you would come and they didn't believe me but you're here!"

Eleven-year-old Amber, the *de facto* adult of the house, had tears streaming down her cheeks. "I . . . I t-thought you would've d-died too."

Caleb leaned back from the hug to look his young granddaughter in the eye. "I didn't. I'm here. I love you all so much. There was no way I could stay away . . . I came to get you as soon as I could."

Turner, nine years old and a quintessential middle child, looked up at his grandfather and, with a voice full of sadness, announced that his daddy and mommy died.

"I know, buddy," Caleb replied, tears filling his own eyes. Even though he knew his son and daughter-in-law received the MMR vaccine and would not have been able to survive the outbreak, hearing the little boy say it aloud ripped out his heart all over again.

In the next instant, Mr. Harris remembered where he was and what he came to do. "Pack up a small bag of your stuff, kids. We need to go ahead and get back on the road."

The three children who were still clinging to their grandfather abruptly disengaged and stepped back. "Where are we going?" Hunter asked.

"Los Angeles. We have supply trains bringing food to the city now, and there are a lot of people in my neighborhood who are still alive. You're not going to stay here by yourselves."

Amber took another step backwards and shook her head. "We're not going." Turner and Hunter joined their sister and all three looked up at Caleb with the same stubborn face that their father displayed as a child.

Grandpa Harris hadn't expected this kind of resistance. "What are you talking about? Of course you're going. You can't stay here."

"Yes we can," replied Amber, sticking up her chin in defiance. "We've made it this long on our own. And we're not leaving Mom and Dad."

"Your mom and dad are dead, sweetheart."

The blunt words didn't faze the eleven year old at all. Such was the life of a pandemic survivor. "I know that. We buried them in the backyard. And we're not leaving them."

They what?! "You . . . you buried them yourselves? In the backyard?"

Hunter nodded and even smiled, proud of his contribution to the effort. "Turner made crosses for them, and I picked flowers, and we all used the shovel to dig the holes."

"Dig the graves," Amber corrected. The little girl who became a mother-figure overnight was nonetheless protective of the memory of her parents.

Caleb understood why his grandchildren wanted to stay, but he also knew that it was impossible. "I'm so sorry about your mom and dad. Believe me . . . remember, your dad was my son. I miss him and your mom too. And I know they're so proud of you for the way you buried them. I'm proud of you. But you have to go with me. We'll come back when this is over, but for right now you have to leave. It's safer in L.A. There are more people still alive and the supply trains will come into the depot once a week." His voice took on a harder edge as he said: "this is not up for debate. You're my grandchildren; I'm your guardian now. Pack a bag . . . we're leaving."

****

The battle of wills complete, Grandpa Caleb and his three young charges grabbed their small backpacks and duffle bags and exited the house. But unlike when he first arrived, the sidewalk and street in front of the Harris home was now dotted with children and senior citizens. Over the course of the past several weeks, after the wave of Shorewood Disease victims died, survivors in the area started to find each other and band together for safety and comfort. All those still alive in the general vicinity of the Shady Woods neighborhood had congregated there, mainly because Shady Woods had a large, well-insulated clubhouse and a real, working well to provide fresh water.

Why the people were there, though, was the least of Caleb's concerns. He was more interested in what they might do. Instinctively, he stepped in front of his three grandchildren to protect them. "Do you know these people?" he asked, not taking his eyes off the crowd.

"We went to school with some of them," answered Turner. "And some of them are from our neighborhood."

"A lot of them are living in the clubhouse," Amber added. "It's warm in there, and we had our first snow last week."

Caleb could see the predator looks in the neighbors' eyes as they darted back and forth between the Harrises and the truck, and the grandfather knew that he needed to get his family out of there as quickly as he could.

"Listen," he said, taking a step forward and keeping a firm grip on his gun. "I need you all to back away from the truck, okay?" When no one moved, Caleb raised his shotgun to point it at them. "Back up. All of you. Now."

The unarmed crowd moved from the Harris' driveway into the street.

"Get in the truck, kids," the grandfather ordered. The former military man kept his gun trained on the neighbors until Amber, Turner, and Hunter were all inside the vehicle.

"Step back farther," he said to the crowd. "All the way to the other sidewalk."

Once he had a bit of buffer space between himself and the less-than-friendly looking bystanders, Caleb walked around to the back of the truck and lowered the tailgate.

"I have a box of food and two cases of water," he said. "NATO shipped them in to Los Angeles on a supply train. I'll leave it here for you all if you promise to let us go without any trouble." Even though he was the one with the gun, Caleb knew his reaction time wasn't what it used to be and that a crowd, working together, could overpower him. This close to getting his grandchildren to safety, he wasn't willing to take that risk. After unloading the food and water, Mr. Harris walked back to the driver's side of his truck and opened the door.

The smallest member of the group across the street, a little girl of no more than six, looked over at Caleb with big doe eyes and a toothy smile. "Thank you, sir," she said.

Her polite manners in the midst of disaster nearly drove the older man to tears. "You're welcome, sweetheart," he replied. And then, as quickly as he came, Caleb climbed into his truck was gone – this time carrying with him very precious cargo.

FORTY-EIGHT

Several miles away at Cheyenne Mountain, Dehqan Nazari and his men were also starting to feel the effects of the continued blockade. The nuclear bunker had been well-stocked with food and water when they arrived, but supplies were starting to run low and some of the terrorists were getting cabin fever from being stuck inside the mountain for so long.

"What's the point of taking control of a place," Mohamed asked one day, "if we can't actually walk around there? We have weapons; we're immune from the disease. Why do we have to stay here inside of this cave all day?"

Dehqan knew that the younger man had a point. They were safe inside the bunker, sure, but they also needed to start claiming more territory if they ever wanted to do more than shoot down planes. Not to mention the fact that the group would soon run out of food.

Reluctantly, the Afghan native nodded his head. "Okay, Mohamed, you win. Pick two or three men to go with you. Get a car from the employee parking lot, drive into Colorado Springs, and find us some food. Be ready to report on the condition of the city, too. How many people you see, if any of them appear to be a threat to us, things like that."

"Look for those men in the truck, too," added Farzad. The terrorists hadn't forgotten about their visit from the residents of Shining Light.

A smile broke out across Mohamed's face. "Yes! Thank you!" The teenager turned and ran down the hall, looking for his friends. "Joe! Faisal! Kontar! Grab a gun . . . we get to leave the bunker!"

****

Finding any food in Colorado Springs was more difficult than the Taliban foot soldiers expected. Store shelves were empty, restaurants were shuttered closed, and the few downtown homes they broke into also had bare pantries.

"Praise Allah we still have food in the bunker," Mohamed said as the group of four strolled down the middle of a once-busy street in the city.

"No joke," responded Joe, the Saudi-American convert. "Although there's not much left."

Suddenly, out of the corner of his eye, Mohamed saw a little girl walking down a side street. *She's eating an apple,* he thought. *We don't even have fresh fruit at Cheyenne Mountain.* "Hey, kid!" he called out. "Where'd you get that?"

Olive, the same little girl who thanked Caleb Harris, turned around, saw the men, and started running in the opposite direction. Mohamed took off after her and chased her down. He pinned the six-year-old against the side of a building and pulled out his gun, waving it in front of her face.

"I'll ask you again: where did you get the apple?"

Tears streamed down Olive's face. "An o-old m-man in a truck d-dropped it off a couple of d-days ago."

"And where did he get it?"

"L-los Angeles. He s-said there's a t-train." Her voice squeaked out of fear.

"Did he say if he would be coming back?" asked Mohamed.

Olive shook her head. "I d-don't know. H-he didn't s-say."

****

Returning to Cheyenne Mountain several hours later, after finally finding some food closer to Denver, Mohamed let the other men unload their car while he went in search of Dehqan.

"We have company, sir," the Singaporean announced to his boss.

"What?"

"We saw a little girl in Colorado Springs," Mohamed explained. "She was eating an apple. I asked her where she got it and she said some man in a truck dropped it off a few days ago."

"Fresh fruit?" said Dehqan, hardly believing the story. "Nobody around here has fresh fruit anymore."

"That's what I thought. The girl said something about Los Angeles."

"Xiao!" Dehqan yelled. "Are you positive that there haven't been any planes flying in American airspace?"

"Yes. One hundred percent positive."

"The girl also said something about a train," Mohamed added.

The terrorist leader let out a low growl. "Trains. Shit. Of course. I should've known the UN would find a different way to get supplies into the country without risking healthy lives. Shit."

FORTY-NINE

While the arrival of the supply trains was an immediate success, it took the doctors at the ECDC a bit longer to formulate the correct vaccine for the Shorewood Disease. Eleven of the Stockholm Sixteen died, including Dr. Capello's favorite, Margaret. Some of them had longer, more painful deaths than the original victims, but on the twelfth try Dr. Capello and his team hit the jackpot.

"We did it!" Ricardo beamed as he yelled the news into the phone when he called the WPR in Brussels. "We did it! We have a vaccine that now works! It was tested on volunteers twelve through sixteen and they are all still alive and healthy!"

A party broke out at NATO's headquarters, soon followed by the rest of Brussels and other cities and towns around the globe. For the first time since the containment efforts began, church bells rang in celebration and Drs. Capello, Mencken, Delacroix, Ekstrom, and Schroder became the toasts of the world.

The joyful festivities, however, were short-lived. Although the ECDC physicians sent out the vaccine formula to health departments around the world so it could start to be mass produced, public officials soon realized that the Chinese president had been correct in his prediction: people were extremely wary of getting the new government-mandated shot. And they were vocally wary, with television hosts, celebrities, and even some politicians taking to the airwaves to question the mandatory inoculation program. Australia's most popular DJ summed up many people's feelings with a speech on his daily radio show.

"No offense," he began, "but why in the hell would I ever agree to be vaccinated for anything now? Our government is telling me that I need this vaccine so I don't get the Shorewood Disease. Yeah, well, that's what people said about the MMR vaccine too, and look at what happened to everybody in America who listened. They're dead. Make up your own minds, of course, but I'm not touching any government-mandated anything with a ten foot pole. No way."

****

The WPR's response to the backlash was swift and strong, albeit predictable. In those democratic countries with significant public opposition, a mass media campaign commenced to, in Lucy Rodgers' words, scare the people into compliance. Other nations announced that anyone who refused the vaccine would be deemed a threat to public health and jailed, while the least-democratic governments around the world gave their residents no choice. As soon as the vaccine became available, those militaries started going door-to-door to administer it. One dictator declared that everyone in his country would get shot, but that it was up to them whether it was with a needle or a bullet.

Mandatory vaccinations weren't the only thing causing public unrest, though. Tired of the continued personal, political, and economic upheaval caused by the embargo against the United States, people around the globe were upset by the WPR's decision to leave the blockade in place after the ECDC announced it had created a working antidote.

"Out of an abundance of caution, the UN Special Committee on Worldwide Pandemic Response, in conjunction with NATO and the governments of Canada and Mexico, have decided to extend the implementation of the containment zone for three more weeks. This is to ensure, as much as possible, the health and safety of all persons – both inside and outside the containment zone."

Those were the words of NATO's Secretary-General, once again acting as the spokesperson for the WPR. *He deserves a medal, a vacation, and a very large bottle of alcohol when this is all over*, thought Prime Minister Rodgers. *Hell, what am I saying . . . I deserve that too.*

FIFTY

Public anger about the mandatory vaccinations and the continuance of the containment zone was the least of NATO General Brad Davis' worries. He knew that none of the WPR's efforts would matter in the end if he didn't find a way to defeat the terrorists holed up in Cheyenne Mountain.

Because of that, General Davis convened a conference call between the P5+1 political leaders, his senior staff, and Sheriff Jones in the United States. The sheriff's report from his recon mission had been very helpful, if for no other reason than it let people on the outside know a little bit more about what things looked like in America. Josiah's pictures from the Cheyenne Mountain bunker were also of great interest, and General Davis had giant versions of those photos plastered to the walls of the conference room where the group in Brussels was now gathered. Much to Davis' dismay, the old Russian spy, Boris Stanlovich, also joined the meeting.

"We cannot," General Davis began, "re-open the borders of the United States as long as NORAD is under the control of the terrorists. Every day that the blockade remains in place, the world loses hundreds of millions, if not billions of dollars in economic productivity . . . not to mention whatever computer hackers they have inside the bunker get that much more time to work on figuring out our nuclear codes – if they haven't already. What we need now are ideas about how to get rid of the terrorists, and quickly."

Stanlovich, the former Soviet agent, cleared his throat and stood up from his chair. At no more than five-foot-six, Boris was almost as wide as he was tall and waddled like a duck when he started to walk around the room. "When we made the bunker," he said, "we wanted to have it be secure enough to survive a direct hit by a nuclear missile but also close enough to the surface to effectively monitor air and space flight."

"Hold your communist horses, buddy," General Davis interrupted. "*We* does not include *you* as far as this bunker and the US military is concerned."

Boris stopped waddling and turned around to face the general, taking a handkerchief out of his pocket and using it to wipe the sweat from his forehead. "Actually, *we* did include me. Mother Russia sent me as a spy, but I also have an engineering degree and helped design the bunker."

The American military officer continued to glare at the frumpy, sweaty old man standing across the room. "First of all, 'Mother Russia' is not a person. Or a term. Or anything. Secondly, how the hell do you have an American accent when you talk?"

Boris smiled, and Lucy Rodgers grimaced at the sight of the teeth worn down by decades of neglect and vodka. "I got my engineering degree from Purdue," the Russian said. "Also, Mother Russia gave me special training so I would have an accent like the other people in the United States."

"Stop it with the damn 'Mother Russia' shit!"

"Alright, alright," Prime Minister Rodgers cut in, standing up and placing herself in between Davis and Stanlovich. "Let's all calm down. General Davis, you know what type of missions the NATO personnel are capable of undertaking. And Mr. Stanlovich, you can tell us what would work best when trying to remove the terrorists from the bunker."

"Why don't you just blow it up?"

The suggestion of the usually mild-mannered Josiah Jones took everyone by surprise.

"I'm sorry, what?"

"You heard me," the sheriff replied via speakerphone. "Aim your nukes at Colorado Springs and bomb it."

"No offense, Sheriff Jones," said General Davis, "but you have no authority to give me permission to drop a nuclear bomb on our country."

"And who would? Every person in our official presidential line of succession is dead."

The world leaders in Brussels looked around the conference room and all agreed, via raised eyebrows and shrugged shoulders, that the man inside the containment zone made a valid argument.

"Why don't we?" Germany's chancellor asked. "We all heard the recon mission report: dead people everywhere, littering the streets. What was it you said, Sheriff? 'At some point you stop counting the bodies. You'll go crazy if you don't.' It pains me to say it, but the United States as we knew it no longer exists." He took a breath but continued his monologue. "We've all seen the numbers. Reports have it that upwards of ninety percent of the American population is dead. Those who survived are now being held hostage by a combination of our travel bans and a terrorist network that stole their weapons. I mean, come on. Sheriff Jones went up to Colorado Springs. He scouted it out. Every good or decent adult in that city is dead. The neo-Taliban controls it. Nuke their asses until their shit turns green so that the people who remain can start to rebuild the country."

The German leader's speech garnered support from many of his colleagues.

General Davis sighed and attempted to regain the group's composure. "We're not going to drop a nuclear bomb on Cheyenne Mountain."

"Why the hell not?" asked Boris the spy.

"For starters, as you said, the facility was designed to withstand a direct nuclear blast. So the terrorists would likely survive, and in the process we would be condemning Colorado to decades of radiation poisoning. Not to mention looking like the bad guys in all of this."

"We're the good guys," the German leader shot back. "What are you talking about?"

"Take the angry blinders off for a minute and see the big picture, okay?" Brad Davis' frustration boiled over. "We closed the borders of what was then the world's biggest superpower and said that, apart from dropping some food down from airplanes, we didn't care that almost everyone inside those borders would die. And now you want to make it where, even after the blockade is lifted, no one can settle in that large region of the country because we exploded a nuclear bomb on it?" The general shook his head. "No. This is my military operation and it's my country, and I say no."

"So what are we going to do?" Lucy Rodgers asked.

"Why don't we use the trains to our advantage?" suggested the French president. "Send in a commando unit on a train, and then they go into the bunker and kill the terrorists. Why use an ax when a scalpel will do?"

"It could work," replied Lucy, "except we don't have a way to bring the terrorists out of the mountain."

"The complex was never stocked to withstand a siege," Boris said, liking the commando idea more and more. "They should run out of food and supplies soon, if they haven't already. We – okay, *you* – surround the mountain and if they try to come out, we turn their bodies into Swiss cheese."

General Davis had to refrain from rolling his eyes at the 'Swiss cheese' remark. "For all we know," he said, "the Shorewood Disease is still running rampant in the United States. We don't have any troops capable of spending that long waiting outside the mountain, potentially exposing them to the disease . . . the vaccine hasn't really been tested in the field like that before. No." He shook his head. "If we go the special forces approach, we need a way to lure the terrorists out of the bunker."

"And your 'surround the place' idea wouldn't work anyway." Josiah Jones' words crackled over the speakerphone. "They'd see you on the security cameras."

"Can't we cut the power?"

Boris shook his head. "Not at Cheyenne Mountain, no. The backup generators there have backup generators. Remember, the idea was that the US would be the ones inside the bunker and the enemy on the outside."

"What if you had a way to get them to come out of the mountain on their own, and in a shorter amount of time?" said Josiah.

"What'd you have in mind, Sheriff?" asked General Davis.

"I'll go."

"What do you mean 'I'll go'?" Lucy Rodgers asked.

"I mean I'll go. I'm immune from the disease, which means I can travel freely in civilian clothes with no mask. If the terrorists have access to weapons systems then I'm sure they also have internet and know that my town has a lot of survivors. General, you told me about the news articles about Shinin' Light." He paused, choosing his words carefully. "I'll say I'm comin' to talk about the future with them. About how we're going to run the United States once the travel bans are lifted. I'll get them to come out of the bunker . . . maybe say they should come to Shinin' Light and meet the town elders. Once they come out, y'all kill 'em."

"Two things," said Brad Davis. "First of all, and most importantly, they have no reason to trust you enough to come out of the bunker."

"And the second thing?"

"Even if they did agree to a meeting, only a couple of them would go. We need them *all* out of the bunker."

Murmurs spread around the room. "He's right," the German chancellor said. "It won't work."

"You have any better ideas?" Prime Minister Rodgers asked.

"It's not a great plan," said General Davis, "but it's the best we've got right now. And I'm not comfortable sitting around waiting for the terrorists to cannibalize each other.

There's no telling what kind of shit they could pull with control of all of those weapons. If you give somebody that much unfettered access to our systems, eventually they will crack the codes. We need them out of the bunker." He ran his hands through his hair and stood up. "Sheriff Jones is our best shot."

****

Later that day, Lucy Rodgers walked down the hall to General Davis' office and knocked on the door. "Do you have a minute?" she asked.

"Yes ma'am, of course. Please come in."

The British prime minister took a seat opposite the American general.

"What can I do for you, ma'am?"

"Do you think it will work?" Lucy asked. "Sending in Sheriff Jones and having him get the terrorists to come out of the bunker?"

General Davis sighed and leaned back in his chair. "I hope so. It's not the best plan in the world, but it's the best one we've got."

"And what happens after that?" Rodgers pressed. "Let's say it works and the terrorists die and we reopen America's borders. Keeping any semblance of order there will be a bloody nightmare."

Davis nodded and shrugged his shoulders. "You're probably right. But there's not much we can do about that. I imagine there will be some help from other countries' militaries and a lot of self-policing for months, if not years, until a proper government can be established."

"Self-policing?"

"Sure. Isn't that what should have always been happening?" Brad Davis couldn't help but break military character for a minute and speak his mind. "At what point did the government stop being a collection of citizen leaders and turn into this separate, competing entity? I mean, I've always believed that democracy done correctly is when the people are the government and the government is the people."

Lucy smiled. "You know what that sounds like, General?"

"A much less eloquent version of *The Federalist Papers*?"

"Maybe. But I was going to go with a campaign speech."

"Campaign for what?" asked the general.

"President. In case you haven't noticed, your old one is dead. And America will need some form of central government to handle national defense and make sure that this Taliban shit doesn't happen again. Not to mention the drug cartels in the southwest will be trying to set up their own little fiefdoms. When the ban is lifted, there will be a power vacuum. We'll need a good person to fill it."

Davis dismissed the British leader's comments with a laugh, but then grew serious again. "All I care about right now is the success of the special forces mission. I'll leave the country building to y'all.

PART III

FIFTY-ONE

At the UN relief staging area on the outskirts of Monterrey, Mexico, in a converted train depot, most of the people bustling about assumed that the railcars they were loading were for another round of supplies being sent to survivors inside the containment zone. However, it was hard not to notice that only a select few workers were allowed near what would become the seventh and eighth cars in the train's line. Behind a guarded screen, a group of engineers was busy retrofitting the old boxcars for their new and extremely important mission.

Wanting the cars to look like the others, the weathered metal exteriors were left alone but lined on the inside with Kevlar-reinforced steel . . . the same material protecting the outside of the Humvees that would be loaded in the boxcars. Electricity was added as well to the seventh car to ensure communications could occur between the railcars' passengers and NATO headquarters. Oxygen tanks, protective bodysuits, some food and water, and a massive arsenal of weaponry were also ready to be loaded onto the train. And inside a small room behind the security screen, plotting their mission, was a team of Navy SEALs.

Originally based in Virginia Beach, the SEALs were on a training excursion overseas when the virus struck in the United States. This mission would be the American sailors' first on their home soil.

"Okay," the group's commanding officer began, standing beside a whiteboard and facing his team. "The powers that be at NATO have given this the name Operation Lincoln." He scribbled the two words on a whiteboard with a dry-erase marker.

"Lincoln, sir?" one of the men asked.

Lieutenant Sean Garrison nodded. "General Davis did the honors. Something about a quote by Abraham Lincoln that if the US ever fell apart, it would be because it was destroyed from the inside." He paused. "I don't think this situation is quite what Lincoln had in mind, but that's the name it was given so that's the name we have."

The twenty-nine year old graduate of the University of Texas' ROTC Program snapped the top of the dry-erase marker up and down in a nervous habit. *Pop-click. Pop-click. Pop-click.* "Now, those two railcars out there are being retrofitted to seal the interior and prevent any exposure before we arrive at the launching point. We've all gotten the vaccine but we still don't want to take any chances. Remember, we're the first people testing out the Shorewood vaccine in the field. It worked in a controlled environment but, well . . . like I said, we don't want to take any chances." *Pop-click.* "Our launching point is Pueblo, Colorado. That's the closest train station to Cheyenne Mountain The Humvees are also being sealed airtight and will transport us and our gear approximately forty-two miles north from Pueblo to the Cheyenne Mountain facility."

"Do we anticipate any resistance?"

Pop-click. Pop-click. "None is anticipated, no. Our asset on the inside will be meeting us in Pueblo to be outfitted with necessary tracking and communications devices, and at that point he should be able to give us an update on the location of any enemy combatants. Our latest report indicates that all surviving civilians have remained loyal." *Pop-click.* "Any other questions?"

"Capture or kill?" asked Seaman Lewis Swain, the lieutenant's newest squad member.

"Excuse me?"

"What is our objective, sir? Capture or kill? Dead or alive?"

"If any of them happen to survive," *pop-click*, "we'll deal with it. But as far as I'm concerned, it's hunting season."

FIFTY-TWO

North of the border in Texas, Mary Jones stood in the doorway of her bedroom and watched her husband pack clothes for his trip. Josiah wasn't taking much with him to Colorado – just the bare essentials. But a lifetime of hunting wild game meant that the sheriff didn't have any problem throwing together his makeshift ruck sack. Camouflage clothing, portable cooking devices, extra ammunition, and capsules that could make water safe for drinking all made their way into Josiah's oversized, Army-green backpack.

"You just gonna stand there and watch or do you wanna help?"

Mary leaned against the door frame and crossed her arms over her chest. "I'm just gonna stand here. I don't see why you're goin' – you're just invitin' trouble."

Josiah tossed an extra pair of socks into his bag and then walked toward the bathroom to get his toothbrush. "We can't let terrorists run loose on our military bases. Someone who can't get the virus has to go up there and help the SEALs take back the bunker."

"I understand that," Mary replied. "I just don't see why that someone has to be you."

"Because I can," the sheriff replied. "Because I told the people at NATO that I would. And because all that is necessary for evil to triumph is for good people to do nothin'."

Mary rolled her eyes and turned to walk down the hall away from the bedroom. "I hope you're enjoyin' it up there on your soapbox," she said over her shoulder. "Just know that the higher you go, the bigger targets you and your family become."

****

After a restless night of sleep, Josiah woke with the break of dawn. After quiet time with his Bible and breakfast with Mary, the sheriff kissed both of his sleeping sons on their foreheads, grabbed his duffle bag from the hall, and walked out of his house. When Josiah opened his truck's door and started to climb in, he noticed that his dog had already beaten him to it. Upon seeing his owner packing the truck with guns, food, and camo gear, Gus decided that they must be going on another hunting trip and jumped in the crew cab. A sharp pang of guilt tore through Josiah's chest when he saw the dog's big amber eyes and chocolate face smiling at him from the passenger seat.

"No, I'm sorry big guy. You can't go this time." Sheriff Jones walked around to the other side of the truck and opened the door. "Out," he ordered.

Gus stopped his smiling and sadness filled the overgrown puppy's eyes. Eventually, the Labrador Retriever lowered his head and jumped down out of the truck.

"Good boy," Josiah said, petting the dog on his head and giving him a quick rub behind the ears. "You take care of the family while I'm gone." Jones then commanded the dog to 'stay' before walking back around to the driver's side of his truck.

Mary was there waiting, just like Josiah knew she would be. Despite their argument from the night before, the sheriff knew that their relationship was bigger and stronger than this one event. He also knew that the longer he lingered in the driveway, the greater the chance that he wouldn't ever leave. After saying his final goodbye, Josiah climbed in the truck, cranked it, and drove away.

****

Mary stood at the end of the driveway, not even bothering to wipe away the tears that were streaming down her face. The recon trip had been one thing; but that was travelling in a well-armed group whose objective was to remain unseen. But this? *This is insane*, Mary thought. *This is walkin' into the lion's den wearin' a sign that says 'eat me'.* Mary sniffed back more tears and gave in to wipe some of them away as they rolled down, over, and off her chin. She had said those very words – the lion's den and the 'eat me' sign – to Josiah the night before. She hated fighting with her husband, and their fights were rare, but Mary couldn't stand to let him leave without speaking her peace. They had gone to bed angry that night, something both apologized for when they woke up.

"I'm sorry we fought," Josiah said that morning, carrying a breakfast tray of pancakes and orange juice into their bedroom and placing it across Mary's lap. "I'm sorry it has to be this way. With so much death and destruction everywhere." Josiah sat down on the edge of their bed. "But I'm not sorry I'm goin'. I prayed over this . . . you know that. God put me here for such a time as this. It has to be done. To protect you and the boys."

Tears had welled again in Mary's eyes. She cried more in the past forty-eight hours than she did in her entire life combined before then. "Come back to us," she pleaded. "Come back to me."

Josiah had brushed the tears off of his wife's cheeks. "I'm going to do everythin' I can to make that happen."

Mary then swallowed the lump in her throat and let out a deep breath. "Don't be a cowboy," she had ordered him. "Don't pull any hero stunts."

The sheriff sighed. "The world needs a hero right now, honey."

As Mary stood in the driveway and watched Josiah's truck fade into a dot on the horizon, she realized that she still didn't have a good response to that statement. The world did need a hero . . . she just wished that the hero didn't have to be her husband.

"Come back to me," she repeated moments earlier while Josiah finished loading gear into his truck.

He had walked over to stand right in front of her, his six feet dwarfing her five feet four inches. Placing his hands on her cheeks, Josiah had gently kissed Mary's forehead and smiled. "I'll try. I want to. You know I want to." He paused. "But remember, even if I don't, I'll see you again in Heaven." Josiah had then leaned down and kissed her. "I'll see you 'round the bend, pretty lady."

Mary couldn't help but smile through her tears. That was the same thing Josiah said to her on their first date. "Don't say things like that," Mary had replied, repeating her same response from their dinner and a movie twenty-two years earlier. "You sound like a dork."

"Be nice to the dorks," Josiah had grinned as he continued the reenactment. "They'll run the world one day." He then paused, breaking the memory. "Or maybe the dorks will save it."

Sheriff and Mrs. Jones kissed again before he stepped away and started to walk toward his truck. "I have to go."

"I love you, Josiah Jones."

"I love you more, Mary Jones."

And then he climbed in his truck and was gone, leaving Mary to stand in their driveway and watch as the dot on the horizon disappeared.

FIFTY-THREE

Every so often on the journey from Monterrey, Mexico to Pueblo, Colorado, a member of the SEAL team in Boxcar Seven would unlatch a small metal covering on one of the car's walls and peek out the bulletproof side glass window. The most frequent looker was Lewis Swain, a Texas native.

"Waddaya think, Swain, that if you keep looking you'll see your folks as we go by?"

"Trevino," Lieutenant Garrison rebuked sharply.

"Sorry, sir, just messing with the kid. Come on, we all have to have a bit of a humor about the shit we deal with every day."

"Trevino," the lieutenant repeated. "That's enough. If we were rolling through Long Beach, you'd be doing the same thing. Shut up and leave him alone."

The California native didn't dare push his luck twice. And Seaman Swain, for his part, kept looking.

A few minutes later, the nineteen year old closed the window hatch and returned to the box that he had been using as a seat during the trip.

Quietly, where even the man sitting next to him could barely hear, Lewis said, "I didn't think it'd look like that."

"Like what?"

"So . . . normal."

The petty officer next to him let out a short laugh. "What'd you expect it to look like?"

"I dunno. Different. More like other places we've been. Rundown. Bombed out. You know."

"It's still the same place, bro. The people just all disappeared."

****

Sheriff Jones was waiting for the SEALs at the train station in Pueblo when they arrived. After joining them in Boxcar Seven, the men commenced planning Josiah's infiltration of the nuclear bunker.

Lieutenant Garrison spread a map across a folding table in the center of the railcar that now doubled as mission headquarters. Josiah and three other men stood by the table, while the remainder of the SEAL team was positioned around the boxcar's walls, guns in hand in case any unwelcome guests arrived.

"These are the most recent plans that we have for the mountain," Lieutenant Garrison began. "When everything was realigned in 2006-2008 and NORAD headquarters were moved to Peterson Air Force Base, the Air Force drew up a new map of who entered where and when and that sort of thing. Command told me it's more of a traffic map than a real facilities layout, but I think it'll be good enough for our purposes. We also have satellite photos, but of course those can't tell us anything about inside the bunker." His eyes scanned the room. "Any questions so far?"

The men all shook their heads no.

"Alright. So this here," he said, pointing with his index finger, is the main mountain. The base facilities are literally built straight into that. This motherfucker was designed to survive a direct hit with a nuclear bomb, so we gotta know everything important is buried pretty damn deep." He paused. "That's where you come in, Sheriff."

Josiah nodded. "Right."

"You get inside the bunker as our eyes and ears."

"Speaking of," a sailor said, handing Josiah a pair of glasses. "Wear these. They have a camera and a microphone embedded in them."

"I don't wear glasses."

"The lenses are fake," the SEAL assured him. "They look real but you'll still be able to see like normal."

"No, you don't understand. I'm sayin' I never wear glasses as in the terrorists are gonna figure out that they're fake."

"He has a point," said Lieutenant Garrison. "If these rag heads can shoot down a plane, I'm sure they can pull up Jones' Facebook page or the town website and see that he never wears glasses. We need a different way to put a wire on him."

Sheriff Jones and the SEALs brainstormed ways to let Josiah wear at least a microphone, if not a camera, but all of their suggestions fell flat. Under his clothes wouldn't work because the terrorists would know to check there. Shoes would be too far away from his mouth to catch the sound.

"What about his hair?" asked Lewis Swain.

The group of men looked over at the young seaman in confusion.

"His hair?"

"Yes sir," Swain said. "Glue it down in the top center of his head and brush his hair over it so you can't see it. He's a tall dude . . . unless they have a giant down there, no one will be looking down on the top of his head.

Garrison thought about the idea for a minute and then nodded. "I like it. Can we do it, Branson?"

The SEAL team's resident technology expert walked over to his crate of gadgets and rummaged around in it before pulling out a small plastic box, the kind civilians used to hold fishing lures. "Yes sir, I think so. It'll be a bitch to remove – you'll have to be really careful with that, Sheriff – but yeah, I think it'll work. Good idea, Swain."

Once the microphone was glued to his head, Josiah was handed yet another piece of equipment.

"Here, put this on," said Petty Officer Second Class Trevino. The Californian smart aleck was holding out a black ski jacket.

"I already have a coat."

"Now you have a new one," the sailor insisted.

"That's your weapon of last resort," explained Lieutenant Garrison.

"A jacket?"

"It has special fibers woven in. If we get the signal, we'll be able to detonate it remotely."

Sheriff Jones had one arm through a sleeve but stopped when he heard the word 'detonate.' Taking the piece of clothing off and tossing it away from him, he yelled: "it's a bomb?!"

"Don't freak out," Garrison replied, picking up the jacket and holding it out toward Josiah. "Here. Put it on."

"There is no way I'm walkin' in there wearin' a bomb," Sheriff Jones declared, crossing his arms and shaking his head. "How is that a bomb anyway? I don't see anythin' different about it."

"Well, that's because you're not supposed to be able to see anything different. It's in the clothing fibers," the lieutenant explained again. "The explosive materials are all made of plastic so as to be undetectable by machines. It's kind of like the gun that you can make from a 3D printer . . . you've seen that, right?"

Josiah nodded his head yes.

"Okay, well, the Pentagon has some Research & Development folks whose whole job is to sit around thinking up weird new shit, and this is one of those things. You can answer your phone through your watch and have a car that drives itself . . . you think we can't make a bomb that looks like a coat?"

"Yeah, I guess you have a point there," the sheriff conceded. "Gives a whole new meanin' to the term 'bomber jacket.'"

Petty Officer Trevino smiled. "Uh oh . . . the sheriff's got jokes!"

The group's laughter filled the boxcar and they all enjoyed a much needed moment of levity.

"Put it on," Lieutenant Garrison insisted after the laughter subsided. "We can't have you going in there completely unarmed. And if things go wrong, if somehow we get into a very bad situation, we're going to need you to do as much damage to their nerve center as possible."

The sheriff exhaled deeply and closed his eyes.

"Sheriff? Do you understand what I'm saying?"

Josiah opened his eyes and reached out to take the jacket. "I do," he said, and then put on the weapon disguised as clothes. "I get it."

FIFTY-FOUR

On a hill overlooking the access road to Cheyenne Mountain, Josiah unbuttoned his jacket and shirt enough to be able to reach in and pull out the small chain necklace he was wearing. Attached to the necklace were a gold cross that his mother gave him and a Saint Michael medal from his grandmother. Grandma Bradley, his mom's mom, was a staunch Catholic and not a fan of her daughter's family moving to live among 'those Protestant heretics' in Texas. But Grandma Bradley had a soft spot for her grandchildren, and on the day Josiah was sworn in as a sheriff's deputy she gave him the Saint Michael medal. "He's the patron saint of police officers," she said with a smile and tears in her eyes. "He'll keep you safe."

Although Josiah wasn't quite sure what he thought of the whole patron saint thing, some combination of superstition and family loyalty kept him wearing the necklace all these years. The sheriff rubbed the cross between his thumb and index finger and closed his eyes to pray.

This is it, Lord, he said silently. *I have no doubt . . . this is what you put me here for.* He paused. *God, I won't pray for my safety. I know that's probably a lost cause at this point. But Lord, if you could keep my family safe. . . . Lead us in defeatin' these two enemies of disease and terrorism, and when this battle is over God – should I not make it through – if You could please comfort and guide Mary and the boys. And let Your will be done.*

Josiah opened his eyes and breathed out deeply. "Amen," he said, then put the necklace back inside his shirt and buttoned it closed again. He stood up and brushed the dirt off his pants. "Let's do this."

****

The sheriff's heart was racing and his palms were so sweaty that he could barely grip the steering wheel as he completed the last leg of his drive from Pueblo to Cheyenne Mountain. Whereas during his first visit to the bunker the sheriff parked down the road, this time he drove straight up to the entrance – past the employee parking lot and the guard gate and right up next to the large, tunnel-shaped entrance. Josiah knew that the terrorists could see him now and that there was a strong chance they would shoot him without ever giving him a chance to explain himself. *God help me*, he prayed.

Exiting his truck, the sheriff walked up to the small, regular-sized door beside the larger tunnel opening and looked at the security camera. He then held up a sign with his message written in English on one side and Pashto on the other.

I COME IN PEACE. I WANT TO MAKE
AN ALLIANCE. I AM UNARMED.

After holding up the sign long enough for anyone to read it, Josiah took a few steps back and waited.

Approximately fifteen minutes later, he heard locks on the pedestrian door being unlatched.

"No sudden movements," a voice called out. "And keep your hands where I can see them."

Josiah did as he was told, all the while reeling from the fact that the voice on the other side of the door sounded like it belonged to an American.

With his hands up in the air, Sheriff Jones watched as first a gun, and then a man, and then two more men with guns came outside.

"What do you want?" asked Joe, the American-accented young man.

Emphasis on young, Josiah thought. *He can't be older than twenty.* "My name is Josiah Jones," he answered. "I live in Shinin' Light, Texas, which is about ten hours south of here. Almost my entire town survived the disease outbreak . . . we don't believe in gettin' vaccines."

"He did not say 'who are you'," another terrorist commented, this one looking even younger than the first and speaking with a heavy foreign accent. "He said what do you want."

The American terrorist placed a hand on his colleague's shoulder. "It's okay, Mohamed. Let him speak."

"You probably know that a group of us from Shinin' Light drove up here a couple of weeks ago," Josiah continued, still holding his hands in the air like a captured criminal. "We heard on the news – back when we still had TV – that a group of terrorists had taken over NORAD, so we came to check it out."

"Why are you here now?"

The sheriff's arms were beginning to cramp and he slowly lowered them down to his sides. "Like my sign said, I wanna make an alliance. Think of me like the ambassador for my town. We want to kinda join forces with y'all and figured it'd be good to work out the details before they open up America's borders again."

The three terrorists eyed Josiah skeptically, and his heart began to race even faster. *Please believe me. Please believe me. Please believe me.*

The man who had been silent up to that point took a radio out of his back pocket and spoke several sentences in a language Josiah couldn't understand. After receiving a reply, the man nodded his head. "Take off clothes," he ordered.

"Excuse me?"

"We need to search you for weapons," the American terrorist explained.

"And I have to be naked for that?"

"Do it!" the hotheaded kid ordered, pointing his rifle at Josiah's head.

"Okay, okay. Calm down."

****

After his rather cold strip search in the November Colorado air, Sheriff Jones was escorted inside the Cheyenne Mountain nuclear bunker. The one called Mohamed swiped a badge and punched a code into the wall to open a massive, twenty-five ton door, only to reveal yet another door a few feet down the hall. Josiah's head was on a swivel the entire time, trying to memorize everything in case he later needed to make an escape.

Once through the two blast doors, which were bigger, thicker, and heavier than any bank safe Josiah had ever seen, the terrorists led their visitor into a hallway with various other tunnels branching off in different directions. The four and a half acres of main chambers were connected by those tunnels and supported by steel frames and spring shocks to protect against earthquakes or potential bomb blasts. Of course, Josiah didn't know any of that – all he saw was a maze of whitewashed hallways decorated by the occasional Air Force logo, fighter jet picture, or recently added pro-jihad graffiti.

After about a ten minute walk, the men arrived in the command room, aptly named the Missile Warning Center.

Dehqan and the rest of the terrorists were waiting for him.

"Farzad says you want to be allies?" the Afghan man said, wasting no time.

Josiah nodded. "I do."

"And why should I believe you?"

Josiah took a deep breath, trying to remember his rehearsed speech. "At some point you have to make that choice. You have to choose to believe me. To trust me enough to work together." He paused. "Look, the containment zone covers more land than you could ever hope to manage. It's in all of our best interests to carve out a new map. So when the blockade is lifted we can tell the outsiders that we have those areas under control. As for my group, we want Texas. Lookin' at a map," Josiah said, pointing to one on the wall, "it makes sense for us to take New Mexico and Oklahoma too."

Cold, gray eyes stared back at Josiah. "Why would I give you all of that land?"

"Cuz then you wouldn't have to worry about your southern border. If you start with Kansas and Colorado and move north, you'll have a big chunk of land . . . includin' the oil fields up in the Dakotas." Josiah paused. "We protect your southern border and y'all protect our northern border. It's good for everybody."

Dehqan still wasn't quite sure what to think of the other man's plan. "I thought you Americans loved your country. Why wouldn't you turn the land back over to whatever government will run what remains of the United States?"

Josiah leaned his hip against the table beside him and crossed his arms over his chest, preparing to spin a web of lies that he hoped would catch the terrorist. "We're not all that different, you and me. We both want to live in countries that honor God and promote a religious way of life. We have different religions, sure. But the US government got too big and too nosy."

The sheriff paused, trying to gauge the other man's reaction. *Looks like he's buyin' it so far.*

"Look," he continued, "I've got my truck parked outside. There's a supply train about forty miles from here. It's got food and gas and all kinds of other stuff that y'all can use to restock. Why don't y'all come with me, we'll load up with supplies, and you can see that I'm not out to trick you or anythin'."

"I thought the closest supply train was going to Los Angeles," said Dehqan.

That statement took Josiah by surprise. *How does he know about the trains?* "Umm . . . no. I drove past one in Pueblo on my way up here."

The Afghan leader remained unconvinced. "We saw people walking around in Colorado Springs with food brought to them by a truck from Los Angeles. They didn't say anything about one here in Colorado."

What the heck? Sheriff Jones tried to think on his feet. "Uhh, no, they're comin' closer. Maybe at first it was just to L.A. But I passed through some other places on my drive here and the other survivors I saw – there weren't many – but those I saw said that word has gotten out about trains goin' a bunch of different places now." Josiah mentally crossed his fingers and hoped the terrorists wouldn't stop to think through how word could get around when there was no phone, internet, or television service.

Dehqan was tempted by the American's offer, but something still made him nervous. "Why don't you just go get the supplies and bring them back to us?"

"Some of this stuff is way too heavy for one person," Josiah reasoned, having that answer already prepared. "Plus it'll go a lot quicker if y'all help me."

The Taliban leader stood in front of Sheriff Jones, eyeing the American skeptically as he considered the proposal.

"You can take three men with you. Mohamed, Joe, and Kontar. The rest of us stay. If you come back with the promised supplies, then we'll talk."

FIFTY-FIVE

Outside the nuclear bunker, positioned up on the ridge overlooking the tunnel entrance just like Daniel Jones had done weeks earlier, Lieutenant Garrison was listening to Josiah's conversation underground. Upon hearing the group leader's suggestion that Jones leave with a few men and then return to Cheyenne Mountain, Sean knew that his mission plan had gone out the window. *There's no way we can leave that many of them alive inside the bunker. Josiah is our one bullet . . . we have to wait for the perfect shot.*

Putting his wrist to his mouth, Garrison said into his radio: "hold your fire when they come out. I repeat: hold your fire when they come out. We're going to wait until they return with the supplies."

Petty Officer Trevino, poised beside the lieutenant on the ridge, turned to him and said: "do you think the sheriff has enough sense to leave his jacket behind?"

"I don't know. I hope so, but I don't know. Get on the radio and call our guys in Pueblo. Tell them they've got thirty minutes to get those boxcars unloaded and looking like the rest. We can't have anybody getting suspicious when the sheriff shows them the train."

****

After Josiah Jones and the three terrorists left the bunker, Dehqan and the remainder of his crew returned to the command center. Xiao had stayed behind, both to monitor the security cameras and to work on the project that continued to elude his grasp: hacking into the NATO mainframe. Xiao knew that if he could gain access to the enemy's computer and phone systems, the battle would be over before it ever truly began.

"They're all gone?" he asked when his colleagues were back in the control room.

"Yes," Farzad replied with a nod. "He said the supply train is about forty minutes away, so we probably have around two hours until they get back."

"Still no luck with the NATO system?" Dehqan asked, walking over to stand behind Xiao's chair.

"Still no luck." The computer expert shook his head. "This thing is as close to hack-proof as I've ever seen. Ideally, I'd have a whole team coming at it at once from a bunch of different potential openings, but with just me it's going to take a lot longer."

"Okay, well, keep working at it," Dehqan responded, patting his colleague on the shoulder for encouragement. Noticing something new on the workstation, he added: "what's this?"

Xiao looked over at the jacket in his boss' hands. "Oh, it belongs to the American. He was wearing it when he came in but got hot so I told him to just set it down there."

A little voice in Dehqan's head started screaming *danger!*, but when he looked at the jacket, checked the pockets, and patted it down, nothing seemed out of the ordinary. "Hmm. Okay," he said, putting the piece of clothing down on the table next to his computer expert. "Make sure he takes it with him when he gets back."

FIFTY-SIX

Just shy of two hours after Josiah and his passengers left, Lieutenant Garrison's radio crackled through the air.

"Jones' truck is approaching," the lookout announced. "Turning onto the entrance road now."

"Everyone into position," Garrison said. "Do not engage until I give the order."

The lieutenant knew his men were highly trained – the best in the world – but at that moment he was more nervous than he had ever been on a mission and knew that they likely were too. One slight slip in patience and control could lead to disaster for his team and the operation. The SEALs hadn't planned on spending this long outside the pressure-sealed boxcar, and he knew their oxygen supplies would begin to run low soon. They were supposedly protected from the Shorewood Disease by the new vaccine, but Garrison knew that ditching their protective gear would just add another layer of unnecessary complication to the SEAL team's mission. *Please God*, Sean prayed, *don't make us have to do that.*

****

With only Josiah aware of the military eyes watching them, Sheriff Jones's truck rumbled along the final stretch of road before pulling to a stop in front of the bunker's entrance. One of the terrorists with him – Josiah thought his name ironically sounded a lot like the Jewish 'cantor' – got out of the crew cab and walked over to the garage door-like gate. Looking up into the security camera, he smiled and gave two thumbs up.

Some top secret codes these guys have, thought the sheriff, shaking his head. But the next thing he knew, the pedestrian door to the side of the large gate unlocked and opened. Out of America's most secure military facility and into the early afternoon sunlight walked the terrorist leader, his deputy, and six other men. All of them shielded their eyes upon seeing the sun for the first time in days, if not weeks.

Breathe, Josiah told himself, willing his heart to stop racing or at least slow down enough that he could speak without his voice shaking. *Breathe. You're a law enforcement officer; you're trained for this.* A split second later, though, the panic returned. *No I'm not*, his mind warred back. *I'm a small town sheriff. I write speedin' tickets and bust kids for shopliftin'. I don't stare down international terrorists while holdin' the fate of my country in my hands.*

By that point, Dehqan had arrived to stand next to Josiah's truck. "You look like you're going to be sick," the younger man commented. "Some reason why you would be nervous?"

"I'm just tired," Josiah lied. "It was a long drive up here from home. Everythin' we got is in the back of the truck," he continued. "Food, water . . . "

"It's good stuff, Dehqan," said Joe. "And you should see this train. He was telling the truth – it's packed full of everything we might need."

Dehqan stood silently for a minute while cutting his eyes back and forth between the sheriff and his own men. Finally, Nazari smiled. "Good work," he said, placing his hand on the American's shoulder. "You've proven yourself. Let's get this stuff out of the truck."

****

High above the bunker entrance, Sean Garrison was watching the scene below unfold through binoculars. Every thirty seconds or so, he would repeat his order to 'hold,' just in case anyone got too antsy or trigger happy.

When Garrison saw who looked to be the leader give Sheriff Jones a pat on the shoulder and a smile, the lieutenant knew the time had come.

"Branson," he whispered into his radio. "Did we get confirmation that the jacket is still inside the bunker?"

"Yes sir. No one on the base team reported seeing the jacket when Jones returned to the train."

"Prepare to engage," Garrison ordered, and all across the ridge Navy SEALs inched forward and trained their sights and their guns on the crowd below.

Sean picked up a second radio from the ground beside him. "This is Lieutenant Garrison," he said, talking to his men assembled back in the main boxcar in Pueblo. "Detonate the jacket."

"SEAL Team," Garrison said in his full voice. "Execute."

****

The hail storm of artillery started raining down around Josiah from all directions, engulfing him in a storm of whizzing bullets and screaming men. The sheriff instinctively ducked down behind his truck, hoping the spray of ammunition would somehow miss him. He heard the terrorists' reaction more than he saw it, but at that point Josiah wasn't too afraid to admit that he was too afraid to open his eyes. Torn flesh, the thumping sound of bodies hitting the earth, yelling in a variety of languages, and cries of pain rang out through the air . . . all accompanied by the background 'click click click click click' and 'sheeeuummm sheeeuummm' sounds of automatic rifle fire streaming in from above.

The first bullet struck Josiah in his ankle, having ricocheted off the ground under his truck. Sheriff Jones cried out in pain and grabbed at the injured leg, only to feel another hit of speeding metal pierce through his right shoulder. The truck was no longer a sufficient barrier, Josiah learned, as the men positioned above him unloaded round after round and magazine after magazine on their targets below. Deciding he needed to get out of the firestorm if he had any chance of survival, and despite every instinct in his body telling him to freeze and not move from the fetal position he now found himself in, Josiah used his good arm and leg to push himself up into a crouched position. Hobbling forward, dragging his injured left ankle behind him, the sheriff set off in the direction of the access road and away from the bunker.

****

At first, Dehqan wasn't sure what was happening when the sound of automatic gunfire erupted all around him. Unlike the teenagers and rookie members of his terrorist cell, though, Dehqan's battle experience meant that his reaction time and instincts were much quicker than the others currently under attack by the unknown assailants above. Nazari was three steps back toward the bunker's still open door when he realized that it was a set-up. The sheriff was a traitor. Two more steps brought Dehqan within inches of the doorway and safety before his legs gave out beneath him. Looking down, the terrorist leader saw blood pouring out of his thigh and stomach.

It was at that moment that Dehqan saw the traitorous infidel, Sheriff Jones, limping down the road away from the firestorm. *Oh no you don't,* Nazari thought, using what remained of his strength to lift his rifle and point it in the direction of Josiah. "Allahu Akbar," Dehqan said through gritted teeth as he squeezed the trigger. "God is great."

A second later, Lieutenant Garrison returned the favor, sending a bullet through Dehqan's skull and turning out the lights.

FIFTY-SEVEN

With both the terrorists and the virus defeated, the UN Special Committee on Worldwide Pandemic Response set about the difficult task of reopening and rebuilding the devastated United States.

Central America's borders had been open for over a month, and Mexico and Canada were freed from restriction after Dr. Capello's vaccine was distributed in those countries. How to manage the opening of the United States, however, was an entirely different issue. Americans trapped overseas were the first allowed to return, transported in via plane, car, and some even on the same railroad tracks that had previously carried supplies to survivors. NATO and UN troops that were guarding the borders were sent inside the US to help preserve peace and security . . . much like Allied soldiers did in Japan and Germany after World War II.

Experts in public utilities and farming were also given special license to travel to America and were offered financial bonuses if they agreed to stay and reestablish a class of professional, skilled workers in the country. "Homesteading for the Twenty-First Century," Lucy Rodgers labeled it with a smile.

Traditional homesteading was also revived, and prospectors and squatters flooded in from around the world to take advantage of the 'free' land. But with the American population decimated down to levels not seen since the Civil War, immigration was a welcome blessing.

The people of Shining Light, for their part, didn't try to seize control of Texas like Josiah made the terrorists believe – although a few residents said it wouldn't have been a bad idea. Mary Jones forbid it, though, and no one dared cross the widow of the man who saved their lives.

All six hundred residents of the tiny town turned out for Sheriff Jones' funeral, including a tearful Mary and stoic

Daniel and Isaac in the front row. Members of the SEAL team who participated in Operation Lincoln wanted to attend as well, but they were ordered to exit the containment zone immediately following mission completion. They did send a flag, though, folded in the traditional manner and with a note attached: 'on behalf of a grateful nation.' Airdropped along with the US flag was a baby blue one from the United Nations that read: 'on behalf of a grateful world.'

A small wooden cross was all that denoted Josiah's grave, a temporary marker that the people of Shining Light planned to replace with a more elaborate headstone as soon as they could get a factory up and running again. Josiah Jones deserved that much, at least. 'The Savior of the Republic' was what people were calling him. Without his actions at Cheyenne Mountain, without his willingness to enter the terrorists' headquarters and lure them outside, the world's greatest experiment in democracy would have ended. The shining beacon of freedom snuffed out. Ronald Reagan's city on a hill, no more.

But the republic was saved. Carved into the cross marking Josiah Jones' grave were three words: *Husband. Father. Patriot.* "That's all he would have ever wanted it to say," said Mary when she told Pastor Jenkins what to put.

"It's fitting," the preacher had replied.

The funeral service and graveside burial had ended hours ago, the slight drizzle of the morning clearing away to leave not a cloud in the sky. Shining Light's residents had returned to their homes, each beginning the process of beginning again. And Mary and her boys were back at their ranch. Daniel and Isaac locked themselves in their rooms with the doors shut and music blaring, hoping against hope that the sound from the stereo would block out the pain in their hearts. Mary, for her part, sat alone in the living room, staring at the two triangle-shaped flags on her fireplace mantel. Window blinds drawn shut, lights off, with the dark, empty room matching the feeling in her soul.

The morning after the funeral, when Pastor Jenkins arrived at the cemetery, he noticed a fresh set of footprints on the dirt track leading to the section where Josiah was buried. *Somebody came in the middle of the night,* he thought. The pastor followed the footprints along the path in the direction of Josiah's grave, and a bittersweet smile crossed the man's face when he realized who the prints belonged to. Tears welled in his eyes when he rounded a corner and his guess was confirmed. Lying beside the grave, having spent the night there, was Josiah's dog Gus.

EPILOGUE

The morning of the inauguration of America's new president dawned bright and beautiful in Washington, DC. Fourteen months after the terrorists were killed at Cheyenne Mountain and thirteen months after the United Nations dissolved the containment zone, the international committee overseeing the rebuilding of the United States was officially handing over power to the country's newly elected leaders.

Standing just inside the Capitol building and looking out at the assembled crowd was President-elect Brad Davis. The former Army general hadn't wanted a big fuss over his inauguration – "we've got too much work to do," he had argued – but the rebuilding committee and the rest of America's new politicians insisted that there be a ceremony on the Capitol steps, just like with previous presidents, as a sign that the United States was back on track.

"I don't think pomp and circumstance is really the most important thing we can do to signal our return to the world," the elected chief executive said.

His wife Faye had stepped in then and, as usual, resolved the matter. "Even George Washington gave speeches, dear."

With that, the ceremony was set.

"Are you ready?" Faye now asked, as she and their daughter Kaylie walked up to stand beside him.

"As ready as I'll ever be."

The First Family then made their way out into the January cold, down the carpeted steps, and onto the assembled podium. While Mrs. Davis and Kaylie took their places beside the judge who would administer the oath of office, Brad stole a quick glance at the small clock resting on a shelf inside the podium. *12:01pm*, he read. *It's official. I'm the president.*

The crowd gathered for the Inaugural Address wasn't all that large – mostly members of Congress, staffers, and foreign dignitaries who had come as a sign of support. Certainly not the hundreds of thousands who showed up for the inauguration events of presidents past. But, then again,

America didn't have nearly as many people residents as before, *and those that did survive have work to do. Like me,* President Davis thought. Lucy Rodgers was there, though, as were the other members of the small WPR leadership committee and all five members of the ECDC's research team.

A minute after he entered the stage, with the Oath of Office complete, President Davis took a deep breath and stepped up to the microphone to deliver his speech.

"My fellow Americans," he began, smiling at the words. "How wonderful it is to be able to say such a thing. For a while there, I know many of us wondered if anyone would ever be able to say it again. But enough with the past. We've spent too long already in those dark months of despair."

"We have a chance to start over," the president declared. "To begin anew. We are devastated, yes, but we are not defeated. We are weakened, but not broken. We are here. We survived. And we owe it to those of us who did not make it to continue on. To rebuild our great nation. Because America is more than land and borders and purple mountains majesty. You cannot defeat, you cannot silence, the United States of America. No more than you can defeat or silence any idea. America is alive and well in the hearts of all freedom-loving people around the world. And you know what?" Davis said with a smile. "When I woke up this morning, our flag was still there. Now let's get to work."

****

Immediately after the inauguration of President Davis, the newly-elected members of Congress gathered in the chamber of the House of Representatives. The first act of the new legislature was a ceremonial yet important one, as Josiah Jones was posthumously awarded the Congressional Gold Medal. The nation's new chief executive was also present at the ceremony, there to give Josiah the Presidential Medal of

Freedom – collectively the two highest civilian honors in the United States. The medals were received on behalf of Josiah by his wife, Congresswoman Mary Jones, and their two sons, Isaac and Daniel.

Congress' second act was equally ceremonial yet equally important: Dr. Ricardo Capello became the eighth person in history to be awarded honorary citizenship to the United States. Dr. Capello was only the third person to receive the honor while still alive; the other two being Winston Churchill and Mother Teresa.

Watching the ceremony from the gallery, Lucy Rodgers smiled. "They've done it," she whispered to herself. "America is back."

Please consider writing a review online!

ABOUT THE AUTHOR

Danielle knew she was born to be a writer at age four when she entertained an entire emergency room with the - false - story of how she was adopted. *The Containment Zone* is Danielle's fourth novel. She is a graduate of Georgetown University (Go Hoyas!) and Harvard Law School. Danielle lives in Georgia with her chocolate lab, Gus.

Find out more about Danielle and her books on her website: www.daniellesingleton.com.

Follow Danielle on Twitter: @auntdanwrites

Like Danielle's Facebook page: www.facebook.com/singletondanielle